When she got home she took out the news clipping again and thought about Karla Hoffman.

Funny, she thought, bringing the picture closer to her, I didn't notice her earrings before. She got up and went to the desk. There was a magnifying glass in the top drawer. When she held it to the picture, the earrings became more distinct.

They looked like small gold rings with tiny pearls along the bottom. She put the magnifying glass down and thought for a moment.

Then she went right to her bedroom and to her jewelry box. They were there. Stephen had bought them for her years ago, and they were very similar. They were too similar.

It was bone chilling.

ANDREW NEIDERMAN
REFLECTION

WORLDWIDE

TORONTO • NEW YORK • LONDON • PARIS
AMSTERDAM • STOCKHOLM • HAMBURG
ATHENS • MILAN • TOKYO • SYDNEY

First published November 1986

ISBN 0-373-97027-7

Copyright © 1986 by Andrew Neiderman. All rights reserved.
Philippine copyright 1986. Australian copyright 1986.
Except for use in any review, the reproduction or utilization of
this work in whole or in part in any form by any electronic,
mechanical or other means, now known or hereafter invented,
including xerography, photocopying and recording, or in any
information storage or retrieval system, is forbidden without
the permission of the publisher, Worldwide Library,
225 Duncan Mill Road, Don Mills, Ontario, Canada M3B 3K9.

All the characters in this book have no existence outside the
imagination of the author and have no relation whatsoever to
anyone bearing the same name or names. They are not even
distantly inspired by any individual known or unknown to the
author, and all incidents are pure invention.

The Worldwide design trademarks, consisting of a globe surrounded
by a square, and the word WORLDWIDE in which the letter "O" is
represented by a depiction of a globe, are trademarks of
Worldwide Library.

Printed in Canada

*For our daughter, Melissa,
who has Nanny's eyes
and Nana's vision.*

1

CYNTHIA WARNER SMILED to herself after she read the first line of her horoscope in the morning paper. "Good preplanning brings financial success." No kidding, she thought. She shook her head and then sipped from the mug of hot coffee she held just below her chin. It amazed her how many people had such faith in these things and read them religiously. She had to admit, though, that even though she was skeptical, she always read it.

When she gave it serious thought, she realized that she could empathize with the followers of astrology. All of us have this desperate need to know our futures, she thought, me included. And don't we all sit back and wonder what different choices we would have made had we known what we know now about ourselves? Would I have married Stephen? Would I have become a real estate agent, or would I have competed with Jason to take firm control of the family's business?

Questions like those could become tormenting. Perhaps it was better to leave it all to fate, fate and good effort and yes... good preplanning. Thank you, Jeanne Dixon. She laughed aloud. She did feel somewhat giddy this morning. She felt that way because she was optimistic, and there was nothing that made life as full and as rich as waking up feeling optimistic.

The feeling wasn't unwarranted. Stephen had already called from the Palmer Building to tell her that the Bloomfields, clients interested in the old Rose Hill House, would be at her office a half hour earlier than expected. They were that anxious. Stephen, on the other hand, was cynical about it. It wasn't characteristic of him to be that way, but as of late his being uncharacteristic had become a characteristic. She tried to ignore it. She didn't want anything to damage her natural high.

She had listed the Rose Hill House only a little more than a month ago when Ralph Hillerman had come to her office to tell her he was going to definitely move his father into an adult residency very soon. Presently, the old man lived in the big house with Patsy Marshall, a widow Ralph had hired to care for his father; but she was going to move off, and the old man had degenerated considerably during the past month or so.

"After all, he's nearly ninety," Ralph told her. He sounded as though his father had abused him by living so long.

Reflection

Less than a week after she listed the place, the Bloomfields called. She sent them photographs, and they called again for more details. Soon after, they made today's appointment.

Cynthia looked up from the yellow Formica kitchen counter. Stephen and she had designed the house, and she had insisted that the kitchen be open and airy. She liked waking up and coming into its brightness. There was a twelve-foot bay window on the east side to welcome in the light of the rising sun. On bright days like this one, when the thin, maple shutters were folded back, there was no need for any lights. Jason always complained about the room when he was in it during the early morning hours. He thought the yellow flower wallpaper was too busy and the light beige tiled floor did little to subdue it.

"You need sunglasses in here" was his frequent comment. Stephen used to laugh, but lately he was in agreement about it and had been suggesting they call in Jason's decorator.

"If I ever agreed to it," she told him, "it wouldn't be Jason's decorator. He is so swishy. He makes my skin crawl when I'm near him."

Stephen didn't disagree, but that didn't stop him from bringing it up again. He had brought it up as recently as yesterday. She'd simply ignored it.

The counter opened onto the dining room in their long, brick ranch-style home, and from where she was sitting she could see herself clearly in the full-length wall mirror on the far wall. As it was, the room was large, fifteen by twenty, and the mirror exaggerated it. Sometimes she felt a bit silly when there were only the two of them dining.

For a few moments this morning as she looked at herself in the mirror, she felt as though she were staring into the window of another house, looking at a total stranger. Only two days ago she had gone to Nikki's Salon and had her hair stripped and dyed blond. Then he fluffed and blew it out until she looked like Melissa Grant in her cover girl shot on *Cosmo*. Stephen had commented favorably about the model's look, and Cynthia thought this dramatic change in her appearance might jolt their relationship back on track.

Before this she had been wearing her dark brown hair pinned back or brushed straight down over her shoulders. When she pinned it back, she thought it emphasized the smooth lines in her neck, the sharp sculptured curve in her chin and jawbone and the depth of her hazel-green eyes. That was the face Stephen had fallen in love with, the face he had called, "Indian perfect, dramatic like a tribal princess perched atop a palamino horse, your hair dancing in the breeze, the western vista spread out around you, embracing you in your heritage and natural beauty."

Once upon a time he could talk like that, spin words poetically, capture a feeling or a mood in a phrase and turn it over and over like a fine jewel. It was why he was such a successful insurance salesman, why her father was happy when they married and he could come into the family business. He had the gift of language, and he could tell people what they wanted even before they wanted it. Everyone admired him. Even Jason admired him and suffered no apparent jealousy when Stephen was quickly promoted to vice president of the Palmer Agency.

Of course, after their father died, her brother, Jason, became the president of the firm, but it was as if he and Stephen were partners. Jason never seemed to make a serious or important decision without Stephen's approval anymore. They had such a good business relationship that Cynthia was often jealous of them. She used to wish that Jason would feel more threatened by Stephen. She couldn't remember them ever having a serious argument, at least none that she knew of or that was conducted in public.

"You spend more time with Jason than you do with me, if you think about it," she once told him, but he just shrugged it off. When she gave it more thought she realized it was hard to have an argument with Stephen. He had a way of isolating himself, retreating into a shell of thoughts. She imagined that he treated Jason the same way, and if there was one thing that Jason couldn't tolerate, it was being ignored.

She was wise enough to know that she wouldn't enjoy working with them, so she eschewed the insurance business and went for her realtor's license instead. She took over an office at the Palmer Building, a modern two-story structure constructed on a two-acre lot her father had bought years and years ago just outside of Woodridge, a small upstate New York Catskill community. From her office on the second floor she could look out at Ulster County and the beautiful Shwangunk mountain range. Sometimes she just sat there staring out at the gently sloping hills and blue sky, either hypnotized by the vista or stimulated by it to think deeply philosophical thoughts.

She was starting to do that now, but Shirley Watson, her cleaning girl, turned on the vacuum cleaner in the entranceway, and the noise snapped her out of her reverie. She considered her appearance again. How would these clients today take to this new, glamorous hairdo? she wondered. They were coming up from New York City; the husband was a corporate attorney. They should be cosmopolitan enough, she thought. It was just that she had detected that they had a stereotype image of what people were like in the Catskills: countryfolk whose idea of a good time was the Saturday-night bingo game in the firehouse. Toby Bloomfield had said, "We're looking for an escape, a place so quiet that the crickets keep you up at night."

And yet they wanted something big enough to house a number of guests on weekends, their own private retreat. What was better for such purposes than a retired tourist house, a turn-of-the-century structure that was in rather good shape, situated on a back country road with nearly twenty acres of flat land and rolling hills. There was even a lake on the property, big enough for rowboats and light fishing. She explained to the Bloomfields that the Rose Hill House had begun as a farmhouse and expanded into a tourist house. "As farming became more difficult and tourism became more profitable."

"How interesting," Toby Bloomfield squealed over the phone.

Ordinarily that might have put Cynthia off, but the Rose Hill House was interesting. Old man Hillerman had built and operated it with his wife, but like so many of the small resorts in the Catskills, it had died a rather abrupt death in the midsixties and become a haven for memories and dreams, a monument to a bygone era when the railroad was in existence up here and moderately priced family vacations were in vogue.

Carl Palmer, Cynthia's father, had begun his agency insuring such places because most of the other agencies were afraid of something they had prejudicially labeled, "Jewish lightning," a fire in a resort when the Catskills had a bad season. There was never a fire at the Rose Hill House, but Ralph Hillerman, like the children of many other resort families, had no interest in continuing with the traditions and the tourist business. He became a professional businessman in his own right, and the Rose Hill House—named after his mother, Hillerman shortened to Hill for advertisement reasons—became a drain and a burden to him. As long as his father, who had survived his mother by ten years, was vigorous and feisty, there was little he could do about it. But now with the old man nearly senile and confined to a wheelchair most of the day, the options were reduced. For the Hillermans the Rose Hill House had to come to an end.

Cynthia couldn't help feeling sorry for the old man, even though she agreed with Ralph's decision. She had met Ben Hillerman briefly when she went up to inspect the property. He made her feel like an undertaker measuring him for a coffin, and she was happy when Patsy took him to the kitchen to eat.

"He knows why I'm here," she told Ralph.

"Oh sure. Despite his condition, you'd be surprised at how much he understands," Ralph Hillerman told her. "But he's drifting in and out of reality more and more now. It would be cruel to prolong this any longer, even though they don't come any tougher. He and my mother made this place work no matter what the cost. I hate to see it the way it is now. It's a shadow of itself, just the way he is."

"Of course I can't see it the way you do," Cynthia said, "but I feel the Rose Hill House still has character. You can sense it. There's wisdom in these old walls and real drama. Think of the different people who had stayed here." She inhaled as though she could smell the history in the old tourist house. Ralph smiled and shook his head in admiration of her enthusiasm.

"I never heard a real estate agent talk about property the way you do," he said. "You make it sound alive."

"Well, it is, in its way," she said, and she believed it. That was her edge, what made her successful. She did much more than pay for her share of the space and facilities she took up at the Palmer Building. She never gave Jason the opportunity to present her with a statement of liabilities, and Stephen had to admit to her financial acumen. But she wasn't as happy about all this as she could be.

When she told Paula Levy, her best friend, about it, Paula said, "You're too successful. It makes Stephen feel unimportant, maybe even unnecessary. Believe me, men like to feel essential. As soon as you show them you can do without them, they whimper. You can hear it in their voices, in their sarcasm."

Paula, divorced, remarried, separated and currently reconciled, wasn't someone to hold up as successful when it came to her relationships with men, but her coldly analytical way often cut to the truth. Like most everyone, Cynthia thought, Paula could see what was wrong with other people faster than she could see what was wrong with herself.

Lately Cynthia had been thinking that Paula might be right on the money with her theories. Just as Paula had predicted, she was beginning to detect a note of ridicule and sarcasm in Stephen's words. It was a tone that was more characteristic of her brother, Jason, than of her husband. It was even in what he told her this morning when he called about the Bloomfields.

"Your big-time New York clients want to play in the mountains," he said. How did he know it was only play? Why did he assume she'd be unsuccessful, or was Paula right—was he hoping she would fail? Was Stephen, with all the success he and Jason were having, jealous of her?

She knew Jason didn't expect her to ever sell the Rose Hill House. Maybe he was responsible for making Stephen so cynical about it. It was a big property, a real estate agent's dream sale of the year. Still, wouldn't it be wonderful if Stephen believed in her and encouraged her? It was amazing what a little optimism could do for a couple, the light it could add to their lives. Why couldn't Stephen see that? What blinded him?

She put the coffee mug in the sink and went into the dining room to inspect her full figure in the mirror. Perhaps the cherry-pink skirt and frilly, blue blouse were too bright and too informal for these clients. This was big money, and she didn't want to appear inexperienced. Everyone said she looked like a woman in her late teens or early twenties as it was. Very few strangers guessed she was thirty, and clients who spoke to her on the phone first always had this surprised look on their faces when they finally met her in person. It was as though they expected her to go get her mother. She did have that deep, Lauren Bacall voice.

A youthful appearance ran in her family. Her mother's skin was smooth to the day she died, and her father never really looked his age. Jason was the same way, only in his case she wasn't sure it was an asset. At thirty-two he still had the look of a college freshman—smooth, light skin with soft, very light brown hair. He shaved daily, but he could go for nearly a week before the evidence of a beard would show. Once he tried to grow a mustache. She figured he wanted to look older, but all he produced was a pale peach fuzz that was impossible to detect from more than ten feet away. He had her hazel-green eyes, or rather, she had his since he was two years older. He wasn't much taller at five-foot-ten, and his slim, almost fragile build sometimes made them look like twins.

Stephen looked his thirty-five years. He was six-foot-one and wide shouldered. Recently he let his tight, athletic build slip, but he still had a strong, authoritative voice and a commanding presence. He was so dark skinned that he always looked tanned, and he had licorice-black hair and a beard that was so heavy he had long since given in to the two-hour shadow and grown a full beard. He kept it beautifully trimmed. Cynthia was happy with it because she felt it gave his face strength and brought out the brightness in his brown eyes.

She remembered the week he grew it, because that was the only time she could recall Jason being jealous of him. He had told him it made him look straggly and disheveled. Appearance was such an important thing to Jason. He had even implied that Stephen's beard would hurt business. But she had encouraged him and he had kept it. Now she wondered if her encouragement about anything could make a difference when it came to the business and his work with Jason.

More and more these days Cynthia felt she had not only fallen in love with a different face, but with a different person. She had never expected him to be so monomaniacal about his work. He and Jason were in the process of building the biggest agency in the tri-country area. They had taken on fifty new companies and had expanded from life, home and car into more exotic realms like racehorses and even the fingers of a pianist. The agency had grown from a company of two agents to ten, not including Stephen and Jason. Now they were talking about opening a branch office in Orange County, as well. She hated to take Jason along when they went to dinner or a show. Inevitably they would talk shop and leave her to fend for herself.

It was the eighth year of her marriage, and she and Stephen had been talking about children for the past two. The discussion hadn't gotten any more intense. She didn't want to be the only one pushing for it. Paula had told her that unless the husband and the wife wanted children with the same fervor, they could become an instant burden for one or the other. It made sense.

Again, listening to Paula, she had developed a similar philosophy when it came to the lovemaking between her and Stephen. Her signals had to be received and returned with the same enthusiasm, or she would turn over and wait for another occasion. Lately she was doing that more and more, so she experimented with the new hairdo and waited to see his reaction.

He was surprised she would make such an abrupt change, but the surprise didn't translate into immediate pleasure. He did look at her in a new way, but she thought he looked more amused than attracted. Paula said it was something he would have to get used to.

"Men can't be as impulsive," she told her, "especially businessmen like Stephen and Jason. They have to check things out with their brokers first. Oh, don't worry," she added, "one day he'll just look at you like he did when you two first met and he'll say, 'My God, you're beautiful.'" They both laughed.

If only that would happen, she thought. She looked at her watch, saw that it was time to go and hurried out of the house. She was anxious to start the day.

STEPHEN AND JASON WERE BUSY with some investors when she arrived at the Palmer Building. Judy Dobbs, the secretary who worked for her as well as for Stephen, told her they were having a meeting about Florida condos.

"Condos? Since when have they been interested in condos?" She really meant it to be only a private thought but she said it aloud.

"Oh, it's been a few weeks, Mrs. Warner," Judy said. Cynthia could see the twenty-eight-year-old woman's look of glee. Cynthia knew she had a crush on Stephen. Judy was unmarried and somewhat socially immature, even though she was a good secretary. She had a plain face with dull brown eyes and a chubbiness that produced an emphatic double chin. She was continually on a diet, but she continually cheated on that diet, too. Cynthia saw her as no threat, but she was annoyed with the teenagelike pleasure she obviously got from knowing something about Stephen that she didn't know.

"Really," Cynthia said. She didn't continue the conversation, but she couldn't hide her unhappiness. This involves real estate, she thought. They should have had her in on the discussions or at least told her about it beforehand, but Stephen hadn't even mentioned it.

But she didn't have a chance to pout about it because the Bloomfields were right on time. She had just picked up her phone to call Jason's office and interrupt them when Judy buzzed. Cynthia told her to send them in immediately.

She liked them because there was no look of surprise on their faces; no doubt in their eyes when they confronted her. She thought they were both probably in their fifties, but they had a youthful vibrancy that was infectious. Toby Bloomfield had a slim, well-proportioned body. She wore designer jeans and a blue, light cotton sweater. Sid Bloomfield, dressed in a tight-fitting black sweatshirt and jeans, was tall and slim, too. In fact they looked like graduate students from a Jack La Lanne health spa. They talked quickly and excitedly, and they had an optimism that matched her own this morning and foretold a definite sale.

They liked the area; they liked the ride up. It was much less in travel time than they expected. No problem to hop up here for a weekend. Why, they could even shoot up for an evening in the middle of the week if they wanted to. And the village... it was just as they had envisioned: one main street, small mom and pop stores, little or no traffic, laid-back and quiet.

"Like a Norman Rockwell painting," Toby said.

"We call it economic depression up here," Cynthia said. They laughed, but they were laughing at everything. She had never seen such a giggly, middle-aged couple, and she found herself feeling somewhat jealous of the joy they took in each other. She wondered whether or not Stephen and she would have that kind of closeness when they were the Bloomfields' age, especially since they didn't have it now.

On the way out she wanted to stop at Jason's office and make some comment about the meeting they were having, but the Bloomfields were so anxious for her to take them to the property, she couldn't hesitate for a moment. As soon as the Rose Hill House came into view, Toby Bloomfield became animated. She clapped her hands and moved about in the car like a child brought to Disneyland for the first time. Her husband was a little embarrassed by her excitement, but he was obviously just as pleased himself by what they were seeing. They went about the place like people who had found their long-lost home. Never had they expected to find anything so perfect on their first try.

"That's why we came up here so early," Toby told her. "We have other listings to examine, but now I don't know if we'll even bother."

Mrs. Marshall greeted them at the door. Ben Hillerman was still living there, but he was confined to his room on the bottom floor. They went through the remainder of the house—the large kitchen and big dining room, the two sitting rooms and the large living room with the fieldstone fireplace that took up an entire wall. They checked the upstairs rooms and even climbed up the small attic ladder to take a peek into the area that now housed some old furniture, knickknacks and family heirlooms.

"I wouldn't be surprised if Ralph Hillerman left some of that stuff here with the house." Cynthia caught the way the Bloomfields looked at each other when she said that and she thought, "frosting on the cake," an old trick she learned from her father—hold back on some goody until the end and then just slip it in casually.

Afterward the Bloomfields went out to walk over the grounds and look at the lake. Cynthia left them alone for a while. She knew the way houses were really sold. If you were too anxious to sell it, used too many high-pressure techniques, people were often frightened off. It was better to let her clients ease into the sale like someone easing into a hot bath. Customers usually talked themselves into something faster than she could talk them into it anyway, once the preliminaries were done. These two were well on their way toward doing it. She watched them from the kitchen window that faced the rear of the property and turned away when Mrs. Marshall came in to get something.

"How's Mr. Hillerman doing?" she asked. Patsy Marshall was a diminutive woman with gentle, kind eyes. Cynthia could understand why Ralph would be upset about losing her.

"He sleeps most of the day now. He has only two or three hours of real lucidity, although when he's lucid he has an amazing memory for details from the first half of his life. Don't ask him to remember what he did yesterday, but fifty years ago . . ."

"How sad."

Mrs. Marshall shrugged.

"Maybe it's the mind's way to remember only when you were younger, stronger and healthy. Sometimes when he drifts off I think he's better off. It's less painful than his realizing what's happening."

"I suppose you're right," Cynthia said. She started to think about how difficult it was sometimes to recall some of the happier moments of her own youth. Her thoughts were interrupted when she and Mrs. Marshall heard the old man call from his room. Cynthia went along with her to see him.

She remembered him only vaguely from her youth, but when she had seen him the last time and when she saw him now, he looked shriveled and small, his face drawn and sallow, his eyes opened too widely. It was as though he had seem the coming of his own death and was startled by what it meant. He had fallen asleep in his wheelchair, apparently waking without calling for Patsy and then getting himself into his dresser drawers, pulling out old papers, letters and documents. Most of them were scattered about; he had attacked them with vehemence, either out of anger or frustration.

"Hello there, Mr. Hillerman," Cynthia said. He looked up at her and nodded as though she had been there for days. "Looks like you had an accident, huh?" she asked, smiling. He didn't reply; he looked around the room as though just realizing where he was.

"He goes through these papers every once in a while," Mrs. Marshall said, looking up from the floor. She was on her hands and knees gathering it all together.

"What's he looking for?"

"Who knows? Something different each time probably," she said.

"Is that a newspaper clipping?" Cynthia asked, pointing to something just to her right.

"Yes."

"It looks very old."

Mrs. Marshall picked it up and studied it for a moment.

"You're right. This says 1935. Someone put it in this plastic sheet to preserve it."

"Laminated it," Cynthia said. "Otherwise it might have crumpled into nothing years ago. What is it about?" She looked at the old man because she felt the intensity of his stare while Mrs. Marshall read the article.

"News story about a murder," she said. She turned it over and then sat back on the floor. Cynthia watched her read. When she stopped and looked up at her, there was a strange expression on her face.

"What is it?"

"She was a tourist, killed right here, but..."

"Yes?"

"Well, look at the picture of this woman, the woman who was killed. Doesn't she look a lot like... like you?" Mrs. Marshall said. Cynthia reached for the clipping slowly and studied the picture. There was a very strong resemblance, strong enough to give her the chills. She looked at old man Hillerman again. This time she thought she detected a slight smile in his face.

"Makes me feel as though I lived before," Cynthia said.

"They say everyone has a twin somewhere at some time," Mrs. Marshall said. "There's yours. Or, there was yours." Cynthia nodded and looked at the article again.

"'FAMILY DISPUTE TURNS VIOLENT,'" Cynthia read, quoting the headline. She looked toward the old man to see his reaction, but his eyes were closed. "Mr. Hillerman, who was this Karla Hoffman?" she asked, but he didn't open his eyes or respond. He looked asleep. She read some more and then turned to Patsy Marshall. "According to this, the murder came as a complete surprise to everyone. No one knew the brother and sister were having difficulties, not even her husband."

"I never heard that story."

"Me, neither." She took a step toward the old man. "I wish he would talk about it. Mr. Hillerman?" He didn't even wince.

"Who knows if he'd remember anything anyway?" Mrs. Marshall said. She continued gathering the papers together to put back into the drawers. Cynthia nodded and looked at the picture again. She was more than simply fascinated with the resemblance; she was hypnotized with the look in the murdered woman's eyes. It was as though the picture came to life in her hands. She felt a great need to keep it in her possession.

"Maybe his son will remember something," Cynthia said. "If you don't mind, I'll take this and ask him about it."

"I don't care."

They heard the Bloomfields call from the front entrance. Cynthia stepped farther into the room.

"I'd appreciate it if you wouldn't say anything about this that my clients might hear. People are funny about things like this. There's a house in Glen Wild in which two people committed suicide and no realtor has been able to sell it since."

"Don't matter to me who buys this place. I'm leaving in less than a week."

"Thanks," she said. "I'd better get back to them," she added when they called for her again. She headed out, but when she reached the mirror in the hall she stopped, looked at the picture of the murdered woman, looked at herself in the mirror and shuddered. It was enough to end the run of optimism she was having because it threw a pall over the house and made the shadows that lingered in the corners look ominous. Despite what she usually told prospective clients, it was impossible to ignore the impact of the events that occurred in a house and separate them from the structure itself. It depressed her, but when she met the Bloomfields on the front porch that depression was short-lived.

"We'll take it," Sid Bloomfield said.

Reflection

SHE DECIDED not to show the article to Stephen or to Jason. She knew they would mock her interest in it. Jason, especially, would say it wasn't "Palmeresque," a term he invented to describe the way Carl Palmer's children should behave. To be fascinated with something that was so coincidental it was almost supernatural would be illogical and silly. After all, "we have an image in this community, a responsibility toward who we are and what we've accomplished." That was Jason's credo, and more and more it had become Stephen's, as well. She was disgusted with his attitude; it was almost as though they were a different breed of humanity.

Cynthia hated to be ridiculed. At times she thought Jason drew a sadistic pleasure from that fact. He had a knack for "getting her goat," as her mother used to say. Jason and she were never very close as children. Even though they were relatively close in age, they had no common interests. Her theory was that Jason skipped childhood. He was studious, a loner, precocious, and at the age of ten, already bored with childish things. She remembered him winning the science-project contest when he was only in the eighth grade. It was a county-wide contest that included older students right up through the senior year. She remembered him reading *Crime and Punishment* in the ninth grade while his classmates struggled with the novella, *The Pearl*.

Sometimes, when she was desperate about her homework, she would go to him for help. He was never really a big brother to her; he was always more like a tutor. But he didn't have the patience to be a good tutor. He couldn't understand why she would have any difficulty grasping concepts he understood instantly. Later on, when he was in college and she was finishing high school, he blamed her slower academic pace on her "female flightiness."

As long as she could remember, Jason did have a lower opinion of women. There was a distinct difference between the way he would talk to their father and the way he would talk to their mother. Her mother chose to ignore it, but even when Cynthia was a little girl she could detect the note of disdain in Jason's voice whenever it came to academic things or business.

The only girlfriend she recalled him having in high school was that Lydia Morris, a pimply-faced, chunky girl with a weird fascination with biology. Cynthia would never forget the day she came home from cheerleading practice and found the two of them in the basement dissecting a cat that had been hit by a car on their block. Lydia said they couldn't waste the opportunity. When Cynthia told her mother, though, she chased them both out and had the area disinfected. Jason never forgave her for telling on him.

He had very few friends in high school, and he participated in few extracurricular activities. He wasn't athletic or very interested in sports. He didn't even come to one basketball game to watch her as a cheerleader. Instead he ridiculed her for it, but his ridicule was subtle. He implied that that was all she was capable of doing.

After college he was different, especially when he became an executive in the firm. She always had the feeling that something had happened to him during that last year in school, something that made him take a more objective look at himself. He had matured and become stable and strong. Although he was still quite arrogant, she found she admired him for his quick business sense and his fastidious manners.

Too many of the boys she had gone with proved uncouth, coarse and narrow-minded. Jason was a true intellectual. He had become engrossed in the firm, but he never lost his love of music, theater and books. She had to admit that he had a good influence on Stephen in this respect. Even though she was often left out of their conversations because she wasn't familiar with the authors or the music they discussed, she welcomed the change in conversation. It was when they could be most interesting.

At dinner parties they often commanded the attention of the gathering. They seemed to have the best political insights, the clearest perception of the significances in the manifestations on Wall Street and the most awareness of the latest current events. What one didn't know, the other provided. What was it Sally Rothman said? "For you it must be like being escorted by monarchs."

They did move like princes through this community. Other businessmen had taken to asking their advice on various matters. She was sure she didn't know half the extent of their investments in local and state projects. And whenever she discovered something they were doing and then confronted Stephen about it, he would say, "But, Cynthia, I thought we told you about that" or "But, Cynthia, you were there when we were discussing it." For all she knew she might have been. She had probably tuned herself out as she had done so many times before. At the end she would think, why should I care anyway? It's not my passion. Let them become entrepreneurs or whatever.

She enjoyed what she was doing: traveling the countryside, looking for and at new listings, meeting people and learning about their lives, their histories, the histories of their homes and their property. For her it was an ongoing saga, a never-ending soap opera of the highest quality. Whenever people called her in to sell their homes and property, they invariably felt they had to explain the reasons why they wanted to pull up roots. Some people improved their lot in life, but many fled their failures.

When Cynthia returned to her office, she put Jody Dobbs right on the papers for the Rose Hill House. The Bloomfields wanted to take her to lunch, but she pretended she had a meeting with another client. The discovery of the old newspaper clipping and the photograph of the victim had put her into a very serious mood. The Bloomfields were too flighty. Suddenly she resented wealthy people who could purchase a property as large as the Rose Hill House as quickly and as easily as most people purchased toothpaste.

But it wasn't them so much as it was herself. She was fascinated with the newspaper picture, fascinated with the face of Karla Hoffman. As she studied it in the privacy of her office, she saw more and more of a resemblance. Was her imagination running away with itself or were all the similarities there? How could this be? How could two people from two entirely different backgrounds look so much alike? Was it a toss of the genes, a coincidental combination?

And suppose that were true—it was only a coincidence. Why did she have such a deep, overriding affinity for this long dead woman? She couldn't deny what she felt, and she couldn't flee from it as people could flee from their properties. The more she stared at the amazingly identical face, the more she felt it was telling her something. But what... what?

She looked up quickly at the knock on her door. "Yes?"

"Congratulations," Stephen said. "Judy just told us about your sale."

She put the article under some papers on her desk and sat back in her chair. He stood just inside the doorway. She had forgotten what he had worn this morning, the light blue sports jacket and slacks with his shirt opened at the collar. He looked radiantly masculine and confident, but at this moment, without really understanding why, she hated him for it.

"Thank you. I guess it pays to be optimistic sometimes," she added. If he understood her implication, he ignored it.

"What did Ralph Hillerman have to say? I know he wasn't very optimistic about it."

"Oh my God. I forgot to call him."

"What?"

"I... I just forgot to call him," she said. She sat forward, surprised herself at such a major oversight. She looked at the papers that covered the old news article and realized that it was the story and the picture that had done this to her. It had had the effect of taking her out of reality, out of the present. She looked up at Stephen, who wore this annoyingly amused look on his face, and for a moment she considered telling him about the article. But she was afraid he would turn it around and use it as an example of how important it was to follow a prescribed procedure. That was Jason's new kick these days: following procedures. For all she knew he probably lived his personal life the same way, even brushing his teeth the exact same time every morning. She had told them "following procedures" would stifle her creativity, and Jason had laughed.

"What can be creative about selling real estate?" he had said, and she had reddened, not because he had belittled what she did but because Stephen hadn't come to her defense, as she had expected he would.

"I can't believe this. Wait until Jason hears about it. Talk about dizzy women," Stephen said. He hadn't closed her office door behind him, and she was sure Judy Dobbs was listening keenly to every word. Before the day was over every secretary in the building would know about it.

"Wait a minute," she said, straightening up quickly. "I know why I got distracted. What's this talk about Florida condos?"

"It's a project Jason's been developing... something called time-sharing."

"I know what time-sharing is. What I want to know is how come nobody thought to tell me about it. I thought I had something to do with the real estate end of this agency."

"Well, it isn't exactly real estate the way you think of it, Cynthia. It's more of a business venture."

"A business venture in real estate. It means the same thing, Stephen. I resent not being told about it."

"Sorry. I'll speak to Jason about it, and we'll have a meeting. Nothing's been confirmed yet."

"I had to hear about it from my secretary," she said, lowering her voice.

"Okay, okay, I said I was sorry. You'd better call Ralph Hillerman," he added, backing out. He looked as if he was in a hurry.

"Where are you going now?"

"Jason and I have a lunch meeting with some people over at the racetrack."

"Did it ever occur to you that I might want to come along?"

"Do you?"

"No, not this time, but you could have asked."

"You're right. I've just been going at it so hot and heavy and I . . ."

"Well, maybe you ought to pause for a while, Stephen, and think more about us." She put her hand on the papers covering the newspaper article. Maybe she should show it to him, she thought; maybe he would stay with her and talk about it.

"All right. We'll go to dinner tonight. To Dede's. You love their lobster." He started to close her door behind him.

"Just the two of us!" she said before it closed. Then she pulled the article out from under the papers and looked at the picture again. It reminded her about Ralph Hillerman this time, so she made the call. He was absolutely ecstatic.

"Was my father any problem?" he asked.

"No. They didn't even see him," she said, and then thought about the article and the picture before her. The face stared up at her with an eerie expectation. "What are you doing right now?" she asked.

"Doing? I was on my way to lunch in Liberty."

"You owe me one," she said. "Can you pick me up?"

"Really? Sure. I'll be there in fifteen minutes."

"All right," she said.

After she hung up she sat back and thought for a moment. Something was bothering her about the old news story, and it was more than the uncanny likeness between her and the victim, Karla Hoffman. Some detail...some fact...she looked at the article again and read it for the fourth time since she had taken it from Mrs. Marshall.

"Yes," she said, the heat coming into her face, "that's it." She sat back and stared at her closed office door.

Karla Hoffman had been thirty years old when she was murdered, the same age Cynthia was now.

2

RALPH HILLERMAN WAS one of those men who would look as if he was in his late fifties until he was about seventy-five, when his true age would begin to show. He was sixty-four now, but he was a vigorous and active sixty-four. Considering that his father had still been driving a car when he was eighty-six, Ralph Hillerman was a good example of the importance of genes. He had been running his own heating-oil business for the past thirty-five years, and he had built it into a rather successful enterprise. He had three children, all college graduates and professionals: two lawyers and one dentist. He and his wife lived in a large two-story stone-faced house on Pine Hill Drive in South Fallsburg, one of the more expensive neighborhoods in the township.

Cynthia had known him all her life. She remembered that her father had liked him because he thought he was a clever businessman, serious-minded and shrewd. He was a pleasant enough man, polite and soft of manner. Like her father,

Ralph Hillerman had an air of respectability about him. He was always dressed in a jacket and a tie and always cleanly shaven. Although Cynthia had never been to his house, she had heard that his wife was meticulous and even now spent a large part of her day cleaning and polishing. With all their money, they never hired a housekeeper, even when the children were all there.

"My wife would only clean up after her," he told Cynthia once. He joked about it, but it was obvious to Cynthia that Ralph Hillerman's wife had a strong influence on him. He kept his office neat and clean, and although he drove an eight-year-old car, it looked practically brand-new. She loved getting into it. The cloth seats were spotless, and the inside of the car carried the scent of an expensive men's cologne.

"I can't believe the good luck," Ralph said after they pulled away from the Palmer Agency. Cynthia had gone out to wait for him. Their building was still surrounded by undeveloped land and the fall colors were at their peak. Besides that, they were experiencing some of the famous Indian summer for which this part of the Catskills was famous. Mornings were brisk and cool, but the afternoons warmed the day into a kinship with the summer past. At night the temperatures dropped again, but usually remained ten degrees or so above freezing. In the morning the heavy dew would make the grass glisten as though covered with ice.

To Cynthia this was the best time of the year to advertise and sell a house and property. The area was deceptively beautiful because it was quiet and pretty. The summer tourist season was over, and any newcomer wouldn't be as aware of the way the area changed during the busy resort months. Streets were sparsely traveled; stores looked quaint and quiet; nature looked unabused. There was a picturesque, storybook quality to the area that recommended it to prospective real estate customers.

"I told my wife," Ralph went on, "that the Rose Hill House would probably end up like so many of the other old tourist places, an eventual eyesore."

Cynthia smiled. She hadn't been able to get a word in. The sale had made him ebullient, bringing even more color into his healthy-looking crimson cheeks. His robustness was infectious, and she was able to put aside her heavy thoughts for a moment.

"I can't envision the Rose Hill House an eyesore."

"Oh, believe me, it wouldn't take long. We've already lost control of a good part of the grounds. I don't know if you're old enough to remember how my father kept that place. If the sun didn't go down he'd never stop. Thank God he can't realize how bad it has become." He paused and looked at her.

"Heck, I'm goin' on and on here, and I really haven't properly thanked you. You're a damn good businesswoman, Cynthia, damn good."

"Thank you, but this was one of those times the product sold itself. It just happened to be what these people were looking for."

"You're modest, but I know you had a lot to do with hooking them."

She laughed, and a few minutes later they pulled into Liberty, one of the busier villages in the county. Because of the fine weather, there were more people than usual on the streets. She felt a liveliness in the air, and she realized she was proud of herself for what she had done. It was an accomplishment.

Ralph took her to Chucky's, a restaurant on Main Street. It was a small place, but it was well-known for its pot roast sandwich. However, Cynthia wasn't very interested in food. She ordered a salad and a club soda. She had always had a slim, attractive figure with a narrow waist and hips. Her posture and her air of confidence gave her a model's elegance. Some people, especially envious women, characterized her demeanor as arrogant, part of what Jason called being Palmeresque.

As soon as they had ordered, Ralph wanted to know all about the Bloomfields. Cynthia had expected that. It was part of her theory about the sale of houses. Owners who weren't in desperate financial straits acted as though they were handing one of their children over to a new family. In their own minds they were trying to imagine how this new family would fit in their surroundings. Some people wore their homes like clothing; it was difficult to think of someone else being warmed and sheltered in it.

"Well, they don't sound like your typical rooming-house owners," Ralph concluded. "They'll probably turn the place into a Club Med."

Cynthia laughed.

"Oh, I don't know, Ralph. You really can't tell about some people." He grunted, but he was convinced his own predictions would come true. Cynthia thought she would take advantage of the pause in the conversation. She told him about the mess his father had made with the papers in his room and the discovery of the newspaper article.

"He had that? I didn't think my mother permitted any copies to be in the house. I never saw it—that's for sure."

"Why not?"

"It was a forbidden story. I was just a teenager when it happened, but I remember my mother putting the fear of God in me about it. It worked because I pushed it out of my thoughts all these years."

"Why did she do that?"

"Why?" He sat back and smiled as though he could see it all before him. She envied the obviously good memories. "We were in the heyday of good seasons then. Our reputation was great. The grounds were gorgeous; my mother was a fabulous cook, and the house was kept spick-and-span. Don't forget the railroad was encouraging tourism in the area to stimulate its passenger business. My father was even talking about another expansion. You know," he said, sitting forward, "I often think we might have become a major Catskill resort like the Concord or Grossingers, if we'd had the right capital investment and some of the luck."

"Maybe you should have stayed with it."

"Naw, naw, I could see the future. I knew what was coming."

He was quiet for a moment, and she wondered if that were true—if he had been able to foresee and predict. It made her think of the story again.

"But getting back to this news article. Your mother wanted you to forget it?"

"People are funny about things like that. You know what I mean. What's that place you told me no one can sell because of the double suicide that occurred in it?"

"The Martin house."

"Right, right. Well, you can imagine what a brother murdering his sister at our place would do to the reputation of the Rose Hill House. We weren't to blame of course; but you do get tainted." He smiled and then laughed.

"What's so funny?"

"My grandmother, my father's mother, was still alive then. She was from Hungary and always talked about the gypsies and the evil eye and that sort of thing. She told me if you talked about the dead, especially those who died violent deaths, you could stir up their spirits. Anyway, any mention or even the vaguest reference to the murder by anyone in the Rose Hill House was taboo, worse than a string of four-letter words. I said something about it once to a kid, son of a tourist family, years later, and it got back to my mother. She put my father on me, and he beat the livin' bejesus out of me. I was about seventeen at the time, too. My father was a strong man. Why, when he got mad..."

"But you're not afraid to talk about it now, are you?"

"No. I just don't remember that much anymore. Honest. I guess I did what they call repression. After what my grandmother had told me, I usta have nightmares about it once in a while." He smiled at the memory and sat forward. "What did the Bloomfields have to say about it? How did they react?"

"They don't know about it. I told Mrs. Marshall not to say anything, either, and she said she wouldn't."

"Oh." He thought a moment. "Then maybe we shouldn't rile it all up again. At least not until the sale is finalized."

He bit down softly on his lower lip, as though to prevent himself from uttering another word, and she felt a terrible sense of disappointment.

"You're right, but I honestly believe if these people knew about it they'd think it was more reason to buy the house. They're intrigued with its history; they think it has character. Stories like this one are fascinating to people nowadays."

"I'm sure they are."

"There's no reason why we can't talk about it. As much of it as you can remember, that is."

"I suppose not. What do you want to know?"

She pulled the news clipping from her pocketbook.

"I kept this. I hope you don't mind."

"My, you are interested, aren't you? What makes an old story like this one so special? Turn on your television set, pick up a newspaper tomorrow...murders like that one happen every hour on the hour these days."

"I guess you don't remember what Karla Hoffman looked like, do you?"

"No. I didn't pay much attention to the adult guests in those days and as I said..."

She pushed the clipping across the table, with the photo facing up. He looked at it and then took it into his hands to inspect it even closer. Then he looked at Cynthia and smiled with a slight nod.

"Think she looks like you, is that it?"

"Doesn't she?"

He compared her to the picture again and shrugged.

"There's quite a resemblance, but your family background and hers don't..."

"No, there's no possibility of our being related. At least I don't see how there could be."

"They say we all came from the same parents." His smile widened, but she could see that the comparison of faces didn't strike him as being a very significant fact. "So, what about it, Cynthia? She looks like you. What does that mean?"

"I don't know exactly." She thought for a moment. When someone as fatherly as Ralph Hillerman questioned her now, she did wonder if she were acting silly. "I just have this... this need to know more about her and what happened," she said slowly, like one in a dream. "Don't laugh," she added, "but it's almost... mystical."

"I'll be damned." He sat back, the half smile on his face again as he considered the picture more seriously. She could see he was trying to revive his memories. The waitress brought them their food before he spoke, but she could almost hear his thoughts—he was wondering if she weren't a little wacko.

"Tell me what you remember. Please."

"Well, if I strain my memory..." He looked at the article again. "No one knew there was any such animosity between them. They seemed like a quiet threesome."

"Threesome?"

"Her brother always came along with them. But there wasn't anything wrong with that. My mother wouldn't have rented them rooms if she suspected any problems. Believe me. Actually, now that I recall, they were quite respectable. They owned a small but growing clothing factory in the city. Not a sweatshop, a quality place."

"So what went wrong? What happened?"

"I don't really know. One night there was some argument and the knifing. I slept through the whole thing. I didn't even hear the police arrive or anything."

He took a large bite of his sandwich. Cynthia had been eating her salad as she listened to him attentively, but she took the opportunity to finish what more of it she wanted when he began to eat. She was a great deal hungrier for the remainder of the story. He sat back, thinking again.

"I guess of the three of them, my mother liked the brother the least. She got that from my grandmother who had a way of sizing up the guests. Like a gypsy," he added, "with some kind of crystal ball, she would make her pronouncements about people, her predictions."

"Do you think it's possible that her husband might still be alive?"

"Couldn't tell you that. Like I said, once it was over, the story was drummed out of my consciousness. I wouldn't ask any questions about them. Once the excitement ended I lost interest anyway."

"He'd be about seventy-five," Cynthia said, looking at the article.

"It's certainly possible."

"But you don't remember much about Karla?"

"No, not really. I certainly never connected her face with yours until you put the picture right in front of me. I mean we're talking fifty years ago."

"I know," she said. He continued to eat his sandwich, but he ate a little faster. Cynthia looked as though she might cry. "Is there anyone else around who might remember her?" she asked quickly.

"What are you after here?"

"I don't know for sure, but I do know I have to satisfy that need to know as much about her as I can." He stopped chewing and stared at her. "Indulge me, Ralph. Then you won't have to give me a bonus for selling your property so quickly. This will be my bonus." He laughed.

"All right. Let's see. Sure. Sammy Segar was a policeman then. He's still around, lives with his son and daughter-in-law in Devine Corners. He'd a hafta have been in on it. I suppose you go see him; he loves to talk about the old times."

"Thanks. Do you mind if I keep the article?"

"No. That's okay. I've got a number of old things up there of some value, I suppose. My mother had a lot of great old pictures. What I'll do is go up to the house during the next few days and sort through some of the stuff. I'll probably donate a good deal of it to the county museum in Hurleyville." He started to eat again and stopped. "Hey now, there's a place for you to go."

"The county museum? But this wasn't a famous case or anything."

"No, but they've got those stacks and stacks of old newspapers in their library. They go back to the 1800s."

"Of course," she said. "And I'm friendly with Miss Weintraub, the county historian. I should have thought of that."

"Surprised you didn't. Maybe you're not as hot over this as you think you are."

"Oh, I'm hot enough about it," she said, smiling. She put the article back into her pocketbook. "I wonder," she said, "if, during his more clear-minded moments, your father would remember much about the whole affair. For a moment there today, he seemed almost as though he wanted to say something."

"My guess is that even if he could remember anything, he wouldn't talk. My mother's influence is too strong, even now."

"Would you mind if I tried to talk to him about it sometime?"

"Well..." He was surprised at the anxiety in her face. "It's okay with me, but you'd better remember what my grandmother told me."

"I forgot already."

"Stirrin' up the spirits."

"Oh, yes, yes. I'll be careful about that."

"Who knows," he said, "it might be too late already."

He had to laugh emphatically to let her know he was only joking.

JASON CAME TO HER OFFICE only moments after she returned from her lunch with Ralph Hillerman. She suspected that her brother had asked Judy to signal him as soon as she had come back. Cynthia didn't like to think of herself as being paranoid, but she was feeling spied upon more and more lately. Jason made great demands on the staff. They sensed his expectations and responded with the kind of loyalty that nurtured his power over them. Cynthia felt his stamp on everyone. There was an air of perfection about everything, even the smallest of tasks. Phones were always answered properly; messages were always taken accurately and correctly. She couldn't help resenting it. Sometimes she felt as though she were surrounded, deliberately kept off to the side like some poor relation, tolerated but not really respected, a shadow of Jason left to linger in a corner.

Sometimes Jason moved like a shadow. He spoke softly and carried himself with a quiet grace she often envied. Recently, however, her brother's eyes displayed an uneasiness that had attracted her interest. He seemed distracted and too thoughtful. Whenever she spoke to him she felt he was looking through her, beyond her, around her. Afterward she would be left with an eerie, cold feeling, as though she had just had a conversation with a corpse.

As usual Jason was impeccably dressed in his coordinated Pierre Cardin brown jacket, tie, slacks and shoes. His ring, their father's ring, the flat black onyx with the diamond in the center, glittered on his fourth finger. It had been Carl Palmer's pinky ring, but Jason's hands were so much smaller than his father's.

Jason's hair, the same dark brown shade of Cynthia's natural color, looked as though he had stopped at his barber's for a comb-out. She suspected him of doing that occasionally anyway. Ever since she could remember, Jason was terribly concerned about his appearance and his personal possessions. While other mothers were continually after their children to pick up their things or clean up their rooms, Jason was after his mother to improve on the way his room was cleaned and his things were handled. Cynthia recalled the hours he would spend in his room organizing his socks and underwear, folding his shirts and pants and shining his shoes. He hated to see anything out of place.

Because of his fastidiousness he was often ridiculed by other students in school, but none of that seemed to matter to him or bother him. Cynthia had always admired her brother for his ability to turn off people when he wanted to or when they were somehow distasteful to him. Jason often based everything on his first impressions, and he rarely changed his opinion of someone, especially negative opinions of her friends.

Even so, they had few confrontations. He, like Stephen, shied away from doing any verbal battle with her. They usually retreated, sidestepped, apologized or rationalized. She had begun to get the feeling that they had conspired to "handle" her, secretly priding themselves on their success. It was frustrating, but she couldn't point to any one thing and pounce.

Studying the photograph and realizing the similarities between herself and Karla Hoffman had made Cynthia more aware of the similarities between herself and her brother Jason. Looking at him now, she imagined that if she didn't pluck her eyebrows, they would be like his. They had identical noses, and both of them had their mother's soft, thin mouth. Jason's cheekbones weren't as pronounced as hers and his eyes weren't set as deeply, but they often had the same look.

Their differences were underlined in the way Jason's face changed expression and in the way he held his mouth. Jason's smile was often sardonic; his thoughtful look more intense, even hypnotic. When he was angry his face was all eyes; they would widen and burn with a catlike fury. Opponents would feel they were about to be clawed, which was most ironic, for Jason was not a very physical person. He disliked men who patted and touched one another incessantly, "like adolescent boys in school locker rooms." Nothing made him cringe as much as a man putting his arm around his shoulders during a discussion. His handshake was quick and smooth; he'd slip his fingers in and out of someone's palm so fast that the person wasn't sure they had really touched. If a man held his hand too long, his shoulders would rise and he would turn away as if to say, "I refuse to look or to speak to you until you release me."

Only Stephen could violate these pet peeves of Jason's, but he didn't violate them often. Stephen was very sensitive to Jason's moods, even more sensitive than he was to hers, Cynthia thought. It bothered her, but she justified it by thinking that perhaps it was because she wasn't as finicky as Jason and didn't take out her bad moods on others the way Jason often did. Anyway, she thought, Stephen and Jason had been working together so long and were so intent on their similar purposes that it was understandable Stephen would be so in tune with Jason. She resented it only because he wasn't in tune enough with her.

"Stephen tells me that both congratulations and an apology are called for," Jason said. He closed the door softly behind him and approached her desk.

"I wish you would reverse the order of the two."

He laughed. Jason always has perfect posture, she thought, but smiled to herself recalling a vivid dream she had once. In it Jason was a peacock.

"It wasn't Stephen's fault, it was mine. We don't mean to neglect you. I was so involved in this idea that I didn't think to talk to you about it. Stupid of me because here we obviously have a resident expert when it comes to real estate," he said. He sounded sincere, but that made her even more resentful. He never lost his cool, never lost the advantage.

"You two always do such a nice job of apologizing for one another," she said. He smiled and waved his hand backward, a characteristic gesture that looked more as if he was chasing away flies than anything else. It was his way of signaling the end to a discussion of that subject. Arrogant and usually annoying, she thought.

He sat in the chair just to the right of the front of her desk and crossed his legs.

"You must tell me how you pulled off this sale. An old tourist house like the Rose Hill... it's something of an accomplishment, Cyn. Once this gets out you're going to have triple the listings."

"There's nothing to tell. The right customers came at the right time."

"False modesty? Come on. You're a Palmer. You're good at whatever you do. Dad would be proud of you."

"Bullshit, Jason. He'd be shocked. He never had any faith in my business abilities."

Jason laughed.

"Well, Dad had some old-fashioned ideas good for his time. Anyway, Ralph Hillerman must be ecstatic. You took some load off his shoulders. I was thinking about contacting him about a partnership we want to form involving a parking lot in Manhattan. Maybe he'll be interested now. It looks like a good investment."

"What parking lot? Where?"

"Oh hell, there I go again. Carl Samuels wrote me about this. I'll show you his letter. If you have time later, come in and peruse that and the prospectus on this time-sharing investment in Florida. I'd like to hear your impressions."

She let herself relax because he did sound sincere. Suddenly that saddened her, however. Why was it that her brother could be more understanding than her husband when it came to her feelings? They weren't as intimate. It made her wonder about the bond of family and the way Jason always talked about being Palmeresque. Maybe there was something to it; maybe there were facets of herself that she never realized. Maybe she was more like Jason than she cared to be. Or maybe . . . maybe he was more like her.

These thoughts brought her quickly back to Karla Hoffman. If she had had such a dramatic reaction when she was confronted with the picture of the murdered woman, what would be Jason's reaction? Impulsively she pulled the old news clipping from her purse.

"I want to show you something I found up at the Rose Hill House. Old man Hillerman had thrown his papers out, and the woman who takes care of him handed me this."

She put it on her desk, and he leaned forward to pick it up. He read it and looked at the picture. She watched his face as he did so, but she detected very little change in his expression. Finally he shrugged and put it back on her desk.

Reflection

"Obviously you are impressed with the physical resemblance."

"Aren't you?"

"I never told you this, but when I was in college I met a girl who looked a lot like you. Actually I got to know her well. It was during my senior year. Of course, she wasn't at all like you. She was what people today refer to as an 'airhead,'" Jason said. She saw a new look in his eyes, a cross between anger and hurt. "But the physical resemblance was strong."

"Are you saying I have a common face? Because the same would apply to you."

"No, it's not that," he said, snapping out of whatever memory made his eyes glisten. "I'm just trying to tell you that as remarkable as this might seem to you now, it's really no big deal. The world is full of people who look somewhat alike."

"I don't agree. I find it intriguing, and I want to find out more about her, more about the story."

"How you waste your time is your own business, I guess."

"Exactly."

"Did you show this to Stephen?"

"No. And I don't intend to," she added quickly. "I know what he'll say—he'll just agree with you."

"You judge him too harshly, Cyn. He's a lot more sympathetic than you think. He brags about you incessantly at meetings. Actually I find it sickening at times."

"Couldn't tell that by me," she said dryly. "Anyhow," she added putting the clipping back into her purse, "this is a private thing right now, and I'd appreciate it if you wouldn't make it the subject of one of your frequent tête-à-têtes."

"Okay. If that's the way you want it," he said, standing up. "See you later then. Congratulations on the sale. Oh," he said, stopping at the door. "Heard you're going out to dinner tonight to celebrate."

"Yes," she said, and then held her breath. If Stephen had invited him along...

"Stephen asked me to go, but I have an appointment in Middletown. I'm meeting with the key investors in the new Sandburg Mall. Might be something big in it for us."

"I'm surprised Stephen didn't worm his way out of our dinner date to go along with you."

"He mentioned it," Jason said, "but I wouldn't permit it. I don't want my sister neglected," he added, smiling. "Especially after she's made such a killing on the real estate market."

At that moment she hated him for making it sound as though he had given her her husband for the evening, out of the goodness of his heart. Did he think he had that much control? Maybe he did, Cynthia thought sadly.

"Thank you, Jason. Thank you for thinking of me," she said. It came out surprisingly sarcastic, and she thought she sounded more like Jason than herself. It only brought a wider smile to his confident face.

"That prospectus is in my office," he repeated, and left her.

She sat back and stared at the closed door. She didn't understand why, but she felt terribly frustrated when she knew she should be excited and happy. The resulting anxiety drove her back to the old news clipping and the picture of Karla Hoffman. She hadn't had it in her possession that long, but she felt as though it had become an important part of her. She was being drawn to it by more than mere curiosity. It was eerie, but fascinatingly so. Jason was wrong to brush it off so quickly.

As she studied the picture now, she thought that Karla Hoffman's expression had somehow changed. It was a ridiculous idea. She knew that. But the smile around the dead woman's eyes... was that there before?

SHE WENT to Jason's office to read the prospectus on the time-sharing investment. She wanted to be critical about it; she was in that kind of mood. But after she read it she found she couldn't be. She had to agree with him when he talked about the location, the growing population and the investments in developments, businesses, restaurants and the malls in the area. He behaved as though it was important to him that she approved, so she put aside the indignation she had felt for being ignored.

Before she left Jason's office Stephen buzzed to remind her that she had to take him to Al's Foreign Car Service Station, where he had left his 380SL.

"I have to leave early," she said. "I want to pick up some stockings and some things at the drugstore." He wasn't happy about it, but he left when she wanted to.

"Why did you have to ask Jason to go out with us?" she asked him as soon as she pulled away from the agency. He didn't respond, and when she turned to him he looked puzzled. "I thought it was important for us to be alone."

"I don't know what you're talking about, Cyn. I didn't ask him."

"He knew about it."

"I mentioned it to him, but I didn't ask him along."

"He said you did. The only reason he's not joining us is because he has some business meeting."

"He must have been teasing you."

"Don't you think that after all these years I would know when my brother is joking?"

"Well, I didn't ask him along," Stephen said emphatically. "When I see him tomorrow I'll find out what he was up to."

Reflection 61

"No," she said. "I don't want to start something. He'll realize that it was bothering me that you might have asked him."

"So?"

"Just forget it. I want to be happy. I should be happy," she added, as though she had to convince herself more than she had to convince him.

"All right. If that's what you want. It's not that important anyway." He sat back and closed his eyes.

When she looked at him she thought, Stephen is changing. He's becoming more and more like Jason. It wasn't always like this, she thought, and she remembered. She remembered Stephen when they first met, how physically vibrant he was. She laughed at the memories of their one-on-one basketball games, the way he played tennis with a racket in each hand, the time they went bowling at the Kiamesha Lanes and she threw five gutter balls.

Jason had little in common with Stephen then, and he never accompanied them anywhere. It was only after Stephen and she were engaged that Jason paid any attention to him. She thought they weren't going to get along. They were so unalike in manner and dress, and they had few, if any, common interests.

She couldn't help believing that her father's death had been the catalyst to bring Jason and Stephen together. In those days she was happy they were getting along so well. She was afraid for the business. Her father had been such a strong personality. She dared not say it, but she had real doubts that Jason could maintain the clientele her father had developed. So much of what they did depended on warm personal contact with people, and Jason was far too standoffish. He needed Stephen because Stephen was so outgoing and personable.

For her to have come between them then would have been wrong, she thought; but now she believed that Jason had taken advantage of her compassion and understanding. He began to make greater and greater demands on Stephen's time until he turned him into the same sort of workaholic.

But she couldn't help feeling pity for Jason, even though it would kill him to know it. In so many ways he had been dependent upon their father. He lived with him up until the day he died. He was there for more than fifteen years, moving in soon after their mother had died. Suddenly he was alone again, and she thought it would be cruel to cut Stephen away from him just when he needed a brother the most. So she tried to ignore the hours he spent at Jason's house, the trips that they had to take together, the long phone conversations they had on weekends or on evenings when the business end of their lives should have been put aside.

For Stephen there was something else. She was there; their marriage was there; their lives were there to be developed and enjoyed. But this was not so for Jason. What bothered her and what she knew bothered many other people was Jason's failure to develop any romantic interests. At first she thought he saw himself as above the pursuit. It was true she couldn't imagine Jason frequenting singles bars, and he had no other close male friends beside Stephen.

She suspected that his occasional weekends in the city had something to do with an affair or two, even though he never talked about it. She thought he had a need to be secretive. It was simply another one of his peculiarities. Occasionally, when he did describe a play he had seen or a place he had been to, she got the distinct impression he had been with someone else. Of course she asked Stephen about it.

"Why do you suppose he hasn't found anyone or developed a relationship?"

"Your brother's too damn particular," he said. "He's had many good opportunities to go out with nice women, but he always finds something wrong with them. Usually it has to do with their personalities or their mentalities. I've given up trying to find him someone. Remember how your Uncle Morris tried to fix him up with the mayor's secretary in Philly? He wouldn't even go on a blind date; he thought that was too juvenile."

"What does he do in New York?"

"He doesn't tell me."

She didn't believe him, but she didn't pursue it. It was like coming to a door, and knowing if you opened it, there would be something terrible behind it. Why open it if you didn't have to? Instead she accepted the fact that Jason was too particular, and she even pitied the woman he might eventually marry; but she couldn't help wishing that he would find someone to take up some of his endless energy and provide him with new interests.

She dropped Stephen off at the service station and went on to do her shopping. They had determined that they would go to dinner early because they were both feeling hungry. He said he didn't have much opportunity to eat at the track. The lunch was more talk than food, and he couldn't get what he wanted anyway.

By the time she arrived at home Stephen had gotten there before her. He greeted her at the door.

"Ralph Hillerman called."

"Oh. What did he want?"

"I don't know. I didn't speak to him. He left his name on the answering machine."

"Thanks." She was still reluctant to tell him about Karla Hoffman.

"Think it's about the house sale?"

"I don't know. I'll call him and see."

"Right. I'm going to shower and dress."

"I'll be right behind you," she said, and went into the den to call Ralph.

"I must be crazy," he said, "talking about this, but you got me thinking about it. You know how it is...once something gets stirred up in your mind...."

"What did you remember?"

"Well, in those days, makeup, cosmetics, beauticians...the whole thing was suspect to my grandmother. She thought women who tampered with their natural looks were floozies." He laughed. "And women who smoked were loose."

"So?"

"I remembered a comment she made about Karla Hoffman. I remembered it because it stuck with me for a long time after her death and the scandal. I used to spend a lot of time with my grandmother...do errands for her, talk with her."

"What did she say?"

"She said she always knew that woman would have a terrible end. She based her prediction on the fact that she had dyed her hair."

"Dyed her hair?"

"Yeah. Like you. I just thought about it when Marge asked me about you. She always wants to know how you look and what you're wearing. She thinks you should have been a model. So anyway..."

Cynthia had taken the old news clipping out of her pocketbook and placed it before her with the picture up.

"You mean Karla wasn't light haired?"

"No, no. She was a dark brunette, like you were before. Don't know why she did it. I guess people thought blondes had more fun, even in those days. Maybe she thought she was another Jean Harlow. A lot of women tried to be."

"She was a brunette and turned herself into a blonde?"

"Yeah. I don't know if that means anything important to you, but I figured I'd tell you."

"Thanks, Ralph. I'll call you after I speak to the Bloomfields again."

Her face was still flushed for a few moments after she hung up. She stood there looking at the photograph and thinking so hard that she didn't hear Stephen come to the doorway. He was wearing only a towel, but he hadn't gone into the shower yet. He studied her for a few moments before speaking.

"What is it?" he asked. She nearly jumped.

"What?" Instinctively she covered the old clipping with her hand as she turned to him.

"Something to do with the sale?"

"Oh, yes."

"Well . . . anything wrong?"

"No," she said. She didn't add anything else for a few moments. Instead she thought how it was because of Stephen, because of the way he looked at and appreciated that model on the magazine cover, that she had dyed her hair. What had been Karla Hoffman's reason? Was it what Ralph thought . . . an infatuation with a movie star? Or was she trying to rekindle the flames of her romance, too? "No, it's nothing," she said.

"Good. I was looking for the hair blower."

"Oh, it's in the blue bathroom."

"Right." He started to turn away and stopped. "Are you sure everything is okay? You look disturbed."

She started to lift her hand from the old photograph with the intention of talking about it, but it was as though her hand were glued to the document. She couldn't raise it.

"No," she said quickly. "I'm just hungry."

"Me, too." He smiled and went off.

As soon as he was gone she was able to uncover the photograph. For a moment she just stared down at it. That smile she had seen around Karla Hoffman's eyes . . . was it still there? Had she imagined it? Perhaps she was simply imposing her own feelings into the picture, projecting her own expressions into Karla Hoffman.

It gave her second thoughts. Maybe Ralph Hillerman's grandmother was right... maybe it was wrong to stir up the victims of violent death. She would think hard before she would go any further with this mania for learning all she could about the Karla Hoffman story. She put the clipping back into her purse and closed it. When she entered the bedroom, she heard Stephen singing in the shower. He hadn't done that for some time now.

Maybe it's all right, she thought. Maybe everything is a product of my idle imagination. She decided that she had better get a hold of herself and, like Jason, be more Palmeresque. It had its advantages.

She lost herself in her preparations for going out to dinner and thought of Karla Hoffman only for a fleeting moment when she had the strange sensation there was another presence in the room. She looked into her vanity mirror quickly and was surprised at the look on her own face. It was the same expression worn by Karla in the photograph.

3

IF IT WEREN'T for the fact that Stephen was so much wider in the shoulders than was Jason, Cynthia would have thought he had borrowed some of his clothes. Stephen liked brighter colors and more popular cuts and styles. He wasn't afraid to buy something "new" or try something Jason might call "too young." But when he put on this shirt, tie and jacket and presented himself, she had to take a second look. For a moment she thought he looked like a parody of her brother. Stephen even had his hairdo looking more like Jason's than his own. For a few seconds she stared dumbly.

"Like it?" He turned about like a model.

"Since when do you style your hair that way?" she asked.

"I thought I'd try it. Jason's barber says we have the same shape heads. I was with him when he went for a comb-out today, and I figured since it looks good on Jason..."

"The barber's wrong. Your face is more narrow, and your hair is thicker and fuller. I liked it the way it was."

"Really?" He gazed at himself in the mirror. "I sort of agreed with them." His voice was high and thin, like the voice of someone pleading. It was uncharacteristic and weak.

"Them? Jason approved?"

"Jason says Micky's never wrong about hair."

"Do what you want," she said, turning back to her vanity mirror. He stood there watching her. She could see him in the mirror, a hurt look on his face. She really didn't know why she sounded so harsh herself. "It's just hard to get used to something different after I've lived with the other way so long. Your hair has always been your trademark, keeping it the way it was fashionable in the fifties. Everyone always remarks about it . . . how it makes you look so young."

"Sure. I understand. I'll leave it like this for a while and see how you take to it."

"Don't just base it on my opinion."

"You're my wife. No one else's opinion is as important," he said, moving closer to her. She wanted to say Jason's opinion is, but she didn't.

"That's a new jacket, shirt and tie outfit, isn't it?" she asked as she put on her eyeliner.

"Uh-huh. How do you like it?"

"You went to Jason's tailor, didn't you?"

"Well, Jason always looks so sharp. Wherever we go together, people remark about it. It makes me feel a little inferior sometimes."

"I wouldn't have called you a slob exactly, Stephen. Your closet is filled with some very nice things, many of which I picked out for you. You used to like them."

"Oh, no question. I still do. But this is a good fit, isn't it?"

She turned and pretended to inspect it again.

"I didn't think you liked those striped shirts. I always thought Jason was a little too much on the conservative side for you, and I remember you saying button-down collars bothered you."

"They did; that's true, but maybe that was because I didn't have my shirts tailored before, like Jason does."

"Jason is simply spoiled. I don't think he has anything but designer silk shirts. I assume that's silk."

"Yeah." His smile widened.

"Suddenly matters to you, huh?"

"You've often complained that I don't take enough interest in my clothing. And don't deny that you have compared me to Jason on a number of occasions."

"Just to use as a contrast. I didn't mean for you to run out and imitate him."

"It's not that. He's got good taste. Can't fault him for it."

"No, I can't," she said, and suddenly she wondered why she was getting so upset. He did look good. She thought of something else instead. "Do you think I made a mistake with my hair?"

"Not if it makes you feel good, Cyn. Jason likes it, too."

"I don't care what Jason likes. Anyway, he didn't tell me whether or not he liked it. In fact he hasn't said one word about it, and I'll be damned if I'll ask him. I know that's what he wants me to do. He's so spoiled," she repeated.

"He told me."

"I don't care. I did it for you, or didn't you realize that?"

"Well, I...I didn't complain about your hair the way it was, did I?"

"No, but I saw how much you liked this color, so I thought I'd try it."

"It's very nice. I think I told you that."

"You could have been more...oh, what's the use," she said, turning back to the mirror. "I'm stuck with it for a while."

"Sure. It's like my new hairstyle...you've got to give it a chance. If you don't like it, you change. No harm done." He looked at his watch. "Almost ready?"

"Give me five more minutes. You did make reservations, didn't you?"

"Yep. I'll wait for you in the den," he said.

She watched him walk out of the bedroom. It's not just his new clothing, she thought. There was something about the way he held his shoulders and his head that reminded her of Jason. Stephen was never an arrogant man. There were no airs of superiority about him as there often were about Jason. His ability to get along with people of all economic levels and social backgrounds was part of what recommended him to her. She thought he was natural and spontaneous. There was a freshness about him that made people comfortable in his presence. Actually, she half expected that someday he would run for political office. He did have a politician's knack for remembering faces and names, and not only the important ones, either.

She smiled at the memory of the first time they had met. She had reluctantly accompanied her father to the Jeffersonian Dinner at the Concord Hotel. She thought she would be bored all evening, but Jason was off on one of his secret trysts in the city and she felt sorry for her father who would have to go to the dinner alone. It was the Democratic Party's annual affair to introduce its current candidates and raise money for its coffers.

At twenty-six, Stephen was campaign manager for a congressional candidate running in a Manhattan district. He had been working in an ad agency for the years immediately following college, and his work for a number of political figures had attracted some attention. She remembered her father's initial impression of him: "That young man's ambitious. He has the look of the predator. I wanna be on his side."

Fate had it that Stephen was seated at their table. His congressional candidate was at the dais. The speeches seemed long and boring to her, and the prospect of the late meal was not appetizing. She and Stephen had been involved in conversation almost immediately after the seating. When he suggested they take a break and walk through the hotel, she jumped at the suggestion. Her father nodded knowingly and approvingly when they excused themselves.

She had been graduated from college with a major in business, but she was still quite undecided as to what she wanted to do with her education and her life. For the past two years she had been working with her father and her brother at the agency, but she felt that she was more like a glorified secretary than a real part of management. She wasn't that interested in the insurance business anyway. She had been dabbling in real estate, even though no one had or cared to encourage her.

As Stephen and she walked she went on and on about this, unraveling her thoughts and feelings like someone freeing string tangled into a tight ball. The more she talked, the looser she felt. Stephen listened with interest. In fact he was such a good listener that she didn't realize how long she had been talking about herself and her family and their affairs until she looked around and saw that they had walked from the hotel lobby through the long corridors to an adjoining building.

He had put her at ease immediately. And now, when she thought about it, she realized that had been a major reason why it was so easy for her to fall in love with him. Stephen had a way of getting people to be themselves. Inhibitions fell away. They weren't together more than a few hours that first night, but she came away feeling she had known him for years. He must have sensed how much she needed someone to listen and to care.

Her mother had been dead two years. Her father was understanding, but she couldn't help feeling that he had views of women frozen in stereotype. She felt he was humoring her about her career, expecting that she would soon fall in love, marry and then drift off into the realm of oblivion so many married women inhabited.

She wanted to turn to Jason, but he was still quite wrapped up in himself and almost ignored her completely at times. Whenever he did look at her or listen to her, he had this strange, surprised look on his face as though he had just realized she was grown up, she was out of college and she was with them in the real world. Strangely enough, it took her marriage to Stephen to bring her and Jason closer together. As soon as her engagement was announced, Jason behaved as though he was finally willing to admit he had a sister. It was as though Stephen's desire to marry her had legitimized her importance, even her existence.

Sometimes she attributed this to Jason's admiration of Stephen. There was no question in her mind that Jason respected Stephen's communicative powers and outgoing personality. He wasn't jealous or resentful; it was rather more like a missing part that had been brought to the Palmers. She felt Jason appreciated her for bringing it. In those days she thought it was just Stephen's power, his salesmanship. After they had become more familiar she kidded him about his techniques. She told him he sold himself to her like an ad campaign.

"I took Propaganda 101, too, you know." He laughed, but she went on to dissect him. "You tried 'plain folks': comparing yourself to my father, a man whose most precious commodity was his own ambition. You used 'testimonial': telling me of the approval you won from your most famous clients. And then you used 'bandwagon': subtly suggesting the different women you knew who were interested in you."

"So why did you continue with me if you knew I was such a conniver?" She could see he was impressed, even a little annoyed that she was so discerning.

"I was flattered. I figured if you were trying so hard to sell yourself to me, you must think I'm very important."

"That was it?"

"I found you attractive."

"Go on. It's beginning to sound better."

"And sexy and interesting and sensitive and loving..."

"Stop, stop, you're killing me with the truth," he said, and they laughed.

How much they laughed in those days. Their relationship grew quickly. He was considerate and adoring, making her feel more like a princess than the daughter of a relatively small-town insurance salesman. Every time he came up from the city, he brought her a gift. The gifts began to get more and more expensive until he eventually bought her a diamond ring.

Her father loved the way Stephen proposed marriage. He did it through him. She had no idea he was going to say anything that night; she didn't know he had the ring in his pocket. They were all sitting in the living room. Jason had just poured her father a snifter of brandy. When she thought back to that night now, she realized that if anyone had an air of expectation, it was Jason. She always wondered if he knew what Stephen was about to say.

"Mr. Palmer," Stephen began, "I want to ask your daughter to marry me. What do you think of my chances?"

"Well," her father said. He turned the snifter around in his fingers and acted as if Stephen's question was one that took a great deal of study. Jason stood by, a wide smile on his face. Then all three men turned to her. "Cynthia is the romantic type. I wouldn't ask her until I was in the right atmosphere." Jason laughed.

"He's right," she said, her indignation showing in her brightened eyes and flushed cheeks. "So don't even think of asking me until we get to the restaurant and the candles are lit and we're alone with music in the background."

"The right song, the right food, the right amount of wine and anyone can be seduced," Jason said. His eyes were glassy, and he spoke like a man who had sold his soul. She recalled how his attitude almost put a damper on things.

"You left one thing out," Stephen said. He rescued the moment. "You have to have the right two people."

The right two people, she thought. There was Stephen in the restaurant humming "As Time Goes By" and pretending to be Humphrey Bogart in the film *Casablanca*. There was such laughter in his eyes then. She fell in love with his energy as much as with anything else about him.

But now the music was different—the rhythms were harsher; the voices were shrill. There was tension where there had never been tension before. Maybe it started the day her father had died, and she and Stephen and Jason sat in her father's living room again, sat in the long silence after all the people had left and they were alone. Both of them, her brother and Stephen, looked so small to her then. Her father had been such a presence. Without him they appeared diminished... a fleet without the mother ship. It seemed ludicrous to imagine either of them assuming what her father had been, and yet, perhaps together... it made her sadness that much greater to think of what was to come.

"Are you going to be all right?" Stephen asked, but he asked Jason, not her. She had almost responded, until she looked up and saw that his attention was on her brother.

"I'll be all right," he said. "Go home," he added, looking directly at her. It sounded like a curse; his face had become hard, his eyes narrow and piercing. He hadn't been this way when their mother died. He had been more stoical, almost indifferent, rushing from grief like a man emerging from a cold lake. He wrapped himself in his work. This time he made her feel guilty about leaving the house, leaving him alone with her father's shadows lingering in the corners. She was afraid the echo of his own thoughts would drive him mad. But Stephen disagreed.

"Jason's a great deal stronger than you know," he said, and she wondered how he knew more about her brother than she did. Was it a knowledge that only men could share about one another? Was she as incapable of understanding him as she would be if she tried to understand a creature from another planet? Sometimes Jason made her feel that way, and lately Stephen was doing the same thing.

"Cynthia, I'm starving!"

"Coming," she called, and patted her hair. The new color was doing more than change her looks; it was changing her personality. It was like that science-fiction terror story she read in which this mad hairdresser was changing the nature of the personalities of some of his customers by washing strange chemicals into their hair. After all, she did feel more aggressive and less patient, didn't she?

Maybe the color had changed her vision. The light hair shade made her eyes look bigger. Perhaps she could see more now, see the way she had been placed in a corner, especially at the agency. Judy Dobbs's expression lingered in her mind. "Oh, it's been a few weeks, Mrs. Warner," she mimicked at the mirror. Did all the secretaries and the other agents see her the same way? Was everyone in that place humoring her? She vowed to find out and do something about it, even if it meant not being Palmeresque.

Anyway, if what she suspected was true, it was Jason's fault, she thought. He had a way of making everyone else around him seem so unimportant. He used to spare Stephen, but now he was including him, as well, only poor, trusting Stephen didn't see it that way. He didn't have her vision... for all his intelligence and business acumen, he didn't have her insight when it came to people. She would have to show him; she would have to point it out for him brutally, if necessary. Only she would have to do it without becoming like Jason.

It was important, at least temporarily, to become someone else. Maybe that was why she was so eager to learn about Karla Hoffman and see so many similarities in their lives. To others it might seem like a silly infatuation with coincidences of the past, but to her it served like a form of therapy.

She studied herself in the mirror for a long moment and then turned off the vanity light. It had the effect of dropping her abruptly back into the present. She got up quickly and walked out of the bedroom.

FOR THE FIRST TIME in a long time, their conversation was solely about themselves. With just the two of them sitting at a corner table, the candlelight flickering over his face and making his eyes dazzling, she felt herself sink into the warmth of Stephen's company. The restaurant was busy, but the din of other conversations and waiters serving meals was shut out. It was as though they had dropped a curtain around themselves, and for a while they could peel back the layers of time and return to the fresher, happier moments of their lives together. Both their voices were soft. Their tone made everything, even the most mundane topics, seem exciting. They talked about things they wanted to do with the house, an upcoming vacation and... the prospect of children. He surprised her with his enthusiasm.

"I don't want it to sound as though I have every aspect of our lives planned out like some battle strategy. That makes it so mechanical, unromantic. But I would say we're coming to that point. What do you think?"

"Are you prepared to accept the full responsibilities of fatherhood, even if it means cutting back on your pursuit of an empire?"

He laughed.

"I know I deserve that. Jason is a slave driver, and his ambitions are infectious."

"That's because he has nothing else."

"Perhaps.... Where do I sign?" He reached out and took her hand. "Because there is nothing I want more than making you happy."

This was the old Stephen, she thought, considerate, devoted, loving. Maybe they could turn it around; maybe she had overestimated the effects Jason and the business were having on him and their marriage.

"I'll show you when we get home," she said. He laughed again.

Later they did make passionate love. It was good because she felt he was totally involved. Too often, even when he had shown some desire, she had sensed an aloofness about him. When she looked into his face she saw that same expression that Jason seemed to have more and more often lately—the far-off look of someone seeing beyond or through her. It was as though Stephen and he were both in some kind of hypnotic state. Perhaps they were hypnotizing each other, although as far as she could see, it was Jason who was doing all the hypnotizing.

After they made love she fell into a deep sleep and was only vaguely aware that the telephone had rung very early in the morning. It seemed more like part of a dream. But when she was fully awake and realized that Stephen had already gotten up, showered and dressed, she knew that someone had really called. She heard him in the kitchen and called to him.

"It was Jason," he told her, his face animated with excitement. "We're flying to Atlantic City. This project involving the Sandburg Mall is coming together. We were just lucky he was right on top of it."

"So why can't he handle it himself?" she asked. She sat up and pressed her knees up against her breasts.

"We're talking big money here, Cyn. Maybe half our assets."

"Then maybe you're moving too fast."

"You can say whatever you like about Jason, but one thing he doesn't do is move too fast."

"He's not infallible, Stephen."

"I know. That's why I have to go along," he said, smiling. He came over to the bed to kiss her, and she got a whiff of his cologne.

"That's not your scent," she said. "That's Jason's."

"You said you liked it."

"But I liked yours, too."

"So now I have both. A little variety never hurts. Don't wait dinner for me. Jason doesn't think we'll get back before nine or ten tonight. Oh," he said, turning in the bedroom doorway, "he said he had a message for you. He said Karla Hoffman called. Who's Karla Hoffman? He made it sound important, telling me twice not to forget to tell you."

"He said that?"

"Uh-huh."

"That bastard. He's making fun of me, that's all. It's just like him."

"You'll tell me about it when I get back."

"If he doesn't tell you first," she called behind him. After he left she phoned the office, but Jason wasn't in or he told Sally Kaufman, his secretary, to say he wasn't there. She suspected the latter, and that got her even angrier.

Because her mood of contentment was destroyed, she showered, dressed and ate some breakfast, muttering aloud like a paranoid in a mental institution the whole time. It was as though Jason had sensed her happiness and interfered. The only thing that calmed her down was that Judy Dobbs had three new prospective listings for her by the time she arrived at the office.

Ralph Hillerman had apparently done a great deal of talking during the afternoon and evening, bragging about the sale. She thought he must have made some phone calls to friends who couldn't move their properties. A fourth call came in before she left the office to inspect the new places. Travel and work took up most of her day, and it wasn't until midafternoon that she remembered she wanted to contact Clara Weintraub over at the county's historical center and museum.

"I can be over there in fifteen minutes," she told her after explaining what she wanted, "if that's not an inconvenience for you."

"Not at all," Miss Weintraub said, and added that she would do some investigating for her in the meantime. Cynthia took some shortcuts she knew. Her work as a real estate agent had taken her from one end of the county to the next, familiarizing her with all sorts of secondary roads and streets. Actually she was at the museum in less than fifteen minutes.

The building in which the museum and the historical center were housed had once been a small elementary school. Much of the structure had been rebuilt, yet it retained its old-time school styling with its light orange brick siding, its large windows and big light oak front doors. The big school bell was still out in the front. Cynthia thought the place was the perfect repository for things old and forgotten. She realized that this would be the first time she was ever in it.

Miss Weintraub greeted her at the door. The sixty-year-old retired schoolteacher had an air of history about herself. She looked like someone who had refused to cross over into modern times. Cynthia always felt she looked like and fit the role and personified the stereotype of a typical schoolmarm. She wore thick-rimmed granny glasses and kept her hair tightened into a bun behind her head. The dark gray strands were pulled back so tightly they made the skin in her forehead and temples look as though it were about to tear away. Cynthia had had her as her teacher in the fourth grade, and her image of Miss Weintraub then wasn't much different from what it was now: a spinster, her face kept bland and almost sickly white without the use of any makeup, even the use of lipstick to flesh out her worm-colored lips.

But she was a well-liked, pleasant person, commanding the same kind of respect people had for tradition and the flag. She was always, and would forever be, Miss Weintraub, even to men and women relatively close to her in age.

"The library's upstairs," she told Cynthia, and pointed to the small winding stairway. "That's where the historical society keeps its old books and old newspapers."

"Oh. I've never been here before. It's nice," Cynthia said.

Miss Weintraub smiled as though Cynthia had uttered the password. Then she started toward the stairway. The walls of the lobby were covered with old oil paintings, maps and charts. Actually Cynthia thought it looked somewhat cluttered, but she imagined that they had a space problem. The building was relatively small for a museum and a library.

"Organizing the documents is an ongoing project," Miss Weintraub said. "And I'm afraid we're not as far along as we would like." She paused and turned to Cynthia, who was right behind her on the stairway. "You have to remember that the filing and the inventory of all this is being carried out by volunteers. The county doesn't give us much of a budget. It's not important to anyone until they need something."

"Like anything else," Cynthia said. Miss Weintraub liked that. She smiled and patted her on the hand.

"Come along, my dear."

"Whatever I can find, I'll appreciate."

"I did locate one story, but I'm sure there is more. You're welcome to come back and go through the cartons. We're open Monday, Wednesday and Friday and Sunday afternoon from one to four."

"Thank you. I might just do that."

"I cleared a place for you at the table," Miss Weintraub said.

Cynthia paused to consider it. The long wooden table was covered from end to end with old papers, documents and books with faded covers. There were cartons all around, and some were even under the table. She saw that a few cartons were filled with old picture postcards. Others were filled with books and magazines. The room itself, only about a twelve by fourteen, was narrow and crowded. She saw the evidence of some organization in the books and magazines that were stacked on the shelves to her right.

"This was in the old *Republican Watchman*," Miss Weintraub said, spreading a sheet from the paper before her. "I don't know if you remember that paper."

"Yes, I do. My father used to get it in the mail," Cynthia said. She looked down at another photograph of Karla Hoffman. This one was a full figure shot and her face wasn't as clear, so the resemblance wasn't as obvious. The picture looked as if it had been taken on the Rose Hill House grounds near the gazebo. Measuring the murder victim against the height of the gazebo and a nearby lilac bush, Cynthia concluded that she and Karla were about the same height. But what struck her as more significant was the pose Karla had taken.

She had turned her head to the right, away from the eye of the camera and lifted her chin. Whenever Cynthia looked at herself in the mirror or took a picture, she often did the same thing because she believed her left profile was better. She also had a fear of developing a double chin as her mother had done, so she often lifted her head enough to tighten the skin under and around it.

It was difficult to tell much about Karla Hoffman's figure because of the baggy blouse and fluffy long skirt she wore, but Cynthia didn't think there was much difference in weight. She found a strong similarity in posture and the way she held her hands at her sides, the fingers pressed against her thighs. Cynthia thought she had a picture of herself in a photo album that was remarkably like this one. She had taken it on vacation in Canada when she and

Stephen had stayed in that quaint hotel in Niagara-on-the-Lake.

The article rehashed the same details that were in the article old man Hillerman had, only this one had a few more lines about Karla Hoffman. She was born in Brooklyn, went to public school and then went directly to work in the family's garment business. The article didn't say what kind of work she did, whether it was in management or in the factory. In the last paragraph the reporter wrote that the authorities were still trying to determine the motive for the killing. Apparently her brother said little and her husband could offer no insights.

"Does it help you any?" Miss Weintraub asked.

"Some. I don't suppose you remember hearing anything about this case, do you, Miss Weintraub?"

"No, I was too young. I don't even remember anyone talking about it. In fact there was a reporter from the *Times Herald* here a month ago doing research on famous crimes in the area. We talked about Murder Incorporated, of course, and a few other famous stories, but he didn't mention this one. I'll keep my eye out for any other papers and issues published at the time," she added, seeing Cynthia's disappointment. "If I find anything, I'll call you right away."

"Thank you so much, Miss Weintraub."

"May I ask what it's all about?"

Reflection

She considered her old schoolteacher a moment, and then she opened her pocketbook and took out the other news clipping.

"I found this at the Rose Hill House while I was showing it to some clients."

"Oh?" Miss Weintraub looked at the portrait photograph and then looked at Cynthia. "I see what piqued your interest. A remarkable likeness. No relation, I assume."

"None."

"You know," Miss Weintraub said, handing the clipping back, "I taught elementary school for nearly forty years. In those days all you needed was a two-year degree from what we called a Normal School. Imagine, 'Normal.' How could you be normal and be a teacher?" She laughed. "Anyway, I've seen hundreds of young people in my time, hundreds, and often I would think I saw amazing resemblances in children." She smiled and leaned closer to Cynthia. "I used to wonder about goings-on, if you know what I mean."

"Yes," Cynthia said, smiling.

"But I suppose there's someone, somewhere, who even looks like me, poor thing."

"Don't say that, Miss Weintraub."

"Anyway, you've made this into a little personal project, is that it?"

"Something like that, yes."

"No harm."

"I hope you're right," Cynthia said. "Thanks again."

She was pensive all the way back to her office. When she arrived, she found that there were four more new listings called in for her consideration, but her excitement about that was short-lived. Judy mentioned a message from Stephen.

"I left it on your desk, Mrs. Warner," she said. She practically sang it.

The message was simple. He and Jason weren't coming home until tomorrow. He left a phone number and sent his love. He knew he and Jason were going to do this, she thought. It wasn't the first time, but she was tired of it. She dialed the number immediately, determined to let him know how unhappy she was. The hotel operator rang their room, but neither he nor Jason was in it. She left a message for Stephen to call her at home and then she left.

When she got home she poured herself a Scotch and soda and put on a tape of the *Nutcracker*. But she hadn't listened to it for more than a minute when she realized it was the tape that Jason had bought Stephen, one of them anyway. God, he even dictates our music to us, she thought, and Stephen accepts it. He accepts everything. She put on one of her hits-of-the-year tapes, recordings that Jason despised. They sounded better than ever to her.

Then she took out the news clipping again and thought about Karla Hoffman.

Funny, she thought, bringing the picture closer to her, I didn't notice her earrings before. She got up and went to the desk. There was a magnifying glass in the top drawer. When she held it to the picture the earrings became more distinct. They looked like small gold rings with tiny pearls along the bottom. She put the magnifying glass down and thought for a moment.

Then she went right to her bedroom and to her jewelry box. They were there. Stephen had bought them for her years ago, and they were very similar. They were too similar.

It was bone chilling.

4

THE FIRST CALL was from Paula Levy.

"What I want to know," she said, "is why I have to go to the shopping market and learn about your fantastic real estate sale by overhearing a conversation between Beverly Davis and Lisa Kaufman. When they turned to me I had to pretend I knew something about it."

"You have a right to be mad," Cynthia said. "If there is anyone I should have shared it with, it was you. At least I can be sure you'd appreciate it and be happy for me. Tonight I feel that way more than ever."

"Oh? Is that a tone of female displeasure that I hear?"

"Stephen went to Atlantic City with Jason for a big-deal meeting this morning, and my secretary—you know how sweet she can be—took a message late this afternoon that he called to say he was staying over. I was waiting for my return call from him when you called."

"I see. But surely if he's with your brother, you're not worried about any hanky-panky, are you?"

"I don't know what they're up to, but I have the feeling they had this overnight stay planned out all along. They've been that way lately—two conspirators."

"Well, maybe I'm in luck. I bought two tickets for tonight's Sullivan County Dramatic Workshop production of *Sisters*, and Robert has to stay at the department store until it closes. They're doing inventory again. I swear, if he would inventory me as much as he does that store . . . you think you'd be interested in the play?"

"I don't know. I'm in the mood to stay home and get drunk."

"We can do that afterward. It's better that you get out and be around people when you feel like this, believe me. I'm speaking from years of similar experiences."

Cynthia thought for a moment. She had been pretty intense for the past twenty-four hours or so. Maybe it was a good idea for her to seek some relaxation.

"All right. You talked me into it."

"Great. Pick me up at seven-thirty and wear something seductive. We're invited to the wine and cheese party at the Holiday Club after the show. Guests of Martin Daniels, the director."

"Wait a minute," she said, but Paula had already hung up. Another conniver, she thought and laughed about it. She prepared herself a Lean Cuisine, poured herself another Scotch and soda and ate her dinner sitting at the counter and watching the news on the small television set they had in the kitchen. All the while she kept half her attention on the phone, expecting it to ring. Stephen still hadn't called by the time she was ready for her shower, so she took it with the stall door partly opened so she could hear when he called. He didn't.

Getting more and more angry about it as the minutes passed, she dried off and considered Paula's command to wear something seductive. She decided on her tight-fitting jump suit, the bright blue one that Jason always ridiculed. He called it "glorified coveralls," but any styles created during the past two decades were ridiculous to him.

Feeling even more rebellious, she slipped on her uplift bra and bikini panties. Then when she put on the jump suit, she lowered the zipper a third of the way down into her cleavage. Turning around before the full-length mirror, she could see the distinct outline of her panties and thought she presented quite an enticing appearance. It wasn't in character for her to do this, she thought, but events had driven her to it. At least that was the way she rationalized it to herself as she brushed out her hair.

In fact she was beginning to really like her hairdo now. Maybe it wasn't Stephen who had driven her to it; maybe it was something in herself, some need to bring out imprisoned feelings. She nearly giggled when she put on the wet gloss lipstick and eyeliner. When she stepped back and looked herself over, she felt a sense of feminine confidence she had rarely felt before. It made her buoyant and almost made her forget why she had been so depressed; but when the phone rang at seven-fifteen she was positive it was Stephen.

It was, but not directly. He and Jason were calling her through Jason's secretary, Sally Kaufman. For Cynthia this was insult added to injury.

"Your brother just called me, Mrs. Warner. He said your husband and he have been trying to call you for the past hour and your line's been busy."

"What? I haven't been on the phone. Not for more than an hour."

"That's what they told me," Sally said, her tone of voice revealing her incredulity.

"Well, I'll call them right now."

"You won't get them," she said quickly. "That's why he phoned. He wanted me to tell you they had to leave for an important evening meeting, and they would try to call you when they returned to the hotel later tonight."

"Why they? Why isn't Stephen trying?" she asked, blurting out her thoughts. The fifty-four-year-old secretary who had worked for Cynthia's father, too, was deadly silent. "All right, thank you," Cynthia said. "Wait a minute," she added before Sally could hang up.

"Yes?"

"Did you have any trouble getting me?"

"Pardon me?"

"When you dialed my number, how many times did you have to call?"

"Just this once, Mrs. Warner."

"Thank you," she said, sounding like a lawyer cross-examining a witness.

After she hung up Cynthia realized that she had forgotten to bring home the phone number Stephen had left when he called the office. She thought the hotel operator had said "Sands Hotel," but after she got information and was given the number she was distressed to discover that there was no one either by Stephen's name or Jason's staying at that hotel. She would have to either call Judy Dobbs or go back to the office. Calling Judy Dobbs was out. She couldn't stand the thought of letting her know any more about her marital problems. She was sure it would become tomorrow's gossip at the office if she did so. A decision against going back to the office was made for her when she noticed the time. It was already seven-thirty. She would have to rush to pick up Paula and make the eight-o'clock curtain.

Paula was out in her driveway before Cynthia brought the car to a stop.

"Sorry, but there was a mix-up with my telephone."

"Stephen called?"

"No. They called Jason's secretary who said they claimed my line was tied up. It wasn't."

"This is starting to get fascinating."

"Thanks a lot."

Paula laughed. Although she was only thirty-three, she had the looks of a woman in her early fifties. Her hair, the closest to its natural color than it had been in years, was thinner and drier than Cynthia's. She had it cut short, the strands barely reaching the base of her neck, which, Cynthia thought, emphasized the roundness in her face. Paula's constant battle with her weight problem was most evident in her face. She had long since lost the fight against a double chin and her cheeks were puffy. The dark circles constantly under her eyes had a way of announcing her moods and her energy level. They darkened considerably when she drank too much coffee, popped too many pills and smoked too many cigarettes. Paula was a heavy smoker, often holding the cigarette in the corner of her mouth and closing one eye to block out the rising smoke. It gave her a hard, tough look that Cynthia considered quite unfeminine.

But Paula freely confessed her weaknesses and her addictions. In fact she was eager to do so, feeling somehow relieved by admitting her faults.

"I should have been a Catholic," Paula told her. "I get so high from confession."

Yes, she drank and smoked too much. Yes, she craved too much sex and got little sleep. Yes, she didn't eat the right foods, and she was letting herself slip further and further; but how hard it was to do anything else.

Cynthia often wondered what drew them together. They were different in many ways, although Paula respected career goals, even idolized her for her business sense and financial independence.

"I'm such an idiot when it comes to those things," she said. "The bank issued me a rubber checkbook as a reward for having the account with the most bounce."

Cynthia had to laugh. Perhaps it was Paula's lighthearted and satirical view of things that attracted her to Paula so much, she thought. She seemed capable of taking a great deal of disappointment and unhappiness without showing the pain. Cynthia wished she could be as thick-skinned and aggressive. Paula was often witty and quite sarcastic with people who were too engrossed with themselves. In fact Cynthia was always rather nervous whenever Paula was in Jason's presence. Fortunately her friend checked her caustic wit for her sake. But sometimes she wished she didn't. Jason could use a good verbal whiplashing from time to time, Cynthia thought.

Because of her personality, Paula had few friends. What she really had were a number of acquaintances. Cynthia was her only true friend, but when Cynthia gave it some thought she realized she didn't have all that many real friends, either. Over the past eight years she had given herself mostly to Stephen and to her career. They knew a great many people; they probably knew as many people as any local politician, but they weren't close with any. Now that she thought of it, this was probably the biggest reason why she clung so hard to Paula's friendship. At least she had someone.

"So? Don't leave me hanging. Domestic intrigue is my speciality," Paula said. "Did you finally get to call them?"

"I couldn't."

"You? Chickened out?"

"It wasn't that. You're not going to believe this, but I left the phone number at the office, and I forgot the name of the hotel."

"Why shouldn't I believe it? It's just like you when it comes to personal things. Don't let it bother you, though. Just think how Stephen will feel when he calls later and finds you're not home. We'll stay out as late as possible just to torment him.

I can see him dialing every ten minutes and your brother saying, 'Damn if I would keep doing that.'"

Cynthia laughed at Paula's imitation of Jason—holding her head back and lowering the tone of her voice as she hit her *t*'s emphatically. It was easy to envision him sitting in the hotel room, a glass of cognac ordered from room service, his tie knot still perfect, his shoes still shining.

"To stay out as late as possible sounds like biting your nose off to spite your face."

"Not if we're enjoying ourselves, sweetheart, and I intend for us to enjoy ourselves." She almost spit out the words, and Cynthia could sense the venom beneath the surface.

"You don't sound as though it's all sweetness and light at your house. I thought you told me things were getting better between you and Robert."

"It varies from day to day. It might even be related to barometric pressure, for all I know." She lit another cigarette. "I'm beginning to wonder if I was meant to have a monogamous relationship. I think I need a harem of hunks. Robert's taking a thousand units of vitamin E a day, and he's still too pooped to pop when I want him to."

"Oh, Paula."

"What can I say, honey? I have an enlarged G-spot."

Cynthia laughed. It felt good, and she decided she had made the right choice when she agreed to go out.

They arrived at the theater only minutes before the curtain. The house was full, and Cynthia thought that an unusual number of heads turned their way when they entered to walk down the aisle. Paula had front-row seats. It made Cynthia self-conscious to see all these people looking their way, and for a moment she debated pulling up the zipper on her jump suit. But then she thought that action might draw even more attention.

There were a great many recognizable faces in the audience. Some people waved and nodded, while others pretended not to be that interested. Cynthia could see that Paula enjoyed their dramatic last-minute entrance. She stalled the trip down the aisle a few times by stopping to talk to different men. They barely had reached their seats by the time the lights were dimmed.

The theater was small, holding only 350 people, but the intimacy of the house enhanced the drama of the play and encouraged a closeness between the audience and the characters on the stage. Cynthia found herself absorbed in the story of two sisters whose lives were gradually taken over by a man who had subtly forced himself into their confidence. He made love to both and caused the older sister to despise the younger one until her jealousy turned to hate and that hate eventually motivated her murdering her. After the man had caused it all to happen, he deserted the surviving sister and left her to her sad fate.

The play was well directed, and the three leads were quite convincing. Cynthia was impressed. By the time the lights came up on the final act, she felt she had witnessed something very significant. She wanted to go off somewhere alone and ponder it, but she knew that would have to wait for a quieter time.

Paula liked the play, too, but she was moved by different things.

"I like the male lead," she said, nudging Cynthia. "That's what I call a hunk. Do you know him?"

"I don't think so," Cynthia said. "We meet so many people at the agency that sometimes it's hard to remember new faces."

"You'd know if you knew him," Paula responded.

The both of them stood up with much of the audience as the actors came out for their third and final curtain call. She hadn't noticed it during the first two curtain calls because she was so deep in thought, but the male lead, Terrence Baker, was looking directly at her. Paula caught it, too.

"He's trying to get your attention," she said. "And he's so gorgeous. Smile at him, for chrissakes."

Cynthia locked her gaze into his. He was a six-foot-two almond-skin man with ice-blue eyes and very light brown hair. He wasn't really a handsome man in the sense of a model or a movie star, but there was something attractive, even sexy about the turn of his mouth and the expression in his eyes. He had a cockiness about him that came from good stage presence and the obvious self-awareness about his power to move an audience. She thought he fed on the applause, the glow in his face growing more intense with every passing moment.

The curtain closed and the houselights came up. As soon as there was illumination, Paula began studying the play program. A number of clients from the agency shouted greetings, and some who had heard of the sale of Rose Hill House called out their congratulations. She saw Bill Workman, state assemblyman from their district. He waved emphatically, but his wife just nodded. Cynthia couldn't help smiling to herself as she recalled Jason's opinion of them. They had met them often at various affairs. Jason called Workman and his wife Mr. and Mrs. Manikin.

Damn, she thought when she realized what she was doing. Even when Jason's not here with me, I let him take over. I hear his words and see people the way he sees them.

"Great play, wasn't it?" Dr. Malisoff said as he passed by. He was the doctor Jason, Stephen and she used. Actually Stephen and she used him because Jason recommended him so enthusiastically.

"It was tremendous. I can't believe I'm in an amateur theater," she said. Dr. Malisoff smiled and looked at Paula, who was still memorizing all the biographical information about Terrence Baker.

"Playing the girls'-night-out game tonight?"

"Jason and Stephen went away on business."

"Oh." There was something in the way his smile softened that unnerved her. It was as though there was a whole story behind that "Oh." She couldn't help but wonder what sort of intimate knowledge Jason's doctor had about him. Perhaps he could take an X ray and see the size of his ego.

Other friends asked about Stephen and Jason. She responded, but she was becoming more and more paranoid about the looks, the nods and the smiles. Was it inevitable that whenever two men went off together, they would get involved with other women or do whatever illicit thing they would barely think of at home? She was happy when she and Paula escaped the theater and were back in the cool, clear outside air. Paula had been unusually quiet the whole way out, but Cynthia just noticed it because of all the attention she had been getting.

"Are you feeling all right?"

"What? Oh, yes. According to this, he just started at the First Nationwide Bank in Monticello," Paula said.

"Who?"

"Who? Terrence Baker, that's who. What do you think has been holding my attention all this time... the local artsy-fartsy types?"

"He was good."

"Good isn't the word. He has such energy. He has got to be great in bed. I bet he makes love as if he's on the stage... curtain call after curtain call after curtain call."

"Oh, Paula," Cynthia said. "Don't you think of anything else?"

"Sometimes, but I'm usually strong enough to put it right out of my mind."

They laughed and got into the car. Cynthia wasn't going to go to the wine and cheese party, despite Paula's personal invitation from the play's director; but Paula pushed the right button to convince her.

"What do you want to do instead, go home and wait by the phone like a dutiful wife?"

"You bastard."

"You know I'm right and besides, both of us know that deep down in our pelvises you want to meet that hunk just as much as I do."

"That is an absolute..."

"Truth."

"No comment," Cynthia said, but when she pulled out of the parking lot she turned in the direction of the Holiday Club. She told herself she did it because she was angry at Stephen, but as she drove on she couldn't help envisioning Terrence Baker's eyes when he looked down directly at her. They served like a beacon lighting the way.

THE HOLIDAY CLUB, a fine restaurant in the hamlet of Old Fallsburg, had a rather large size back room that the owners utilized for catered affairs. Cynthia had been there on a number of occasions, the last one being a Sullivan County Chamber of Commerce fete honoring the Palmer Agency and Stephen and Jason in particular. She recalled the way they both rose from their seats simultaneously when they were called up to the dais, each hesitating to let the other go first. Stephen, cognizant of all the eyes on them, had Jason lead the way. She could still see Stephen standing admiringly to Jason's right as Jason spoke to the group. It bothered her because she knew Stephen was a far better speaker, more personable, literary and distinguished, but conversational in tone. If he wanted to, he could have mesmerized the group and eclipsed Jason. As usual Jason sounded like a stuffed-shirt college professor lecturing his students. He had to be sure everyone knew his theories on how to expand the business community. When Stephen's turn came he simply said, "Thank you. Jason's said it all." Even that received more applause than what Jason received. Afterward

Cynthia couldn't understand why Stephen defended him.

"He's my brother," she said, "but he's such a bore at times. I'm sure they weren't expecting his philosophy of business. He's good only when he shares the center of attention with you," she added. Stephen seemed to wince at that.

"He was sharing it with me. Those were my ideas as well as his," he said. She let it pass. It wasn't worth arguing about at the time.

The Sullivan County Dramatic Workshop had hired a three-piece band to provide music during the wine and cheese party. They were playing when Paula and she arrived, but the early crowd consisted of only the tech crew and some members of the production staff. Other guests were trickling in behind them, and none of the cast had yet come. The director, Martin Daniels, met Paula and her at the entrance to the party room. He was acting as host and gave them a rather overly dramatic greeting. But Paula loved imitating the affected thespians and scooped his arm up into hers as they walked into the room. Cynthia nearly laughed aloud as she twisted him about.

"You do know my dear, dear friend, Cynthia Warner, do you not, Martin?" Paula asked, her head back, her eyes nearly shut. He nodded and smiled.

"I know the name, but I don't think we ever had the opportunity to meet."

"My goodness, man, don't you need insurance?" Paula asked. She raised her voice and he blanched.

He was about three inches shorter than Cynthia and wore his hair flat back with a part on the right side. He looked more like someone out of Karla Hoffman's age than her own. She thought he had a rather soft and effeminate face. His eyebrows were too thin, and his lips were weak looking. His handshake was indefinite, so she imagined he was one of those men who were never sure whether or not they should shake a woman's hand.

"Your play was fantastic. We couldn't have seen better on Broadway," Cynthia said, and he beamed.

"That settles it," he said. "I don't care who has my insurance. I'll cancel it and be at the Palmer Agency tomorrow."

"Actually, darling, Cynthia's in real estate. She leaves the mundane insurance business to her husband and brother."

"Real estate? Then I'll sell my house immediately," he said and Cynthia decided that despite his ostentious ways she liked him. But she couldn't help imagining how Jason would react to him. He would most certainly say something nasty about his bright blue cravat and his slick, flat hairdo. Stephen would be polite, congenial, always the politician. At least that was what she used to expect of him.

She and Paula circulated through the growing crowd, with Paula doing most of the talking. Paula had the knack to make herself feel at home most anywhere, but Cynthia began to feel more and more out of place. She didn't know many of these people, and she had little in common with those she did know. Her conversations were forced and dull, and she was about to suggest they leave when Terrence Baker arrived.

Naturally he was mobbed by his adoring supporters. As soon as he appeared in the doorway, the crowd washed toward him like some thick liquid oozing toward an opening. Paula joined right in with them, surrounding him and following him as he made his way across the room. Cynthia remained back, standing alone in the far-right corner, sipping her glass of wine and watching the activity.

She thought that Terrence Baker was in no way diminished now that he was off the stage. He had a natural stage presence and was one of those rare individuals who commanded attention no matter where he was. She thought this was what most people meant when they talked about charisma. There was a brightness and energy about him that drew people to him almost as though they fed upon him. Perhaps they did, she thought. Perhaps talking to him and touching him and merely being around him generated an excitement within them that they could carry away. She did see that some of the people he touched and greeted became more animated in the conversations with each other.

He had changed into a pair of rather tight-fitting designer jeans, a light blue, long sleeve shirt opened at the collar and a pair of tennis sneakers. He wore a gold rope chain around his neck, the brightness of which brought out the richness of his dark skin. She thought he had a slim, firm-looking torso that reminded her of the way Stephen's used to be before he stopped his vigorous exercise program and developed the same paunch that Jason carried since college.

Jason hated exercise and ridiculed joggers and health club addicts, calling them self-indulgent and narcissistic. He said they were lobotomized by Jane Fonda and the like, and he called them "Fondits," a combination of Fonda and idiots. She always expected Stephen would disagree with him about that, but he didn't. Instead he would say, "Jason has his ways," as if that explained it all.

Terrence Baker noticed her. She saw the way he looked between two people, the way his eyes traveled continually from their faces to her, the way he nodded and smiled at them, only half listening. She couldn't prevent her heart from beating rapidly when he cut himself away from the clump of thespians and moved in a direct line toward her. Paula was on the other side of the room, but she spun around as though someone had stuck her with a pin. It was like a cue for most of the others, as well, because everyone seemed interested in whoever Terrence chose for his conversations. There was an embarrassing lull in the group's chatter. Thank God, she thought when the music started again.

"Hi," he said. "Are you a critic or something?"

"Critic?" She held her half smile, tentative, insecure. "Why do you ask that?"

"You're all alone in a room full of would-be actors and the like. You didn't like the play?"

"Oh no. I loved it," she said emphatically, perhaps much too emphatically. She controlled her tone. "I don't think there was a dull moment in it."

"Great. Please don't think I was fishing for a compliment," he added quickly.

"From what I see you don't have to fish for any."

He laughed.

"I'm Terrence Baker." He extended his hand. She put hers into his, and his fingers closed hungrily, possessively. She liked the feeling; it gave her the sense of a man in pursuit, and despite what she would say to Paula, she missed that. She couldn't help remembering the way Stephen had taken her hand aggressively that first night at the Concord Hotel when they left the dining room. There wasn't any hesitation in him then. How long had it been since they had held hands in public? He was almost like Jason now, eschewing any physical contact.

"I'm Cynthia Warner."

"Hi," he said again. He held her hand for a beat or two longer than expected. "You're not part of the workshop, are you? Not even a frustrated actress?" he added suspiciously.

"How can you tell? I don't look like the dramatic type?"

He laughed again. She liked the way his eyes brightened when he did so. He tilted his head back and held his arms out, reminding her of Burt Lancaster in *Elmer Gantry*. She remembered Jean Simmons saying, "You smell like a man." There was something immediately and refreshingly masculine about Terrence Baker. He wasn't an affected, overtly dramatic person, either. His acting ability came from a natural part of him, and his success came from his ability to express it freely.

"It was the way you were standing here, apart from the others. They're a pretty close-knit group from what I can see."

"I thought you thought I was a critic."

"I tested you. If you were a critic you would have said. Critics are the most popular people at these theatrical gatherings; actors are always coming up to them, hoping for good notices."

Reflection 115

"Well, you're right on both accounts. I'm not a critic, and I'm not part of the workshop. I came with a friend who had a personal invitation from Martin Daniels."

"Good for old Marty. Sweet fellow, don't you think?" She caught his innuendo but she didn't respond, and before he could say any more he was pulled away to be introduced to other people. But even as he went he looked back at her longingly. He rolled his eyes as if to say, "Help!" She smiled and took another glass of wine from the tray as Paula approached.

"He makes a point to come directly to you," she said. "Can I call 'em or can I call 'em?"

"Don't start something, Paula. He was just being friendly."

"Pardon my French, sweetheart, but that's a lot of bullshit. I told you he was looking at you back at the theater. I have a nose for these sort of things. It's my speciality—sexual attraction. The only problem is I'm not as good at it for myself as I am for others." She looked about, put her hand to her forehead and her head back and added, "The tragedy of it all."

"Maybe we'd better get out of here before you get me into some sort of trouble," Cynthia said. She had to shake her head and laugh though.

"Are you crazy? Besides, you wouldn't have taken that second glass of wine if you didn't want to stay. Don't fight it. It's bigger than both of us. Well, on second thought, it's bigger than you."

Cynthia stopped sipping the wine abruptly as though it contained a dangerous aphrodisiac.

"For your information I took this out of nervousness."

"Sure. What did he say?"

"He said hello and asked me how I enjoyed the play."

"That's all?"

"Sorry to disappoint you."

"There'll be more. Those vultures have him surrounded right now," Paula said. Cynthia had her back to him. "But he keeps looking this way. I think he's hoping you'll turn around."

"Will you stop trying to start something. I'm happily married."

"No one can be happily married. It's a contradiction in terms. Besides," Paula said, taking on a serious expression, "maybe this is what your husband needs. You're letting him take you for granted."

For a moment Cynthia said nothing. It was as though Paula had driven right to the core of a nerve.

"I want to go."

"It's early."

"I've got to be at the office early in the morning. With Stephen and Jason both away..."

"You're making excuses," Paula said. Cynthia turned and looked at Terrence Baker, who was now looking directly at her, practically ignoring the people talking to him.

"Maybe I am," she said softly.

"Oh, go out to the bar and have a real drink. I'll join you in ten minutes. Go on, you'll be safe there. It's dead at the bar tonight."

"Paula Levy."

"Just ten more minutes."

"All right, but if you're not out in ten minutes I'm leaving you here."

Cynthia put the half-finished glass of wine down and walked out of the room. Paula was right—the bar was very quiet. There was only a couple drinking at the far end. The bar was in a room with subdued lighting. There were a half-dozen booths against the far wall and a jukebox on the far left. A television set, tuned in to a prize fight, was on a shelf behind the bar. The bartender was absorbed in the bout and didn't see her take a seat at the bar.

"Just a Perrier with lime," she said after he heard her rattle her car keys. He poured it quickly and went back to watching the fight. She sipped the bubbly water and thought about the things Paula had said. Alone with her own thoughts, she could confess to herself. She was rationalizing; Paula was right—she was afraid. Terrence Baker had struck a chord within her. She was fearful of what she felt because she was so definitely attracted to it.

"Boring, isn't it?" she heard someone say, and turned around. He was standing there; he had followed her out or...did Paula have something to do with this? she wondered. For a moment Cynthia almost couldn't talk, feeling as though he had somehow been in on her thoughts.

"Pardon?"

"The dramatic analysis...theatrical autopsies. They can go on forever—people talking about the play until it comes out of your ears. Why can't they just leave it be? It was a thing unto itself."

"I would have thought you would enjoy all the attention."

"At the risk of sounding falsely modest—after a while it gets a bit sickening. Isn't that why you left the party?"

"Actually I wanted to leave completely, but my pain-in-the-ass friend..."

"Paula?"

"So she did talk to you."

"What do you mean?"

"Don't you feel guilty being out here with all those fans of yours in there?"

"To be honest, no. Why are you trying to get rid of me?"

"To be honest..."

"Don't you just hate it when people are honest?" he said quickly. They both laughed. It had the effect of shattering the wall between them. "You know what I'd really like to do," he said, drawing closer. "I'd like to just slip away from here. What do you think of that idea?"

"Are you asking me to slip away with you?"

"That's the trouble with actors—they're not direct enough. They rely on puns, innuendos, symbolism...."

"I couldn't. First, of all, I'm married. And second..."

"Don't go into any seconds. It's enough for me to deal with the first. Now let me see...."

"No," she said, getting off the stool. "Don't even try to deal with it. I've really got to go." She hurried past him and went back into the room. His aggressiveness frightened her only because she felt herself leaning toward going off with him. Paula, talking to Martin Daniels, saw the look on her face and excused herself quickly.

"It's not a full ten minutes."

"I'm leaving, Paula. Right now," she said emphatically. Paula nodded. When they turned to exit Terrence Baker came in. For a moment Cynthia and he faced each other.

"Leaving me to the wolves?" he said.

"Somehow I bet you survive. Good night."

"Good night," Paula added, a look of longing on her face.

"You sent him out to the bar to find me, didn't you?" Cynthia asked as soon as they stepped out of the restaurant.

"Of course not. Why would I do something like that? I wouldn't give up on myself that easily, would I?" Cynthia shook her head and smiled. "Tell me what happened anyway," Paula added.

Cynthia didn't respond. They got into the car, and she started away. Paula lit a cigarette, and then Cynthia laughed.

"You know, you're dangerous to be with."

"I am not, and stop trying to imply I manipulated him in your direction. Believe me, honey, that's a man who is not going to do anything he doesn't want to do. How many men do you know like that nowadays?"

"Not many," she said, and thought about Stephen. "Not many," she repeated sadly.

STEPHEN CALLED about a half hour after she arrived at home. She had already prepared for bed and slipped under the covers, debating whether or not to read for a while. She couldn't tear her mind away from thoughts of Terrence Baker, and when the phone rang she jumped half out of guilt as well as from surprise.

"Sorry to call so late," Stephen said, and she realized he hadn't even tried to call earlier. "We just got in."

"That's all right. I just got in, too."

"Oh?"

"I went to the dramatic workshop play with Paula."

"How was it?"

"It was very good. Why did you have Jason call Sally Kaufman?"

"It was his idea when we couldn't reach you."

"I don't understand that, Stephen. The phone was in working order, and I wasn't on it the whole time you supposedly tried."

"Well, maybe Jason made an error in dialing."

"What do you mean, Jason made an error? Didn't you try yourself?"

"I was showering and he was getting the number for me, and then before he went into the shower he tried again and again...."

"Why didn't you try yourself?"

"Why is that so important?"

She thought for a moment. She wanted to be sure to phrase it just right.

"Because some things between us should involve only us, not Jason."

"Getting you on the phone?"

"All right, Stephen, forget it. What time will you be back?"

"We have an eleven-o'clock flight, and we should be there by three."

"Was it so important you stayed over?"

"We have a pretty important meeting with lawyers at nine tomorrow. This thing is looking very good. I'll tell you about it when I get back and you'll understand."

"I'm beginning to wonder if I can understand anything anymore."

"What's wrong? This isn't the first time I've gone somewhere with Jason. Did something happen at the office? Something happen with that sale of the Rose Hill?"

"No, it's not that. It's just..."

"Just what?"

"Just my time of month," she said quickly. "I'll talk to you when you're home. Good night," she added, and hung up before he could ask any more questions.

She lay there for a long time trying to understand why she was so violently angry. It wasn't because of any one thing. He was right; he had gone away with Jason before, and she didn't have this kind of reaction. Maybe she wanted him to say that he was sorry he had to be away, that even though it was only going to be for one night he still missed her. Whatever happened to that kind of intensity, that kind of hunger for each other?

She saw that kind of hunger in Terrence Baker's eyes tonight, and it had reminded her of what was missing in her life. Now Stephen's nonchalance about their separation from each other underscored it. She thought about Baker again, about the challenge in his gaze, about the way her body tingled when he was near her. She wasn't having that feeling with Stephen anymore, and it wasn't her fault. Lately something had fallen between them. Why? She wasn't sure how, but she felt sure that some way Jason was responsible.

Her thoughts went back to Karla Hoffman. She had learned so little about her and what had happened to her, and yet she felt such a strong kinship to this face in the newspapers. Before she fell asleep she developed a theory about it. Karla Hoffman waited out there, waited to be discovered, but not for herself. She waited for the opportunity to give Cynthia some essential knowledge about herself and her own future. It had to be that. It gave her the reason to go on with the historical search.

When she closed her eyes she pledged to herself that she would do it, no matter what the new knowledge might tell her.

5

WHEN CYNTHIA ARRIVED at the office the next morning, she sensed that all the secretaries had been discussing her. Sally Kaufman was at Judy's desk when she entered, and the look on their faces told her she had been the subject of their conversation. There was also a knowing look on Sandra Bernstein's face and Pat Moffit's face. She thought they all had an expression of pity and disdain. After she gave it some thought, she realized that the inner-office staff had been treating her differently for some time now.

Jason's manner has a way of rubbing off on the people with whom he has contact, she thought. These secretaries sensed just how low in his esteem she was. More and more Stephen and Jason had been leaving her out of the company's major decisions, even though legally she controlled fifty percent of the firm's value and profit. She had permitted Stephen to hold the reins of that control, but perhaps it was time for her to assert herself more forcefully, she thought. Perhaps she had been

Reflection

wrong to devote most of her energies to the real estate end of things.

No matter how successful she was with her real estate work, Jason, and now even Stephen, had a way of making her feel she was pursuing a hobby while they were pursuing serious business ventures. She was convinced that that attitude had permeated the entire Palmer Agency staff. It was true that she was never fond of the insurance business, but she had stepped back so that Stephen could find a place and an identity for himself. She was afraid that if he didn't, he would seek to return to the advertising world, where he did have some identity and self-worth. It seemed to have worked, but she now wondered if it hadn't worked too well.

She had been sensitive enough to realize that a man of Stephen's ego would suffer greatly if he thought people considered him a kept man, someone who had married into a business and had it all handed to him. Up to now she had assumed that was a major reason why he drove himself so and permitted Jason to drive him—he wanted to prove himself. It occurred to her, however, that a new irony had resulted. Instead of people sarcastically calling him "Mr. Palmer," because of her, they could very well be calling him "Mr. Palmer" because of Jason. Was he becoming Jason's kept man?

She made a mental note to bring this up with him, to discuss it fully and see what his thoughts were. There had been a time when they could be very honest and very open with each other. She hoped to be able to return to that, even if it meant he might get a little insulted.

Her schedule for the day looked crowded. She had new listings to examine and new clients to meet, but she had gotten up this morning with Karla Hoffman still very much on her mind. Maybe it was crazy to be this intense about it but she couldn't help it. She decided to put a priority on a visit with the old policeman Ralph Hillerman had mentioned at lunch, Sam Segar. She knew Ralph would be in his office by now, so she called to get the name of Segar's son-in-law and directions to the house.

"Benson, Paul Benson," Ralph told her. "He works up at the dam in Neversink, and his wife is an elementary teacher at the Tri-valley School."

"Do you think the old man will answer the phone if I call him this early in the day?"

"Oh sure. He's seventy-eight or seventy-nine but he's sharp. I haven't seen him doing it, but he told me he still drives a car. You'll like the house. It's a two-story eggshell-white structure with some of that turn-of-the-century architecture you're so fond of: eyebrow attic windows, a separate section with a spiral roof and that heavy hand-carved oak door, like the one on the Rose Hill House. They keep the place in tip-top shape. The porch floor has been redone, and the hand-carved posts look brand-new. Whenever I'm there, either Sam or his son-in-law is doing something around the place. I was there two weeks ago."

"How do I get there?"

"It's about five miles out of Loch Sheldrake. When you get to Crammer's chicken coops on the road to Devine Corners, turn down that road that goes off right and go about a half a mile. You'll see the house on the right. There's a small pond right before it. Benson has about eighty acres."

"Thanks, Ralph. I have a note that the Bloomfields have their lawyer started on the title search for the Rose Hill House. It won't be long now."

"Sounds good. Keep me posted."

Checking out her new listings, Cynthia worked out an itinerary that she estimated would bring her to Loch Sheldrake hamlet around ten o'clock. She called Sam Segar and was pleased with the vibrancy in his voice and his eagerness to meet.

"Anytime, sure," he said. "Got loads of time and no place to go. Palmer, you say?"

"Yes, sir."

"Oh, don't call me sir. Call me Sam. Your father was Carl Palmer, the insurance man?"

"Yes."

"Knew him well, knew him well. I had a policy with him back in forty-eight. Then I had a brother-in-law go into the business. That was no bargain, but with family being family..."

"I understand," she said. She had the feeling he would keep her on the phone for hours if she let him. "About ten is okay then?"

"Nine, ten, eleven, whatever you pick. Only thing I like to do is watch the six-o'clock news. I watch that fella on channel four. You know the one I mean?"

"Yes, sir. I mean, yes. I'll see you at ten," she said. "Thank you," she added quickly, and hung up. Maybe this visit would be a mistake, just a waste of time, she thought, and with all she had to do today it seemed stupid to waste time.

The intercom buzzed before she could debate it any further, and Judy announced "a Mr. Baker on line two. He wants to speak to you personally," she added, the little innuendo in her voice.

"Thank you. Hello."

"Morning."

"Surprised you're up this early," she said. "I thought actors sleep late, especially after a show and a party."

"I'm on a coffee break at my job at the bank. Acting is an avocation. So far it's only cost me time and money. I'm not even cashing in on the fringe benefits I expected," he added, and she wondered if he meant her. She didn't like being thought of that way, but she couldn't help being flattered by the pursuit. Was that what this was now?

"Maybe you should try out for a professional theater production."

"I don't have the temperament. And to tell you the truth, I can't stand rejection."

"Really?"

"You'd be surprised."

"What can I do for you?" she said, deciding to hide behind a more formal tone of voice. He laughed as though he recognized her need to do so. "You've obviously tracked me down for some reason," she added.

"Well, you know I'm relatively new to this area."

"Actually, I don't know much about you. I didn't even read the blurb on the play program," she said. She didn't mean to sound so hard, but she thought it was best to show him she hadn't demonstrated any real interest in him, no matter what Paula might have suggested.

"Well, I am. I took an apartment in Monticello at a place called Terrace Hill Gardens when I first arrived in the area, and I have been living here since."

"Nice, but overly priced as far as I'm concerned. Although there is a dearth of good apartments in this county," she added.

"My feelings exactly. That's why I'm calling you for professional reasons."

"Oh?"

"I wanted to know if you have any listings of houses that might be for rent. With an option to buy, of course."

"Actually, all my clients are interested in immediate sales."

"I see." There was a long disappointed pause that made her feel somewhat guilty.

"Maybe, just maybe, one or two of them might be frustrated enough with their failure to sell and might be interested in renting with an option to buy, but I warn you it's not going to be cheaper than the apartment you're in now, regardless of the inflated rent. There's heat and utilities and..."

"I realize that, but my thinking is I'll get more for my money, and if it's nice enough and I want to remain in the area I'll have one-up on a sale."

"Okay," she said. "I'll look into it, but I can't promise anything. Hold on and I'll have my secretary take your phone number.

"I'd rather you took it."

"As long as she has it, I have it," she said, choosing to ignore his real meaning. "I really have to be going," she added quickly. "I have a number of new listings to examine this morning."

"Sure. I heard you were a go-getter," he said. "Someone with a lot of energy. I thought if I had to put my future into someone's hands, why not someone with a lot of energy?"

What did Paula tell him? she wondered.

"You might be wise to call other agents, too," she said, "so you'll have more chances to find something."

"I'll take my chances with you," he said. She could hear the smile in his voice.

"Just hold on and I'll get my secretary," she said, and put him on hold before he could tease her with another word. She told Judy to take down his information and make a card for him. She didn't come back on the line. Instead she left the office quickly, almost as though she was fleeing from it.

She congratulated herself on her route planning because it brought her into the Loch Sheldrake area at exactly ten o'clock. One of the two houses she had visited on the way was owned by a lawyer who was upset that the house, a modest bilevel, just outside of Hurleyville, was still unsold after two and a half years. It had come to him in a foreclosure, and as far as he was concerned, it was just a drain "because I've been paying taxes on it and keeping it up so it would be presentable for a sale, but we haven't even had a real bite. Let's face it," he said, "this place is going to be harder to sell than the Rose Hill House. It's either too much for low income families or too little house for middle income families."

She thought about Terrence Baker and asked him if he would be interested in renting the house to someone.

"You'd also give him the option to buy it after a year," she said. "I only mention it because it's guaranteed income for at least a year and a potential sale." She felt a little self-conscious pursuing it so hard, but it was a result of the aggressive saleswoman in her and the need to do something to please Terrence Baker.

"I'm not happy about being a landlord," he told her, "but I might go for it if it's only a year and the party is reliable."

They settled on a fair rent to charge, and she told him she would talk to a prospective client shortly. Normally she would never bother with a rental agreement, but she rationalized it by telling herself that events just seemed to fall together, as though fate were driving her toward a closer relationship with Terrence Baker. Was it something she wanted? More importantly, was it something she could prevent?

She put the questions aside as she turned down the road toward Devine Corners and followed Ralph Hillerman's directions to the house in which Sam Segar lived. It was as Ralph had described: a classic turn-of-the-century structure, an old farmhouse, expanded, well maintained, showing evidence that the people who lived in it had an affection for it.

Cynthia had a theory that she had been developing ever since she had started real estate work—

the homes in which people lived were an extension of them, an expression of who they are and how happy or sad they are about their own lives. She often heard people say that pets, especially dogs, take on the personality of their owners. Well, for her, homes did the same thing.

Funny way to think about buildings, she thought, but she couldn't help it. What was more significant was that she was going to one of the older houses in the community to get information about Karla Hoffman. It seemed part of some overall design.

Indeed, as she stepped out of her car she had the sense that she was crossing boundaries, moving back through time, passing into another age. The world behind her went to pause like the video picture on a tape deck. It would wait for her return, wait for her to push the button to start the present moving forward again.

Sam Segar was out on the porch before she reached the front steps. The five-foot-nine- or ten-inch man had barely a stoop to his seventy-nine-year-old frame. He still had a kind of official demeanor about him, a policeman's posture, an energetic and aggressive manner of standing and walking. He stood with his hands on his hips and looked out at her through thin-rimmed prescription sunglasses. He had a healthy head of gray hair for a man of his age, and he had apparently just wet it and brushed it back. Some of the stubborn strands popped up like broken guitar strings.

His face, narrowed and lean with years, was dominated by his rather sharply outlined jawbone and protruding forehead. It diminished his soft-looking nose, the kind of nose that suggested a prizefighter, and it exaggerated the lines of his mouth because the corners were pulled down emphatically. When he smiled, though, his face brightened with personality and warmth.

"Hello there," he said. "You Cynthia?"

"Yes. It's beautiful out here. You know," she added, looking around, "I think this is one of the few roads in this county that I haven't been on for one reason or another. But the views are magnificent."

"Especially when the leaves change color. From the back porch you can see down into the valley and up the mountains over into the Roundout Valley. Come in, come in."

"I love this house," she said, stepping onto the porch and shaking his hand. His fingers were bony, but his grip was still firm and definite.

"Been in my son-in-law's family since it was built. Yep, you got your father's face. I remember him well. Now that I think of it, though, don'tcha have a brother, too?"

"Jason."

"Right, Jason. Used to be I had a handle on every family in the township, 'specially the older families." He saw the way she was looking at the house. "You want a tour of the place?"

"I'd love it," she said. "You know I'm in real estate."

"No. I thought it was insurance."

"That's the end of the business my brother and my husband manage."

"Don't say?"

He took her through the house. She had such an admiration for the colonial style in furniture, the rooms with high ceilings and the big family-style kitchens that she wondered why it was she had settled on a modern decor for her own home. Being a real estate agent, she should have found a good old house with integrity and refurbished it with style and lasting taste. But of course she had built their home before she had gotten deeply involved in real estate as a career, and at the time Stephen had such definite ideas about the house he wanted. Lately he had become so impressed with the ostentatious show of wealth.

Now that she thought about it, Jason wasn't very fond of old houses, either. Didn't he actively participate in the urban renewal venture that resulted in the destruction of so many older buildings in Woodridge? Today there were gaping holes where rehabilitated classic old structures could have stood. Thank goodness there was a growing interest in historic value and the trend was back to rehabilitation instead of removal, she thought.

"So?" Sam Segar said after they settled in the living room, a comfortable room with thick, soft-cushioned chairs and a long French Provincial-style couch. She sat on the couch, enjoying the way the cushions accepted her. "You mentioned something about an old murder?"

"Yes. I'm tracing down a story I came across while selling the Rose Hill House."

"Sold it, you say?"

"Yes." She smiled.

"That's quite a house to sell. I met my wife there, you know."

"Is that right?"

"Uh-huh. In 1928. We got married about a year later. She came up from Brooklyn with her parents and stayed at the Rose Hill House for a few weeks every summer. They had relatives here. She had an uncle in Mountaindale who was a doctor, Dr. Oberman. Way before your time. Good doctor, though. Made house calls any time of the day or night. He was one of the first to have a car. Just a stick for a steering wheel, you know. I was just a kid, but..."

"Anyway," she said, interrupting him as softly as she could, "this murder took place there."

"Where? Oh, the Rose Hill House. Oh," he said. "You must be referring to that brother-sister deal."

"Yes." Her face lit up, seeing that he had the story firmly in his memory. "Her name was Karla Hoffman. Here's an article I found about it up at the Rose Hill House," she said, and got up to give it to him.

"Yeah, I remember this. It was one of the first murder cases I was ever involved with. We didn't have fancy detectives in those days. Not like they have now. There was me and Louis Neselwitz and Buzz Sussman and a guy from the county came down... I forgot his name, and that state cop... name of an animal... Colt, that's it. Something Colt."

She wondered why he didn't say anything about the picture.

"People say I look like her," she said. He studied the picture and then looked at her.

"Yeah, there's some similarity here, but if I remember her right, you're a lot prettier than she was, though," he said, but she suspected he was just being charming.

"Did you know her husband or her brother before the murder?"

"Naw. They were tourists. I mighta seen 'em around from time to time in town, but I didn't know 'em or remember 'em for any reason. I remember how upset Tillie Hillerman was," he said, sitting back, "and how important it was, not only for the Hillermans but for other resort people that we play down the story."

"What did you think of the brother after you had arrested him?"

"Very odd." He stared ahead for a long moment. She feared that he had lost his train of thought, but he shook his head and leaned forward as though to impart some secret detail. "After he killed her, he had Tillie Hillerman phone us. She said he came down to the kitchen, acting very politely, and said something like 'Please call the police. I'm afraid I've killed my sister.' Can you imagine that? He didn't try to get away or cover it up or anything. As I recall, he didn't even want to get a lawyer to defend him."

"And what about her husband? How did he take it?"

"Weird, too, I thought. He didn't go after his brother-in-law for doin' it. In fact he acted as though he felt sorry for him, more than anything else."

"Did he see it happen?"

"No. At least he said he didn't. He came upon the scene and remained with his wife's body and his brother-in-law until we got up there. You know, now that I think about it, I remember that he was the one who got his brother-in-law a lawyer. I can't remember who that was because it was someone from out of town, but I remember Harry Luddington talking about it. He was district attorney then, and he said he thought that both of them were as queer as a two-dollar bill."

"Why would he be so concerned about his brother-in-law after he had killed his wife?"

"Don't know."

"Ralph Hillerman told me his mother didn't like the brother very much," she said.

"I can understand that. He gave me the creeps."

"Why?"

"He was the kind that makes you feel inferior, even though he was the one bein' locked up for murder."

"Did he ever say why he killed her?"

"Lost his temper. That's all he would say. Harry thought he was trying to act crazy so he could get off."

"Do you remember what he looked like?"

"I don't remember him that well. I suppose they looked alike, him and his sister."

"Did anyone suspect that her husband might have been the one to do the stabbing?"

"Why should they suspect that? The brother confessed." He thought for a moment. "Maybe he was crazy. It wasn't anything anyone would plan out. Why plan out a murder you're going to confess to right afterward?"

"Open and shut case?"

"Yep." He handed the article back to her, and then he sat back, a smile coming to his face.

"What is it? You remember something else, something funny?"

"Well, it's one of those silly, scary things. Nobody took any stock in it. I remember it because of the way Ben Hillerman told it to me. Boy, he had this look on his face," he said, recalling the scene. He shook his head. "We were down at the station, you know. That's when the station was a part of what's now the Union Bank Building. We just had a part of the downstairs in those days," he said, and paused as though he had lost himself in the recollection.

"What did he tell you?"

"Huh? Oh," Sam Segar said, leaning toward her. "He pulled me to the side. He grabbed my arm, you know," he said, grabbing her arm for emphasis, "and he says, 'Sammy, Sammy, she told me this was going to happen.' I said, 'Who told you that, Ben?' He was really upset, the murder happening right in the midst of the season and all. He says Karla Hoffman. 'She was sittin' on the front porch that mornin', just starin' ahead, and I happened to be out there and she says . . . like someone makin' a prediction . . . I'm going to die soon.' Just like that. Can you imagine such nonsense? He said it shook him up, but he didn't think that much about it afterward; he didn't even tell Tillie until after the murder. Then she told him what I told him."

"What was that?"

"He imagined it. What else could it have been? No one's got that kind of power, not really," Sam Segar said, and sat back, contented with his own conclusion.

BY THE TIME Cynthia got back to the office, Stephen and Jason had arrived, but Stephen had gone out again to meet with some bankers. She went directly to Jason's office once she learned that. He was working with Sally Kaufman, but he stopped the moment she entered. Dressed in a camel-colored sports jacket, a light brown sweater with a coordinating tie and a pair of slacks, he looked Ivy League.

"Stephen was disappointed you weren't here when we arrived," he said quickly. How well they protect each other, she thought.

"I have a slew of new listings to check out."

"So I hear, so I hear."

She looked at Sally Kaufman, who looked away. Cynthia imagined that she had filled him in on everything that transpired since his absence, no matter how small or how insignificant it might seem. She almost felt spied upon. Had he been given a log of her phone calls? Would he ask her about Terrence Baker?

"I would like to talk to you privately for a moment, Jason," she said, and deliberately glared at Sally. For some reason her loyalty to Jason was annoying now, even though she knew that she, herself, would want such a dedicated secretary.

"I'll be right out front when you want me," Sally said, and sauntered past, indignation showing despite her attempt to look undaunted. The moment the door closed Jason sat forward, spinning his chair so he could look straight at her. His eyes brightened with that familiar fire, the fire she knew would burn in her own when she was annoyed.

"What is it?"

"Why did you tell Stephen about Karla Hoffman?"

"Who?"

"Karla Hoffman, Karla Hoffman. Don't play the innocent now, Jason," she said. She went to the chair in front of his desk and sat down. He was such an actor, she thought as she watched him go through the process of remembering.

"Oh, you mean that murdered girl, the picture in the old newspaper, the girl who looks like you," he said. He had laughter around his eyes now.

"You knew that was who I meant. I told you I didn't want Stephen to know. I thought you said you respected that and you wouldn't say anything about it."

"I wasn't going to. To tell you the truth I put it out of my mind as soon as I left your office. You think with all I have to do around here I'm going to give any thought to some old news story just because the woman happened to look something like you? Really, Cynthia..."

"But you told him. I know you did."

"When he asked me about her, I told him what I knew. I figured since he already knew...."

"He didn't know anything, Jason."

"Look, what's the point of all this? So he knows? So what? I don't understand why it's so important anyway. Don't you have more serious things to think about? You're a successful businesswoman now, and we're running this multimillion-dollar operation and..."

"I don't need you to lecture me on how I should spend my time, Jason." She felt her face redden. She didn't want to get this angry; she wanted to show the same kind of control that Jason always had. His ability to stay cool gave him an advantage over people. She recalled how easy it was for him to frustrate their parents by simply giving them that unemotional, blank look whenever they chastised him for anything.

"All right, I won't," he said. He leaned back in his seat, but she didn't trust his relaxed demeanor.

"So how is the potential in your new prospects? Sally tells me your phone's been ringing off the hook."

She didn't want to do this—she didn't want to change the topic, but she didn't see the point in going on with it, either. He would deny and twist things around until she felt foolish. She already felt a little silly because she couldn't defend her inclination to keep the Karla Hoffman affair from Stephen.

"Some look good and some are ridiculous. I don't know where people get their ideas about the value of their property."

"It's always hardest to be objective about the things closest to you," he said. She sensed that he meant that to apply to more than just her real estate clients and their love of their homes. Was she objective about the things closest to her, especially the people, or was she like some of her clients, blinded by her own illusions?

"Is Stephen coming back to the office?"

"No, he'll probably go straight home. He had to go see Bob White in New Paltz. But he'll be home for dinner," Jason added quickly. "He wanted me to be sure to tell you that."

"Really?" The heaviness of her sarcasm surprised even her. Jason ignored it.

"Yes, and he has a surprise for you. I wish I could be there to see the look on your face."

"What surprise?"

"If I told you it wouldn't be a surprise and he'd never forgive me."

She stood up and looked at him skeptically.

"Whatever it is, I expect you had a hand in it."

"Oh no," he said, raising his hand in a mock oath. "I had nothing to do with it. He surprised me, too."

"That," she said, "would be the biggest surprise of all." She started out.

"How was the play?" he asked before she reached the door.

"Who told you I went?" she asked without turning around.

"Stephen, who else? What do you think, I'm having you followed?" he asked, laughing. She looked at him.

"It was very good, but I'm sure you'd find something wrong with it." The smile left his face.

"That's not a very kind thing to say, Cyn. I think I'm getting the short end of things here," he added. She thought he looked rather sincere and that gave her reason to pause and change her tone.

"Well, it was very good. You ought to try to catch it next weekend when they do it again."

"I understand they have an excellent male lead."

She studied him. Was there something behind that look? Had the gossip begun? She hadn't even done anything.

"Yes, he is good," she said. "For amateur theater, that is."

"Maybe I will go. I'll call you guys later and see how you liked Stephen's surprise."

"How did you like it?"

"Oh no, no way. You're not going to trick me into revealing what it is."

She left feeling tighter, more nervous and more irritable than when she had entered. She had intended to call Terrence Baker to tell him about the house in Hurleyville before she left the office for the day, but she decided to put it off.

Whether out of a feeling of guilt or out of a need to end her sense of depression and conflict, she set out to make one of Stephen's favorite meals—Chicken Kiev. Everything was prepared by the time she heard the garage door go up. She poured herself a glass of white wine and sat at the counter. The moment he entered she knew what Jason had meant by a surprise.

"Ta da," he sang, his arms out.

She stared at him for a moment and then broke into tears as she ran to the bedroom.

Stephen had shaved off his beard, but instead of his face returning to the face she had first known, his added weight produced a chubbiness and a softness that made him look far less masculine. If anything, he looked more like Jason, especially since he wore Jason's hairstyle and Jason's fashion of clothes.

The heaviness around her heart draped her in a terrible sense of doom.

6

AFTER SHE HAD LEFT HIM in the kitchen, he had followed her to the bedroom and stood in the doorway. She sprawled herself out facedown on the bed. Apparently she couldn't control her sobbing. The frustration and unhappiness had been pent up too long. He didn't go to her to comfort her. He stood back as though he was afraid of her, as though she was some kind of lunatic and he couldn't anticipate what she would do next. When she turned to him she saw that the look of surprise and shock was still frozen on his face.

"I didn't have a beard when you first met me," he said when her sobbing diminished. "I thought you'd like this."

"It's not that," she said, sitting up and wiping her cheeks with the back of her hand. "It's your . . . your doing things without consulting me. Everything's a fait accompli around here. I have as much input in your decisions as does that . . . that chair." Her sorrow began to mold itself into anger.

"Well, I wanted this to be a surprise." He turned as if there was a third person in the room, an objective observer who would rule on their differences. It was a technique that Jason had, a way of belittling the other person's argument. "What kind of surprise would it be if I had discussed it with you first?"

"Why did it have to be a surprise? Your new hairdo was a surprise; your new clothing was a surprise."

"I don't know." He shrugged. "Jason said you always liked surprises and..."

"Jason said? Jason said? Don't you know me by now? Do you have to go to my brother for advice about me? What does he really know about me anyway? We were never close when we were younger. We're still not close. We'll never be close!" she added vehemently. Her face reddened with her anger.

"I didn't mean to start a whole family thing here. I'll grow my beard back. I'll grow it back," he repeated, stepping into the room. He took off his sports jacket and went to the closet.

"Don't do it without asking Jason first," she said bitterly.

"Aw, come on, Cyn." He came to the bed and sat beside her. He put his arm around her, but when she looked at him now, beardless and soft, she felt revulsion. She couldn't help thinking that he had been emasculated, that it had been going on for some time. There was even an unfamiliar limpness in his embrace. "I didn't mean to hurt you. Really."

"Well, it did. It does," she added. He tightened his hold on her to bring her to him, but she didn't permit her body to soften. It still felt like a stranger hugging her.

"It's not going to be hard to correct, not with my heavy beard. The barber shaved it this morning, but you can feel the roughness already. Go ahead, feel," he said, offering his cheek.

She didn't run her hand over it because she felt stupid about it all now. How could she explain her anger to anyone? What would she say—my husband shaved off his beard without telling me? It was such a trifle of an action in and of itself. Here people all around her were having marital problems because one or the other was committing adultery or on drugs or alcohol, and she was crying about her husband shaving. How did her problems compare?

"Forget it," she said. "Maybe you do look better without it. I don't know. We'll give it some time."

"That's more like the Cynthia I know," he said. "In fact it's what Jason predicted," he added. He kissed her on the cheek, but she had a terrible sinking feeling because his tone of voice reminded her of a parent talking to a child. Was she a child in his eyes? Jason certainly treated her that way most of the time. Was Stephen assuming his attitude? "I see you made Chicken Kiev," he said, standing and unbuttoning his shirt.

"Oh," she said, "I left a batch in the deep fryer!" She ran out of the bedroom, but the first batch was ruined. It made her emotional outburst seem even more idiotic now. All that good food ruined because her husband shaved off his beard. Fortunately she had made enough to compensate for it.

During the meal Stephen described the mall venture. He sounded more excited about it than he did about any of the other investments. His excitement was infectious, and she found herself feeling a little jealous.

"If it's so good, how come a coupla small-time investors like you and Jason got in on it from the start?"

"Hey, we're not small-time, Cyn. Jason is a very sharp guy. I'd match him up against any of the so-called big-timers."

"I bet you would," she said. He missed or chose to ignore her sarcasm and went on describing their meetings and the project. She listened as attentively as she could, trying to get used to his new face at the same time. Without his beard his eyes seemed diminished and the puffiness in his cheeks made his face look even rounder. She now regretted she had made the rum cake and she told him so.

"If you're going to go beardless, Stephen, you're going to have to trim down some. It makes your face look too chubby."

"Yeah, I know. That was the first thing Jason said when he saw me. I decided that I'd join that new health club in Liberty and cut out the afternoon martinis. Now I know why Jason doesn't like to drink at lunch," he said, and slapped himself on the stomach.

"Good. Now you sound more like the man I married."

He smiled and reached across the table to put his hand over hers.

"I'm not really different," he said. "Maybe I'm a little more occupied with business but I'm not really different. All of this stuff is superficial. Trust me. You're still the most important thing in my life and always will be. My Indian princess."

She felt her eyes tear. Maybe she was simply overreacting, she thought. Maybe all this was very silly. He would thin down and return to his original self, and they would get back on track. He seemed sincere.

"You shouldn't be this high-strung, baby. Maybe you're working too hard. Jason told me your list really expanded since the Rose Hill House sale."

"Working too hard? You, of all people, have the nerve to say *I'm* working too hard?" She sat back, her mouth opened wide.

"I know, I know," he said, putting his hands up. "Kettle calling the pot black, but male chauvinism aside, Jason and I are kinda used to this pace by now, whereas you..."

"I don't buy that, Stephen. For one thing I really enjoy what I'm doing. I don't see it as a job filled with pressure. I'm not trying to win any awards as the greatest real estate agent in Sullivan County, and I'm certainly not gambling large assets on investments as you two are doing. If anyone is pressured..."

"Well, something's got the better of you. You're changing. Maybe you don't see it, but..."

"I'm changing? That's a laugh."

"No, seriously. Try to be objective about it. You're jumping at me for the smallest things lately. I feel as though I should tiptoe past you at times. It's hard, Cyn. I got to keep thinking what does she want now? What does she expect? Like when you got mad because I didn't invite you to lunch with us the other day. That never bothered you before."

She sat there for a moment thinking. Was he right? Was it she who was changing and not he? For some reason the picture of Karla Hoffman flashed before her. Did it come to support her or possess her? She had been more nervous than usual ever since she confronted the old news story. It was like someone getting up in the morning and reading her own obituary. That's bound to have a dramatic effect. Was this why she was so emotional? Why she felt she could cry at the slightest provocation? Or did it go deeper and was the newspaper article only a catalyst for something greater?

Whenever she studied Jason and thought deeply about him, she was always afraid that she had inherited some of his traits. The difference was she kept them below the surface. But they were always there, waiting for an opportunity to appear. No matter how much you didn't want it, you couldn't deny your genetic inheritances, could you? she wondered.

"I just feel left out sometimes," she said. "It's not easy when I'm with the two of you."

"Yeah, but there's nothing new about that, is there, Cyn?"

"I don't know," she said. She stared through him, and saw Karla Hoffman standing in the gazebo at the Rose Hill House. She looked out over the fields, and there was a gentle but almost sardonic smile on her face. Her eyes caught the brightness of the sunlight, and her hair lifted in the breeze.

"Why are you smiling?"

"Huh?"

"You have this weird smile on your face."

"I do?"

"I'll tell you something," he said, "you and your brother are a pair of birds. He'll do the same thing to me sometimes. I'll be talking and talking and he'll be looking at me, but he'll be in another galaxy." She didn't reply and he looked toward the counter. "That cake sure smells good."

"It doesn't matter. You can't have a second piece tonight as you always do. Not with your fat face." He laughed, and she began to clear the table and prepare the coffee. Stephen went out to the den just as the phone rang.

It was almost as though he knew exactly when Jason would call and wanted to be able to talk to him privately. She heard him lower his voice, but she stopped what she was doing and listened keenly. She was sure she heard him say, "You were wrong. She didn't like it." Did he shave off his beard because Jason told him to? Whom did he want to please more, her or Jason? His voice got lower and lower until she couldn't hear any more of the conversation. She had a great temptation to pick up the receiver in the kitchen and listen in on their conversation but she didn't do it.

"That was your brother," he said, returning. "I think he was more excited about what your reaction would be to my shaving than I was."

"What did he say when you told him?"

"Shows you what he knows about women. He was surprised. He said because your father never had a beard, you never took to mine. He thinks all daughters have a father fixation."

"How would he know whether I took to your beard or not? I never discussed it with him."

"I don't know. You know Jason. He's so right about people so often, he just assumes he'll always be right."

"Why can't he find someone of his own to worry about?" she said, feeling like a broken record. They had been through this so many times before without any satisfactory answers. She paused in cutting the cake and turned to him. "When you were in Atlantic City with him, did he even look at any women? There must have been plenty there."

"No, but you can't fault him for that on this trip. We didn't have a free moment. Hell, I didn't even get a chance to play a quarter slot machine."

"Even so, Stephen, people talk about him. You know they do. Don't you ever discuss it with him?"

"Sure."

"And?"

"You'd be surprised at how private a person your brother can be when he wants to be. Besides," he said, smiling, "Jason is in complete control of his needs. I've never seen anyone as secure about himself. Give me that man who isn't passion's slave..."

"Stop it, Stephen. What you really mean is he's so in love with himself, he can't fall in love with anyone else," she said. Stephen thought that was funny. In fact he thought it was so funny, he laughed about it on and off throughout the remainder of the evening.

They made love afterward, but it wasn't as good as the last time, when they had come back from dinner at Dede's. He was very affectionate then. Their foreplay was soft and loving, a true prelude to the act itself. He held her tightly, stroking her and kissing her, making her feel that he was totally involved with her, that he still saw her and thought of her as he drove her and himself to a climax.

This time their preface was short; their contact was quick and perfunctory. When she opened her eyes and looked up at him, his face hovering above her, his own eyes closed, his skin smooth and chalky where the dark beard had been, she couldn't help visualizing Jason. It was a terrible thing because on occasion she had fantasized about an incestuous relationship with her brother. She never told anyone about it. She thought it was unnatural, and it frightened her that she even thought about it. She had no idea why the images ever appeared. She couldn't help but wonder if Jason had ever had the same kind of thoughts. If he had, he would never reveal it. She was sure of that.

Nevertheless it revolted her to think about it, and she couldn't prevent herself from thinking about it now. It stopped her from having an orgasm before

Stephen climaxed and exited. She wanted him to go at it again, but he claimed fatigue.

It had been a long day. There were all sorts of facts and figures in his head. He felt as though he would collapse into sleep. Finally she let him turn over, but for a long time she lay there staring up into the darkness.

This sense of incompleteness that now came over her seemed to be an appropriate way to end this day. Despite Stephen's promises and his loving gestures, her feelings of insecurity lingered. He might very well believe the things he says, she thought, but he couldn't see as clearly as she could. It was just as Jason had said: "It's hardest to be objective about the things closest to you." That applied to Stephen as well as to her. He didn't understand just how deep the changes in him were. They weren't as superficial as he thought.

Or maybe these weren't really changes; these things that were happening revealed her husband's true nature. What he had done in the beginning was hide it well. He was always overly ambitious, as self-centered as Jason and...and what else? She hated to think of the possibilities. What had happened to all those differences between Stephen and Jason? How alike were they?

She turned her back to him and closed her eyes. A vision of his beardless face floated by, but she pressed it quickly from her thoughts. She didn't like feeling sexually unsatisfied; she knew it would keep her awake. Her thoughts turned to Terrence Baker—the look in his eyes when he came into the Holiday bar looking for her, the sound of his voice on the telephone.

It was wrong to think of him this way as she lay beside her husband in their bed, and yet... she had the feeling he wasn't thinking of her. Whom was he thinking of; what was he thinking of? How often did she come into his thoughts during the course of any day now? Whenever Jason permitted it, a voice within her said, and she nodded in agreement. She almost spoke aloud.

She heard Stephen's deep breathing, and she knew he was asleep. Unfortunately she tossed and turned for hours before she fell asleep herself, and when she finally did so, it was only because she permitted herself to fantasize about Terrence Baker.

"I'D BE GLAD TO LOOK at that house," Terrence Baker said. "And I appreciate your finding something so quickly."

She had called him the first thing in the morning when she arrived at the office. Stephen had gotten up before her, dressed and made the coffee. After she showered and went out to the kitchen, she found him reading the *Wall Street Journal*. He was dressed in another new shirt and tie outfit, something he said he and Jason had bought at the clothing store in the hotel in Atlantic City.

"While we were waiting for two lawyers to show," he added. To her it was obvious that Jason had made the choice of color and style.

Stephen seemed more engrossed than usual in his paper this morning, but she didn't mind the lull in their conversation. Her mind was like a video tape recorder, replaying bits and pieces of the recent past. She reviewed almost every word and glance between herself and Terrence Baker. Sometimes his face, especially the look in his eyes, got caught in a freeze frame in her mind, and she sat there with this self-contented smile on her face. It was only when Stephen asked her what was so funny that she realized what she was doing.

She used a Paula Levy story to explain herself, describing Paula's way of humoring the amateur thespians like Martin Daniels.

"I know him," Stephen said. "The man's gay."

"Some people think Jason's gay," she replied.

"There's quite a difference between a man like that and Jason. Jason's intelligent, perceptive, confident."

"Mr. Daniels did a beautiful job of directing this play. He must be perceptive and intelligent, too."

"From what I hear he's got a lot of raw talent to work with," Stephen said, emphasizing the word "raw." It made her think about Terrence Baker again. She thought about him after Stephen left, and she thought about him all the way to the office. It seemed natural then for her to make the call to him the first thing she would do. She was impressed; even this early in the morning his voice was filled with aggressive energy. Could it be that there was never a time when he was down and depressing, or did she hunger for excitement so much she heard only what she wanted to hear?

"Can you be at my office at four o'clock?" she asked him.

"No problem," he said. She had considered having him meet her someplace else, but then she questioned her motives. Why did she want to hide him? It wouldn't be wise to do it anyway, she thought, not with the gossipy secretarial staff this agency had. By bringing him to the office first, she would prove, mostly to herself, that she had nothing but business in mind, even though the fantasies grew stronger and more vivid after each conversation she had with him.

"See you at four then," she said, and hung up without waiting for his final line.

She kept herself as busy as she could during most of the day. She was at new properties, showing three to prospective buyers. One looked like a promising sale and that made her spirits soar. Even so, while she was talking to people and traveling, she couldn't subdue this nagging tickle in the base of her stomach. It was like the feeling of butterflies performers got before a show. She was nervous about her afternoon meeting with Terrence Baker. There was no way to deny it.

I'm behaving just like a high school girl, she thought, and then she thought, what was so bad about that? Sometimes I think those were the best years of my life. The thing is it's dangerous, she told herself. Terrence Baker is no unproven schoolboy. That's for sure.

When she returned to the office, Sally Kaufman made a point of telling her she liked Stephen's new, cleanly shaven face. It was as though she were sent to do so. Judy Dobbs said it made him look ten years younger, which of course would make him look younger than Cynthia was. Jason didn't say anything to her about it. In fact, with her going in and out and his various meetings, they didn't have much chance to talk. Now Stephen and he were in conference, going over figures, talking to investors.

After Terrence Baker arrived she half hoped that either Stephen or Jason would emerge and meet him. She was curious about how they would react to him and how he would react to either of them. He had taken off his sports jacket and rolled up the sleeves of his shirt. His tie was loose and his hair, although not disheveled, was free and fluffy from the breeze. He looked as if he had been riding in a convertible with the top down.

Seeing him now in the daylight, dressed this way, she thought he looked taller and younger. Judy Dobbs lingered in the doorway after she announced him. Cynthia saw that he had a way of encouraging feminine interest. It was in the way he tilted his head and smiled. His gaze was so intense, it could make a woman blush, if not quicken her heartbeat. Judy's neck was crimson, and she kept her fingers at the collar of her blouse. He winked at her after Cynthia told her "thanks" as a way to dismiss her.

"I'll be just a moment," she told him and went back to her paperwork.

"Take your time. I was looking forward to seeing what your office is like."

He looked at some of the wall plaques—awards given to her father, her framed real estate license; a picture of her, Jason, her father and her mother posing in the living room on the event of her parents' twenty-fifth wedding anniversary; a picture of Stephen and her at a dude ranch, taken a year after their marriage.

"Hubby, I take it," he said, standing before the dude ranch photo.

"Huh?" She had been watching him even though she was filling out some forms, but she didn't want him to know it. "Oh, yes. I'd introduce you to him, but he and my brother are locked in battle with some bankers."

"Bankers aren't hard to defeat," he said, smiling.

"Oh," she said, and giggled like a little girl. "I forgot you work in a bank. Exactly what do you do?"

"Small-loans officer. Your husband and your brother won't be battling with me," he said. "At least, not over money," he added, and she felt the heat come into her face.

"Oh," she said when she realized they were just staring at each other. "I guess this stuff can wait," she added quickly, and shoved papers into folders.

All the secretaries looked their way when they emerged from her office. Cynthia imagined Judy had primed them all quickly. The agency was designed so that the secretaries were working in a row the length of the building. The agents had cubicles for private offices and the secretaries were stationed at central locations, each assigned to a group of agents. Sally, at the far end, handled Jason's and Stephen's work exclusively. She was standing near Pat Moffit's desk, and both of them stopped talking to look Cynthia's way.

"I'll be back shortly," she said to the awestruck Judy Dobbs. "We're going to Sid Jaffe's property." Usually she didn't make such a point of telling Judy where she was going, but somehow she felt a need to do so now and to do so loudly. But a little voice inside her said, *The lady doth protest too much, methinks.*

"My car or yours?" Terrence asked when they stepped outside.

"What? Oh no, we go in my car. That's part of the service."

"Sounds good. I'm not one of these male chauvinists that can't stand being chauffeured about by a woman, especially if she's an attractive woman," he said.

"You know," she said when they got into her car, "I hope you're really serious about all this."

"What do you mean?"

"You've obviously been playing romantic leads too often."

He laughed.

"Taking my parts to heart, is that what you mean?"

"Something like that. It can happen."

"Oh, but we're all playing parts. Remember: 'the world's a stage.'"

"I remember, but I also remember who I am and what I'm here to do."

"I see. Yes, of course I'm serious about renting a house. But," he added, "that doesn't mean I can't appreciate a beautiful woman, does it?"

"I'm not a beautiful woman."

"You? Insecure? Never would have thought it."

"There are still some people who are modest nowadays." She looked at him for the first time since they had pulled away from the agency. He sat back into the corner of the seat, sprawling his body so he could look directly and continuously at her. She liked his relaxed and casual manner and despite what she might say, she also liked his arrogant smile. There was something refreshingly masculine about him. Maybe it was just a reaction to Stephen's new ways, but she couldn't help admiring Terrence Baker for his aggressiveness.

"Tell me about this house."

"It's a modest two-bedroom ranch. Perfect for a bachelor."

"How do you know I want to remain a bachelor?"

"The kitchen's small," she continued, ignoring him, "but it has a nice size living room and a nice size den. It has a bathroom and a half bathroom in one of the bedrooms, a full but undeveloped basement and a carport. I wished it had a closed in garage, but you can't have everything you wish, can you?" Her tone was more one of self-pity, but he took it to be the tone of a teaser.

"You can try like hell."

"What?"

"To get what you wish... you can try like hell."

"I'll keep that in mind. Now he's asking three seventy-five, which is reasonable. The heat and the electric might run you another hundred and fifty. The catch is, he's not interested in renting it for more than a year, at the end of which, if you were interested, you could apply all your rent toward the purchase price. What he's hoping for is, once the new prison in Woodbourne is completed about a year from now, there will be more prospective buyers for such a house."

"Is he right?"

"Could very well be."

"You know your stuff, huh?"

"Yes I do. That's why I'm successful at it. That and timing."

"Timing?"

"Everything's a matter of timing—being at the right place at the right time."

"Oh, sorta like fate, huh?"

"No, not fate. Fate means things are more or less predetermined. I mean doing your homework and preparing well. That's what gets you ahead, not sitting around hoping for things to happen. I know too many people who are like that."

"You never believe that things were just meant to be?"

"No. I'm too much of a realist. If something happens, it's because you want it to happen, because you make it happen or because someone else made it happen to you."

"Doesn't sound very romantic. Sounds too... practical."

"That's the way I am."

"In everything?"

She looked at him. He wore a sardonic smile, but that wasn't what affected her. In answering his questions, she felt herself harden protectively. Whom was she trying to convince, him or herself? Did she really believe the things she said? Was that why the picture of Karla Hoffman and the story were so important to her? They made her challenge her view of things, and in a way, made her act out of character. Normally she would have been more like Jason when it came to such things. But she wasn't. Why? Why?

"Where are you from?" she asked. She made it sound as though he were some kind of spy.

"Not from outer space, I swear. From a small town something like this one, in Pennsylvania. That's why I like it here. Of course, I've knocked around a bit. I lived in New York for a few years, and I've lived in Boston."

"What about family, friends?"

"Family's still in Pennsylvania. Male or female friends?"

"Either."

"I've left a few on the trail," he said, and for the first time he seemed to tighten up. She found this even more interesting.

"You make yourself sound quite mysterious."

"Quite the contrary. I'm an open book."

"I'll bet," she said, and he laughed. They were quiet for most of the remainder of the ride, but she felt his gaze intensely on her. It made her self-conscious and she couldn't help touching her hair, pressing the strands back and running her palms over the sides from time to time. Her activity brought his attention to it.

"Why did you change your hair color?"

"How did you know that? I thought they did a good job."

"They did, but I saw you in that picture with your husband and..."

"Oh, right, right."

"So? Why'd you do it?"

She had a temptation to say that she had a theory that it would make things better between her husband and herself, but she was afraid to reveal any of that. She thought the moment that she gave this man the opportunity to come charging at her he would do so; and she wasn't so sure she had the will to resist.

"I don't know. Why does any woman do it? Boredom, I guess. I'm a little sorry I did it now."

"You did look better in the picture."

"Thanks a lot."

"Just being honest," he said. "I can't help it. Anyway, I thought you were the kind of woman who appreciated honesty."

She knew he was teasing her but she was enjoying it. She was almost disappointed when they arrived at the house and their topic of conversation returned to the business at hand.

"Not a bad location," he said. "Nice size, too."

"It's well built. I know the man who owns the construction company that did this one. He gives people a quality building."

They went inside and went from room to room. She watched him examine closets and envision the way his furniture would fit into the available space. He nodded his head after looking over each room and went on to the next. Finally he stood in the doorway of the living room, his arms folded across his chest.

"I think I'll take this," he said. His voice echoed because of the emptiness of the house. "I'm paying four and a quarter for an apartment, and I don't have half this space or half the privacy. I think there's a herd of elephants living above me, and with those walls being so thin..."

"Just so you remember you can rent it only for a year. He wasn't too happy about renting it, but he's tired of just having an expense."

"I understand." He turned to look at her. "I don't think you'd lead me into anything bad, though," he said. The warmth in his voice and the short distance between them brought a flush to her cheeks. She knew she should step back or away, but she didn't move. She was permitting something to happen.

"I'll tell him to draw up a lease. He's a lawyer," she said, her eyes unable to move from his face. She felt herself drawn to him. He sensed it and leaned toward her, his intention obvious. "Don't," she whispered, anticipating his approaching lips, but he didn't stop and she didn't pull away. Perhaps it was because she felt like someone crossing over into a dream and she liked the recklessness and the danger. It didn't seem real.

He didn't put his arms around her when their lips met. She could have ended it instantly by simply leaning back but she didn't. There was something there, some longing, some hunger that she didn't realize existed within her. When their lips finally parted she suffered a sense of disappointment, but she didn't want to admit it.

"Why did you do that?"

"Consummate the deal," he said, smiling. She just stared at him. Did he sense that she was looking for more reason. "No," he added, "I did it because I wanted to. I needed to. From the first moment I looked out into the audience and saw you sitting there, I thought this would be. It's as if I was sent in this direction by something greater than either of us, by fate."

"You shouldn't have done that," she said weakly. She fought to gain control of herself and turn away from him.

"I don't believe you mean that."

"I do."

"That's not what I read in your eyes."

"You've been reading too many scripts," she said. It brought his full, Burt Lancaster-like laugh.

"You make being an actor sound more like being a criminal."

"Maybe it is. I've got to get back to the office."

"Sure. Look," he said, taking her by the hand when they reached the front door, "will you meet me here tomorrow at the same time?"

"No, of course not. Listen, I don't know what you've been told," she began, thinking about Paula Levy, "but..."

"I haven't been told anything by anyone. My messages come from the same place yours do—from the heart."

"What?" She smiled and thought, this was the way Stephen used to talk. "Look," she said, "I think you're having a little fun with me. No," she added before he could speak, her hands up, "let it be. Let's remain friends."

He shrugged.

"We can try," he said, "but I think it's beyond what you or I want. It's what's to be."

The smile left her face. He sounded so serious about it. Could it be that he really believed it or was this a good performance?

"Let's go," she said. She felt herself slipping emotionally so she hurried down the walkway to the car. He lingered a moment, looked back at the house and then followed.

"This is a good deal," he said, getting in beside her, "and it's not that far from Monticello and the bank."

"No. You'll take the Anawana Lake Road. It's a ten-minute ride, and in the summertime you're better off. Less traffic."

"This isn't much more than a ten-minute ride for you, either, is it?" he asked, a twinkle in his eyes.

"You're a devil," she said, shaking her head. "I should have listened to my instincts."

"What did they tell you?"

"Not to get involved," she said.

"Oh, but you are," he said. "You were the moment you sat down in that theater. Some things transcend time and space. It wouldn't have been any different had we met fifty years ago."

She turned to him so quickly he thought he had said something off-color.

"Please," she said, "stop."

He did. He was quiet and so was she, but she wasn't thinking about him, so much as about what he had said. It made her think of Karla Hoffman again.

Do they? she wondered. Do some things transcend time and space? It went against everything she was brought up to believe, and yet when she snuck a look at him sitting so confidently beside her, looking so handsome and so strong, she felt herself believing him. Perhaps the world that she had thought was built on logic and order was influenced by mystical forces after all. Maybe that was why the Karla Hoffman affair was so important to her—it spoke to her across time and space.

She squeezed the steering wheel harder to stop her fingers from trembling as she drove on, heading for what she now thought might be more truth than she could endure.

7

"PAULA LEVY, I want you to tell me and to tell me right now, everything you told Terrence Baker about me. I mean it." Cynthia stepped past her friend and entered her house. As usual it looked like an unmade bed. Paula had a maid clean and straighten things twice a week, but it wouldn't have mattered if she had the maid every day. She never put things back in their rightful place; she never cleared dishes off tables until the tables became obviously cluttered. Magazines and books were usually left strewn about as though she had thumbed through them looking for some secret note left between the pages. She was always reading three or four books at a time, leaving all of them opened and facedown on chairs, tables and even the floor.

Cynthia was sorry to see this because Paula had a beautiful house. It had been built by one of the area's more successful businessmen. He designed the house himself, providing for a great deal of window space. In its time it was a very unique structure. Because it was located three-quarters of the way up a rise, there was a breathtaking view of the village and its surroundings. About ten years after the house had been constructed, a number of people bought the property above and around it and a significant housing development followed. That was when the original owner wanted to sell. Cynthia handled it.

As soon as she entered the house, Cynthia went directly to the large living room. The mantel of the white marble fireplace was inundated with ashtrays, all mostly full; knickknacks, a few of which matched; and a small pile of paperback novels. She threw the jacket that had been left on the couch to the other side of the couch and sat down. Paula, the ash of her cigarette dangling ominously from its end, followed with obvious reluctance.

"Who said I told him anything about you? What's going on?"

"Paula," Cynthia said, elongating the final *a* sound, "I'm warning you. Tell me the truth."

"What truth?" her friend said. She just made it to the ashtray on the small glass table beside the love seat, but Cynthia could see that it wouldn't have mattered all that much if she hadn't.

"What is that thing you're wearing?" Cynthia asked before they could go any further.

"This thing, as you call it, is a dashiki, and it's a wonderful way to hide your excess poundage. Perhaps this color green is a little too psychedelic for most people's taste, but..."

"The truth I am talking about is the truth about what you told Terrence Baker. Now don't pretend you didn't know he called me to find him a place to live."

"How would I know that?"

"You told him I'm a real estate agent," Cynthia said, and pointed an accusing finger at her.

"I didn't. I'll swear it on a romance novel if you want."

"Paula, I'm serious."

"What did you do when he called? You didn't turn him away, did you? Cynthia?"

"I found him a place to rent," she said, looking away. Then she looked up quickly. "Well, it just happened to pop up."

"So quickly? You are good at your work, aren't you?" Paula asked as though she first believed it. "But I didn't send him to you, honest."

"Then how..."

"You're not exactly someone incognito, Cynthia. All he had to do was ask anyone at the bank about you, and he would have gotten enough information to write a sizable who's who entry."

"I suppose so. But even so," she added, "I'm sure you told him something about me."

"All right. I'll admit I told him you went out to the bar during the workshop party. But he came over to me and asked me where did my friend go? He wanted to find you. I didn't send him. You think I wanted to get rid of him?"

"That was it? You swear?"

"Wait a minute," Paula said, taking the cigarette out of her mouth and crushing it vigorously in the ashtray beside her. "Something more happened here, didn't it? Come on, now that you made me truthful, let's hear it."

"He has definite romantic intentions."

"No shit. So?"

"Paula, I'm not looking for an affair, you know."

"How do you know you're not? Sometimes these things just happen."

"You mean like they're meant to be?"

"Yes."

"I think you two use the same swami."

"Tell me some details," Paula said, sitting down beside her. "And make them as graphic as possible."

"He moves too fast."

"Life's short."

"You're not being any help."

"What do you want me to say? You want me to tell you to stay away from him? Stay away from him. But I bet you don't."

"How can you be so sure?" Cynthia asked. She was very interested in Paula's response.

"You have a certain look about you these last few weeks, Cyn," Paula began, her tone of voice changing, becoming softer, warmer. "I know how I appear to most people, but I didn't want to push myself into your personal life if you didn't want me. You look kind of lost, kind of alone. Is Stephen having an affair?"

"What?"

"Don't act so amazed. Adultery isn't a female characteristic, you know. Men have been known to wander."

"Stephen? No, I...I never thought of that," she said, a thoughtful look on her face.

"But things aren't right?"

"His personality is changing."

"It's like living with a stranger. I know the feeling," Paula said nodding.

"No, not a stranger. It's more like living with my brother."

"Really?" Paula's eyebrows rose, and remained peaked. "He's taking on Jason's personality? Well, I don't know what's worse—your husband falling in love with himself or falling in love with someone else. In the end I suppose it has the same result."

"Yes," Cynthia said, "it does."

"Why don't you talk to him about it?"

"I did. I do, but somehow it always seems as though I'm being foolish." After a pause she added, "He shaved off his beard when he was with Jason in Atlantic City."

"Did he? How's he look?"

"I don't know. I got so used to him with it. He looks kinda milky to me right now."

"The way Jason often looks?" Paula asked. Cynthia nodded. "So what are you gonna do?"

"I don't know. Keep after him, I suppose."

"Now listen to me," Paula said, gathering her dashiki about her knees. "You may think I'm being melodramatic and maybe I am, but if Stephen thought you were interested in another man, he might just come around to being the man you want him to be, the man he should be."

"You might be right. Changing my hair color certainly didn't make any impact."

"And just think of all the fun you'll have while you're teaching him a lesson. Why, it's like being too thin and having to gain weight!"

"Jesus, Paula," Cynthia said. "What kind of an analogy is that?"

"It's the best I could think of."

"I'll bet." She looked around. "Look at this place. It's a mess."

"I know, but I am beyond feeling guilty about it. I'm on a higher plane of consciousness."

"That's bullshit and you know it. You're just lazy and irresponsible."

"That's a higher plane of consciousness." They both laughed. "You want a cup of coffee?"

"Yes, but since I like to have mine in a clean cup," she said, standing up, "I guess I'll have it someplace else. I've got to get home anyway. We're supposed to go to the production of *Torch Song* in Middletown tonight. Jason bought us season tickets to the Orange County Council of the Arts."

"He's so culture-minded."

"They meet a lot of clients down there. Jason is always thinking of the business, believe me."

"He reminds me of a nun, only instead of being married to God he's married to an insurance agency." Cynthia laughed.

"Now that's a good analogy."

"One for two ain't bad. So what are you going to do about Mr. Wonderful?"

"Nothing," she said.

"Nothing?" Paula grimaced.

"Just let things go their natural way."

"Now that's promising," Paula said. Then they hugged, and Cynthia left her standing behind in the doorway, looking like a large green mound of Jell-O with a human head over it.

THE THREE OF THEM WENT to dinner in Middletown. They ate at the Holiday Inn. Cynthia wanted to go to Diana's, a homey and unpretentious little Italian restaurant that was family owned and operated. The food always had a down-to-earth home-cooked flavor, and the atmosphere was conducive to relaxation. Stephen and she had often gone there alone and enjoyed it, but Jason didn't want to go there. He said they were overdressed for a place like that. Both he and Stephen were wearing three-piece suits, identically cut and styled. Stephen had picked his up after work, again not telling her about something he had done for himself. Before this started happening he wouldn't so much as buy a pair of socks without asking her opinion first, she thought. In fact she had to do most of the buying for him.

When he put it on and came to her for her reaction, she thought she would try a new tack—she acted totally disinterested. "It's nice," she said, and went on arranging her own coiffure. It was only when they were getting ready to leave the house that she became emotional about something. He was wearing her father's ring. He hadn't put it on until he came out of the bedroom.

"Where did you get that?" she asked.

"What?"

"That ring? Isn't that my father's ring? It's the one that Jason always wears."

"Oh, the ring. I forgot to tell you," he said, holding his hand up before her as though his whole hand were in question. "Jason gave it to me in Atlantic City."

"What? Why?"

"Who knows? You know Jason—when he gets something in his mind to do, he just does it, no matter what anyone else thinks. He said he wanted me to have it. In fact he insisted. He said your father would want me to have it. I thought that was very nice of him, don't you? I couldn't refuse it and since our ring sizes are about the same..."

"No," she said. She stepped back as though she couldn't believe him. "It's something he should have kept for himself. It's not something to just give away to anyone."

"He's not just giving it away, Cyn. And I'm not anyone, am I?"

"But... it's something he should have wanted to give to his own son someday... heritage."

"So I'll give it to our son. Your father could have left it to you just as well as to him."

"It's a man's ring. It belongs with him," she said, more insistently.

"Well, maybe he's come to the conclusion that he'll never get married and have a son. I don't know. He just wants the ring to be in our family now. What should I do, tell him we don't want it?"

"How can he decide now that he'll never get married?"

"I'm not saying that's it for sure. I'm simply suggesting an explanation. Don't you like it on me?"

"I didn't say that. That's another issue."

"Are you going to make an issue of it tonight?" he asked. He looked terrified of the possibility.

"God forbid we should disturb Jason on a night out. I don't care anymore. Let's go," she said, "or we'll be late picking him up and you'll be scolded."

"Very funny."

She was quiet in the car after they had picked up Jason. He sat in the back, and he and Stephen carried most of the conversation all the way to Middletown. The only time she really got into it was when they argued about where to eat. She realized that it wasn't so much her desire to eat in one place rather than another, so much as it was her mood. She felt a need to be contrary.

"Besides," Jason added as an additional argument, "if I wanted a moderately priced meal tonight, I'd have eaten at home."

"He's right," Stephen said. "Diana's just isn't the place for us tonight. We'll go during the week," he said to placate her as he would a child. The tears came to her eyes, but she didn't continue the discussion.

They met people they knew at the Holiday Inn, other people who were going to the Arts program. Jason reveled in that as though it substantiated his point that this restaurant was more suited for the evening. Although she ordered a glazed chicken breast that looked appetizing, she ate little. Stephen didn't seem to notice or care. Usually he would make a big deal of her lack of appetite, finding it difficult to enjoy himself whenever she didn't.

But tonight he was into everything with a fervor. He ate voraciously; he spoke with energy whenever anyone came to their table, and he seemed totally unaware of her silence and unhappiness. Occasionally he turned from Jason to ask her opinion about an idea, but when she didn't respond with interest he went on with his train of thought as though she had.

Jason was his usual self. When people gathered around their table, he held court, espousing his theories as arrogantly as ever; and Stephen supported him firmly. It was during their conversation about the significance of cultural events in relation to people who lived in the area that she sensed another annoying change in Stephen. Jason, picking up on a familiar theme for him, ridiculed and demeaned the upstate New York population.

"I don't care how much money you invest in these programs," he told Clancy Stratton, an administrator at the Orange County Community College, "you won't take the stump out of the stump jumper. Some of these people still think *Hamlet* is something you make with eggs." He laughed at his own joke, but Cynthia was surprised to see Stephen laugh at it just as hard.

"We've still got a full house," Clancy said in defense. "And we've sold out our subscriptions for next year, as well. It takes time to build anything of value."

"What Jason is saying," Stephen said, "is there are still many, many people around here who think culture is something that has to do with yogurt and nothing else." Jason looked at him and then laughed. It was his kind of joke, Cynthia thought, and she thought that Stephen had delivered it as though he were auditioning for him.

"You didn't think that way when you first came up here," Cynthia said softly. Everyone turned on her. "You used to say this was virgin territory, filled with a great deal of promise, especially because of our proximity to New York."

"That was before he lived here awhile," Jason said, and then he gave his familiar back-hand wave to end the argument. When he changed the topic to institutional insurance, she was left in silence again, but it bothered her that Stephen let Jason get away with shutting her up. If he sensed that, he didn't let on.

When they arrived at the theater they found it packed. Jason and Stephen seemed to know almost everyone there. There were conversations across aisles and rows. She compared it to the night she and Paula had gone to the Workshop show. There, she was the center of attention; here, she was like someone tagging along. People said hello to her, but their conversations were directed to Jason and Stephen. She sat back, letting them roam about until the curtain was to rise.

She looked at the program; it was a professional production coming right out of New York. Two plays in one week, she thought to herself; at least this local yokel is getting the culture. When she looked up again, her heart skipped a beat. Terrence Baker had come down the aisle with Martin Daniels alongside him. They stopped at the beginning of her row. Her look of surprise brought a smile to his face.

"So you are becoming a drama critic after all," he said. "Hi."

"Hi," she said.

"Hi," Martin said.

"You're not alone, are you?"

"No, I'm with..."

"Enjoy the performance," Terrence said quickly. The houselights began blinking. He stared at her for a moment and then started away. She watched with a sense of longing as they continued down to the other side of the aisle.

Just before the lights went out completely, he turned and looked her way. He found her looking back at him, waiting for him to do so. His smile lingered in her eyes for a few moments after the lights went out. She sat back, a new sense of excitement settling within her, making her feel like a young girl again.

"Can you see all right?" Stephen whispered. She caught a whiff of his cologne, Jason's cologne, and for a moment she thought of Siamese twins. The stage lights came up, and she distinguished Terrence Baker's head silhouetted before her.

"Oh yes," she said, "I see fine. Really."

They met during the intermission. In the past Stephen would have remained at her side, forcing people to come to them. But Jason was circulating, and Stephen, after he had gotten her a small container of orange juice, was following alongside him. They were like two public relations men working a party, threading their way in between groups of people, saying a few words to this one and that. She watched them like an objective observer, taking note of how Stephen was even parroting Jason's gestures, seconding his wave, his nod, his smile by offering his own waves, nods and smiles. She had to turn away, and when she did she found Terrence at her side.

"See the difference between amateurs and professionals?"

"You could easily be a professional. They're good, but you were just as good."

"I don't know. These people have consistency. They hit the mark night after night."

"You can hit the mark any time you want," she said. She didn't mean it to sound as ingratiating as it did. It brought a wide smile to his face and made her self-conscious. She had to look away to see if Stephen were looking their way, but he was nodding with agreement at something Jason was telling a group of people.

"I'd like to hit the mark at four o'clock tomorrow," he said. He brought his face close to hers to whisper it.

"I spoke to Mr. Jaffe," she said, ignoring his remark. "He had heard of you."

"Good things or bad?"

"He's willing to rent you the house. Must've been all good. You can sign a lease in a few days."

"You and I should really go over it one more time. I'll be there at four," he said. She started to speak, but he turned and went to join Martin Daniels. Men, she thought, they're all so arrogant and so sure of themselves. But she had to smile when he looked back at her. There was danger in his eyes, danger and challenge. His arrogance was different from Jason's or Stephen's. She was attracted to his.

After the play she dozed in the car all the way home. She wasn't interested in listening to Jason and Stephen review their impressions of various people, and since she hadn't really spoken with many of the people they referred to, she had no opinions anyway. As far as she was concerned, they were having another one of their private conversations in her presence. The only thing that caught her interest was Stephen's suggestion that he drop her off first and then take Jason home.

"It's on the way and you look exhausted," he said.

"Fine."

"I'll take Jason home and be right back."

"I want you to see that prospectus I was telling you about earlier," Jason said. "It'll take you a minute."

"Why can't he see it tomorrow?"

"He can, but since he's right there and..."

"Why is something like this suddenly a problem?" Stephen asked.

She wanted to say that it was always a problem; she wanted to say that he should leave his work in the office, and if he was taking her out for the evening, he should take her out and not Jason and the business. But she didn't. She wasn't up to the effort.

"Do what you want," she said. "I'm going to go right to sleep."

She got out quickly when they reached the house. When she looked back she saw Jason getting into the front seat. After they drove away she went into the house. While she was hanging up her clothes, she found a matchbook cover on the floor by the closet. It had probably fallen out of Stephen's pants pocket, she thought, and picked it up. It advertised a nightclub in Atlantic City. And he had said that he had no time for anything. She threw it on the bureau and wondered how many other lies he had told her these past few weeks. Maybe Paula was on to something when she suggested that Stephen might be seeing other women.

Stephen didn't return for nearly an hour and a half. She had fallen asleep, but she awoke when she heard him come in. She looked at the clock and then, pretending to be asleep, she watched him. Usually he draped his clothing over a chair and left putting things away until the morning. Tonight he was meticulous about his new suit. He hung it carefully in the plastic bag and put it into the closet gently as though it was the most precious thing he owned.

She debated telling him about the matchbook cover and then decided it would just seem like another petty argument. He would have some logical answer, and she would look foolish for bringing it up. Let him discover it on the bureau himself, she thought. At least he'll know I found it. She turned her back on him before he got into the bed. He didn't attempt to wake her to say anything, and she felt this terrible sense of emptiness. It was as if what Paula said was right—she was living with a stranger.

In the morning he told her he wasn't going to go directly to the office. He and Jason were driving to

Port Jervis to meet some people who had an interesting proposal involving group insurance for trade unions and the like. She didn't get up while he dressed and ate his breakfast. He said it was amusing that she was "goofing off."

"I'm just kidding," he said. "You should take the day off. You've been working too hard. Even Jason's noticed it."

"Jason? Noticed what?"

"Your irritability, how short you are with some people."

"Me?"

"You should have seen yourself last night, Cyn. Early on, Jason said, 'Don't cross her tonight.' Maybe you didn't notice it, but both of us were tiptoeing around you all evening."

"That's a clever way to explain how you two excluded me from most everything you did and said," she replied, but her voice revealed her doubt. Could it be that they were right—she was petulant most of the evening?

"Not fair, Cyn. Not fair. Anyway, it's amazing how you two know each other so well. He suggested I tell you to take the day off and here you are, still in bed. Amazing."

"I'm not taking the day off. I'm just going in later," she said. He shrugged and blew her a kiss. "Tell that to my brilliant brother," she called after him, but when he was gone she lay back and thought about the suggestion.

Actually she didn't have much enthusiasm for the office and her work today. She felt like crying. It had been a long time since she had felt this low. Her thoughts just naturally turned to Karla Hoffman again. She took out the news clipping and studied the woman's picture.

Of course there was no way to tell when this particular photograph had been taken; the newspaper had simply acquired a recent photograph. But there was something in her eyes that bespoke of her inner turmoil, Cynthia thought. Maybe she was simply transferring her own emotions into the picture, but she couldn't help feeling there was a sadness around Karla Hoffman's eyes. She thought the camera had caught a trembling in her lips, as well.

When she turned to the vanity mirror and looked at herself, she thought she saw the same trembling, the same sadness around her eyes. She wondered if the picture had a power. Was it a kind of mirror, reflecting through fifty years? Was she looking at Karla Hoffman or herself? The question sent a cold chill through her that drove her from the bed.

It was as though she were possessed, and even though she didn't believe in such things she felt driven to pursue the phantoms. She dressed quickly, outlining her plans as she did so. The more she thought about it all, the more it took hold of her. She didn't like what was happening to her, but she couldn't do much to prevent it. She was becoming a monomaniac.

She barely ate breakfast. Stephen had left the coffee on for her. She had a cup and a piece of a doughnut. She was impatient with everything that delayed her movement. Finally, without taking half as much time as she usually did to fix her hair and her makeup, she left the house and drove directly to the Rose Hill House.

There were two vans parked in front of it. Ralph Hillerman had hired them and some men to take out the things he felt were valuable, things he would either keep or sell. The men saw her pull up. They paused to watch her park and walk to the front entrance. Someone said, "Good morning," but she didn't respond. To them she looked like someone in a trance. It wasn't until she entered the building that she realized old man Hillerman had already been moved to the nursing home. Mrs. Marshall was no longer there, either, of course.

She stood in the wide entranceway of the old tourist house and wondered why she had come. What did she expect to find? There was no one to talk to, nothing in particular to see. Two of the moving-van men went by her quickly and disappeared to the left to get something out of the living room. She moved forward to the banister and ran her hand over it. The mahogany still had a sheen to it, as though Ralph Hillerman's mother had been polishing it all morning. She looked up the stairway and then began to climb.

The wooden steps looked their age, but they still felt firm and secure under her feet. It confirmed her belief that the older buildings had more craft, more quality and more endurance. The materials seemed to have absorbed the grit of the men who used them to build the structures.

She didn't know why she was going up the stairs; she felt drawn to do it. When she had shown the house to the Bloomfields, she had tried to move them through the upstairs rapidly. In her mind the downstairs recommended the house more. There the rooms were cozy and interesting. But the upstairs looked more like a boardinghouse. Most of the rooms were of equal size and were indistinguishable from one another because they were painted the same color, had the same number of windows and even had the same commercial furniture. There was one large bedroom that Ralph Hillerman said was their "executive suite," but even that room didn't appear all that different from the others. There were two bathrooms along the corridor and two linen closets. At the end of the hall to the left, there was a door that opened to a small stairway leading up to the attic.

Because so much of the upstairs was similar, she had no explanation as to why she went to the third room down on the right and entered it. Now there was only a double bed with a naked mattress on it, an inexpensive wooden dresser and bureau, and a small night table to the right of the bed. The blue cotton curtain had long since been faded by the sun, yet it still held its shape.

She walked to the window and looked down at the rear of the house. Ralph had had his handyman come up and cut the lawn. It had been a wet final quarter to the summer, and the warm fall kept the grass a rich green. She thought the grounds were pretty, and she could understand why city folk would have enjoyed weeks and months of rest at such a place. Looking closer at the yard, she noticed that an old path through the brush and overgrowth was still visible. It went from the cleared yard area, through the woods to a small pond about two thousand yards from the house. Beyond that was the undeveloped wooded acres climbing upward to the ridge of the mountain range.

The air was clear; the sky was practically cloudless. Through the window the sunlight felt warm on her face, but suddenly she felt a chill run down her spine and she embraced herself tightly. A moan escaped from her lips and she experienced a moment of deep sorrow, even deeper than what she had felt lying in bed this morning and watching

Stephen. She thought she would burst out in tears, but what frightened her the most about it was she couldn't think of any immediate reason for it. She took a deep breath to help herself regain control.

"Well, I guess you're determined to do your research," Ralph Hillerman said. She spun around and saw him standing in the doorway behind her. "Hi there. Didn't mean to frighten you."

"Oh, Ralph, hi." She was embarrassed that she had been caught here and caught in such a trance. He did wear a puzzled smile on his lips and she had no idea how she was going to explain her presence. She couldn't explain it to herself. "Your father's gone?"

"Yes. We took him up yesterday."

"How did it go?"

"As I expected. He was angry when we first got there, and he realized what was happening. Mrs. Marshall had explained it to him and he had even agreed that it was the best thing, but he forgot everything she said and everything he said." He shook his head and smiled. "Then he got caught up in all the attention he was getting up there, and eventually he drifted into a quiet sleep. When I called this morning they said he was doing fine. I should have done it a year ago. It hasn't been easy, even with Mrs. Marshall."

"He's at the home in Walnut?"

"Uh-huh. If I know him he'll still be there when they take me up there, too." She smiled. "Those men downstairs told me you were here. They thought you were the new owner."

"What did you mean," she asked, just realizing what he had said when he first greeted her, "when you said I guess you're determined to do your research? What research?"

"I thought that was why you came to this room."

"This might sound silly, Ralph, but I don't know myself. I just had this urge to come here today."

"Well, doesn't it have to do with the Karla Hoffman story you've been digging?"

"I don't know. Maybe."

"Maybe?" His smile became a look of total confusion. "How can it be maybe, Cynthia? This is it."

"It?"

"This room," he said, his arms out for emphasis. "This is the room in which she was killed. You knew that, didn't you? Why else would you have come in here?"

8

THE NEED TO KNOW as much as possible about Karla Hoffman had never been more intense. After what Ralph Hillerman told her, Cynthia felt as though she had stumbled across the murder itself. The room was suddenly cold and full of shadows. She couldn't wait to get out of it and escape the images of that fatal confrontation. She had no way to explain what Ralph incredulously called, "the coincidence of walking into this room." She wasn't one to talk about the existence of supernatural forces, but why else was she drawn to the Rose Hill House? Why did she go directly to that room?

I was like someone sleepwalking, she told herself. I don't even remember the drive over very clearly.

Suddenly she was afraid. Karla Hoffman had brought her to that house and that room today. She was sure of it; Karla was with her even now, even as she drove away, her hands trembling as they grasped the steering wheel.

Ralph Hillerman, standing on the front steps, had watched her drive off. In her rearview mirror she saw him take off his hat and run his fingers through his hair. She knew she had frightened him. Back in the room, after he told her what it was, her face had whitened quickly. For a few moments she had been unable to speak. She had gasped and embraced herself. He had stood there in the doorway of the room, a puzzled look on his face, his smile slowly evaporating. He looked around the room as though he, too, sensed a spiritual presence.

"Maybe you oughta stop this, Cynthia," he said. "I'm sorry now that I helped you get into it. It might be getting out of hand. Your brother and your husband might get upset with me."

The statement brought the blood back into her face.

"What do you mean, 'upset with you'? You're not dealing with a child, Ralph. Jason is my brother and Stephen is my husband," she said with emphatic deliberateness. "I am my own person, Ralph. I don't need either one of them telling me what I can and what I can't do."

"I just don't want to get in the middle of any family arguments," he said. "It's happened to me more than once, and it's not very pleasant," he added, softening his tone in an effort to placate her. She saw he was very uncomfortable, and she did feel sorry for him.

"Nothing's going to be your fault, Ralph. I don't mean to sound angry at you, and I appreciate everything you told me."

He nodded, but there was an unpleasant moment of silence.

"The Bloomfields' lawyer contacted Tom. They'll be taking title day after tomorrow," he said, wisely changing the topic.

"That's wonderful," she said, and started out of the room. He followed her down the stairs and out the door. "I'm sorry that I upset you up there, Ralph," she told him before she got into the car. "I didn't mean for that to happen." He smiled and patted her lightly on the shoulder.

"Oh, I'm sure you don't mean any harm to anyone. We all get carried away with things sometime. My wife calls herself a golf widow. I suppose I am addicted."

All she could do was smile. Where was the comparison? she wondered. Did he think her interest in Karla Hoffman was the same as a pastime? She figured she had better leave quickly before she said anything else.

Almost as soon as she closed the car door, she felt the eerie sensation she wasn't alone in the automobile. It was as though her contact with Karla Hoffman had been much more substantial than she could ever imagine. The idea unnerved her. She didn't like the possibility that she might have committed an irrevocable act. She thought the best thing to do now was to go straight to her office and get heavily involved with her work.

But when she arrived at the agency and went through her messages, she discovered Miss Weintraub had called. The county historian claimed to have found a related story in one of the old newspapers. For a few moments Cynthia debated whether or not she should call back. Finally she decided it would be quite impolite not to do so.

"You've got me interested," she told Cynthia when Cynthia called her, "so I spent some of my free time looking. It's almost like doing detective work," she said, "and I've always been an amateur sleuth."

"I appreciate your taking the time, Miss Weintraub."

"At my age, my dear, time doesn't have the same meaning. I waste hours doing the most insignificant things. Anyway, what I found is only a small story, just a long paragraph actually. It was buried in the rear of the paper with the news of hamlets and such. Looks like they didn't want to make a big deal of it. You suppose that might be it?"

"Yes, it very well might. The story wasn't a good advertisement for the resort area."

"Um," Miss Weintraub said. There was a long pause.

"What exactly is the story?" Cynthia asked, smiling to herself. These old-time schoolteachers were a breed unto themselves, she thought. Quaint, charming and somewhat eccentric.

"It's about the brother," she said as though Cynthia should have known all along. "Seems he committed suicide in prison only a few months after he was convicted of the murder. Such intrigue. No wonder you were so interested in this story."

"Suicide?"

"I'll read. 'MURDERER COMMITS SUICIDE,'" she announced. "'Leon Bergman, the man who murdered his sister while he and his sister and her husband were vacationing at the Rose Hill House in Woodridge, New York, this past summer, hanged himself in prison.' The rest is about the murder and just goes over what we already know," Miss Weintraub said.

"Was there any explanation as to why he did it? Did he leave a note?"

"Doesn't say if he did."

"What about the husband? Is there any mention of him?"

"Nope. Sorry. 'Cause this article looks like a piece of something chopped and fitted to the space. Maybe you can get hold of the full news story. We don't have that kind of resources here or I'd help you. We're lucky to have what we have. I suppose you'll have to write to Albany or go down to New York or..."

"Well, thank you very much, Miss Weintraub. If you happen to run across anything else..."

"I'll certainly call. Oh, one more thing, Cynthia."

"Yes?"

"I was talking to Martha Kimble whose sister owns the River Tavern in Woodbourne. Do you know the place?"

"I know of it."

"Not a very attractive place now, but in its day.... Anyway, Martha says she makes a nice living. Her sister Lucy, Lucy Morganstern, has a man named Liza Glenn working there. He's been working there for years and years in the kitchen. Cleaning up, odd jobs, you know. I don't suppose you know him, do you?"

"No, no I don't," she said, wondering what he had to do with anything.

"Martha...she has such a good memory... she's in the historical society, you know. She says Liza used to be Ben Hillerman's handyman at the Rose Hill House and would have been working there when the murder took place. He might remember it. He's along in his years, as you can imagine, but he's still got his wits about him. Don't know why, considering the kind of life he lived, but..."

"I see. That's very helpful, Miss Weintraub. Thank you. I will talk to him."

"Yes," she said, and paused again as though she were going to say something else. She didn't, and Cynthia repeated her goodbye and hung up.

For a long moment she simply sat there staring at nothing. The chill that had come over her at the Rose Hill House came over her again. She looked about her office, half expecting to see Karla Hoffman standing there, watching her. Perhaps Ralph Hillerman was right; perhaps she had gone too far and now this thing was driving her mad.

She stood up quickly. She was restless. The day had started out unnerving and the tension hadn't let up. She had no patience for her work and no interest in it. Impulsively, and again with no clear and immediate reason to do it, or clear understanding of where she was going, she left the office, got into her car and drove off. Judy Dobbs had looked up from her desk when Cynthia walked by, but the secretary didn't have time to ask her anything.

Cynthia rode for quite a while along the back roads, roads that were familiar to her as a young girl, as well as a real estate agent. They eventually brought her out near her parents' house, the house in which Jason now lived. She had no intention of stopping there, but she felt a need to drive down friendly streets, to see old landmarks, to feel like a little girl again, to turn back time to a period in her life when everything was much simpler.

But when she reached the house she didn't find peace and calmness; she didn't find the happiness of pleasant memories. Instead her reverie was ended, and she was thrust back into the present. Stephen's car was parked right behind Jason's in the driveway. What were they both doing there at this time of the day when they were supposed to be forty miles away meeting with insurance executives?

She put her foot on the brake and slowed to a stop. The driveway was a long and wide one. It made a half circle in front of the house, a two-story colonial, one of the few of this style in the county. She recalled how as a little girl she used to pretend they were rich cotton farmers, plantation owners in the deep south. It was a beautiful home, rich and stately without being gaudy and ostentatious. Her parents were elegant people; they had class. She thought she had inherited some of that from them, but Jason... Jason was different. He had taken it to an arrogant extreme.

He hadn't touched the house; he didn't change it in any way, but when she looked at it now, she didn't see it as her old home, her place of youth and mud-luscious times. Instead the pillars looked prehistoric and cold. The windows were all dark and gray. The portico had the sheen of ice. For her it had become the entrance to the house of the dead. Jason lived in there with ghosts, but not the ghosts of ancestors. He lived with the ghosts of strangers, lean and hard, stern-faced people. There was no romance in the house at all.

She parked the car and stepped out. Her body trembled both from anticipation and from anger. She was tired of being lied to and manipulated. What were they actually up to? Why couldn't they tell her the truth anymore? Or did they ever tell her the truth? As she walked toward the house she felt numb from the waist down, and she had to look to be sure her feet were touching the ground. It was more like she floated to the front door. Unsurprisingly, it was locked. She debated about pushing the buzzer, brought her finger to the button and then . . . stopped, her hand frozen in midair.

Suddenly all the innuendos confronted her. She had visions of faces wearing sly "I told you so" smiles. She heard people whispering in the shadows. She remembered her own nightmare.

The three of them were in bed, but Stephen wasn't paying any attention to her. He had turned toward Jason. NO! she screamed, but neither Jason nor Stephen seemed to hear or care. She reached for Stephen and pulled him toward her. When he turned around, it wasn't Stephen who was beside her. It was Jason, and when he brought his lips to hers she didn't resist until their lips actually touched. It was then that she awoke.

Stephen was beside her, his back to her. She wanted to reach out and wake him to be sure it was he. That was how vivid her nightmare had been. She didn't do it, but she couldn't go back to sleep for the longest time.

She shook the dream from her memory and considered the buzzer again. What would she do when she confronted them? What if they had already seen her approach the house and now wouldn't come to the door? Should she insist? Pound and scream? Wouldn't she feel foolish if later on Stephen told her they had gone with someone else, and he and Jason had merely left their cars here?

That could be the answer. Everything could be innocent; maybe there was no lying and deceit after all. Things were always on the verge of being one thing or another. Some of this or all of this could be the product of her own imagination.

She started to back away, paused and then returned to the small panel windows on the door. She couldn't leave without at least looking in once. At first she saw nothing, just the long, thickly carpeted entranceway and the portrait of Grandma Palmer that hung on the corridor wall left of the entrance. She always hated that picture. Her grandmother looked so austere, so accusing. Jason took after her, Cynthia thought.

She began to retreat and then stopped. Jason appeared, dressed in his light blue silk robe, a tray of demitasse in his hands. He moved with such deliberate caution, his attention fixed on the tray and the marble stairway. Without looking in her directon he made the turn and began to ascend. She watched him until he disappeared from view and then she stepped back from the door.

She imagined her face was as gray as a layer of gloomy clouds. She felt the blood drain from her cheeks. Her heart skipped beats; her breathing seemed impossible to regulate. She brought her hands to her throat and moved backward off the portico as though she were fleeing from one of Jason's somber ghosts. Her legs trembled as she went down the short stone steps. Then she turned and ran from the house, running like a fugitive from fire, her eyes wide, her lips pulled back, her teeth gleaming like portions of unfleshed bone.

She got into the car and fumbled for the keys. After she started the engine she pulled away quickly, her hands glued to the steering wheel so tightly they felt as if they had left her arms. To her the car was in control of itself, carrying her off. She welcomed the feeling; she wanted to be swept from the scene, swept from the life she had. It wasn't until she pulled onto a major highway that she became fully conscious of what she was doing. The heavier traffic snapped her out of the spell, but she was afraid to look at people for fear they would see the madness in her face and think that she had fled from committing some terrible crime. Indeed, she began mumbling to herself in lunatic fashion, telling herself to calm down, to get hold of herself, to stop behaving so irrationally.

She slowed down, pulled off the road at the first available spot and sat back, her eyes closed, her hands clutched against her breasts. The warmth of full awareness rose up her body and brought a tingling into her legs and buttocks. She put her arms over the steering wheel and lowered her forehead to them.

How long had it been like this? Why hadn't she realized it before? Or was the truth contained in the adage, "There are none so blind as those who will not see"?

The relations between a husband and a wife are so intimate, so personal, so much a part of who and what they are together, she thought. It was terrible enough to think that someone else shared in that intimacy, but for that someone else to be . . . to be Jason. It made her feel incestuous by proxy. Whose lips did Stephen really kiss when he kissed her?

"Oh God," she moaned, "can this be true? Can all this really be happening?"

Maybe it isn't, she thought. Maybe it was still something innocent. Maybe . . .

Reflection 211

"Stop it," she said out loud in the most commanding tone of voice she could muster. "Get hold of yourself, Cynthia Warner. You're your father's daughter. You've got the grit to battle anything. Anything!"

She sat up straight, wiped her face with her handkerchief, put the car into gear again and drove on. When she reached the agency she fixed her makeup before going inside. Judy greeted her with two good messages—prospective customers were confirming their interest in buying the properties she had shown them the day before, so for a good part of the remainder of the day she was busy with that. She went after her work with a monomanical enthusiasm, calling clients, buyers, bankers, newspaper advertising offices. She paused only when she heard Stephen and Jason come in a little after three o'clock. Stephen stopped at her office.

As he stood there smiling innocently, acting as though the world was the same as it has always been, she couldn't help thinking along the lines of *Invasion of the Body Snatchers*. Stephen's face and frame were the same, but there was someone else living inside him, someone alien and unknown to her. She felt like screaming, demanding to know where her husband had been taken. But she pulled herself together.

"How was your meeting?" she asked him, hoping he would end up by explaining why he and

Jason had gone to Jason's house. Stephen's clothes looked as fresh as they did when he left the house in the morning. She imagined Jason ironing his pants and pressing his shirt.

"Great. We picked up quite an account. Jason was very impressive. They were taken by his knowledge and his foresight. Some of the things he came up with even surprised me," he added, smiling. "Your father would be proud of him."

"Did you have lunch?" Her voice cracked, but he didn't notice or care.

"On the way back."

"In a restaurant?"

"Sure." His smile widened. "Where else? Jason wouldn't stop at any roadside stands, if that's what you mean." She closed her eyes and looked away. "Oh," he said, coming to the desk, "I thought you might be interested in seeing this. It's a free handout the real estate people out there put together. Nice layout. Jason said it was effective and he thought you might want to get into something like this, especially now that you have a significant collection of properties to sell," he added. When he dropped it on the desk she saw the watch. The gold band glittered against his dark wrist.

"Where did you get that watch?"

"What? Oh, the watch. I forgot. Jason gave it to me this morning."

Reflection 213

"Why?" she asked. Her voice was so light, the word was nearly only mouthed.

"Leave it to Jason to remember these things. Today is the anniversary of my becoming a vice president at the agency. Thoughtful of him to think of it, wasn't it?" She simply stared. "We're talking a couple of grand here," he said, unhappy with her stoical reaction.

"Wonderful," she said.

"You all right? You look a little pale."

"I'm just tired."

"I told you to goof off today. You're working too hard. You could have taken a break."

"Maybe you're right." She turned to look out the window. She didn't want him to see the tears forming in her eyes.

"I'm planning a vacation," he said. "Jason and I have discussed it. It's just a matter of settling a few outstanding issues and then we go, anywhere we want, anytime we want. How's that sound?"

"Would we go by ourselves?" she asked without turning back to him.

"Of course. If you promise to leave business behind, I promise to leave business behind."

"Then it sounds... promising," she said. He didn't hear the heavy note of skepticism in her voice. He was already thinking of something else.

"Okay," he said, staring out. "How late are you working today?"

"I'm leaving in a little while."

"That's good. What about Chinese food tonight? I'll pick it up on the way home."

"Whatever you want."

"Jason says this new place in Monticello is good. He recommends this dish they call Seven Seasons."

"If Jason recommends it, it has to be good," she said dryly. He nodded.

"See you later."

When the door closed behind him, she felt as if all the air had been sucked from the room. Jason gave him her father's ring. Jason bought him a new watch. Jason picked out his new clothes for him and changed his hairstyle to be more like his own. Jason got him to shave his beard. Maybe he was wearing Jason's underwear.

She could no longer deal with her work; she could no longer remain in the office. She got up, scooped her briefcase off the desk and went out.

"I won't be back anymore today," she told Judy. She didn't look at her secretary when she spoke, for fear that Judy would see her lips tremble.

After she drove away she was surprised at how quickly her mind shifted to more mundane matters. She imagined it was part of the brain's ability to protect itself. She remembered she had to stop at the dry cleaners to pick up some clothing. She remembered some toilet articles she needed, as well. When she went to the department store she walked mindlessly down the aisles, though, looking like someone who had forgotten what she had to buy. After she left she sat in her car in the parking lot and stared out at people getting in and out of theirs. She had this great urge to cry, but she forced it back, swallowing hard as though she were trying to prevent herself from regurgitating.

Finally she started out slowly, but when she came to the highway she paused and turned in the direction opposite to her house. She had looked at the clock on the dashboard and seen that it was ten to four. She could be at the house she had acquired for Terrence Baker to rent in less than twenty minutes. His words rang in her memory, tolling their temptation and causing her to speed up.

When she arrived there, she saw his car parked in the driveway. The sight of it sent an electricity through her body that was both frightening and exciting. It drove away her depression and filled her with a new hope. It wasn't anything she could verbalize, even only to herself; it was simply an erotic drive sending her in the direction of his voice, his eyes, the memory of his kiss.

He was sitting on the front stoop, his back against the door, smoking a cigarette and looking as though he knew she would come. But she didn't think of him as being arrogant or herself as being predictable. She pulled in behind his car, and he flipped the cigarette over the lawn. She got out and he stood up. He didn't smile; his face was dead serious. She walked to him slowly. Neither of them spoke. He reached out and pulled her to him, and when their lips met she felt herself plunging down some dark tunnel, falling freely, welcoming her sense of helplessness.

"It's meant to be," he said, and she believed him.

THERE WAS VERY LITTLE FURNITURE in the house, and the electricity hadn't been turned on yet. The sun was lower in the fall Catskill sky, so even though it was nearly a completely clear sky, the house was weakly illuminated. Cynthia felt as though she were entering an ethereal world, the land of dreams, someplace levels below the conscious mind. Everything carried a symbolic value here. Nothing could be said or done without it having great meaning.

The windowless entranceway was darker than the rest of the house; she saw it as a transition. She even saw something meaningful in the way the front door had opened into it. The lock turned smoothly, but the door itself stuck against the jamb. He pressed his body against it to force it open and then took her hand to lead her through the shadows. They stopped at the small living room in which the sole piece of furniture was the large-cushioned, colonial-style couch. Alone in an otherwise naked room, it seemed to personify the temptation itself. He took her directly to it.

The sunlight filtering through the windows caught the tiny particles of dust in the air and turned them into airy jewels, the dust of diamonds. A strong breeze slipping in under doors and through small cracks in window frames created a symphony of creaks. Somewhere a loose shutter tapped gently against an outside wall. Their own footsteps, as soft as they were, seemed to rise behind them in an echo that rushed into other rooms. All of this made her heart beat faster, making her think that the sound of her own breathing had amplified considerably. She looked to see if he noticed the changes.

But it was he who changed on entrance into the house. His look of seriousness deepened. There was an intensity in his eyes that already had begun to challenge any thoughts of hesitation she might have. He held her hand firmly, and when they reached the couch he embraced her tightly, lifting her into him, driving his lips against hers with a hunger that nearly overwhelmed her.

She had longed for a way to challenge her sadness. She fought back tears and found that her unchecked passion helped her drive back the urge to cry. Her response to him came from an energy that sprang out of her anger as well as out of her desire.

In this giving of herself to Terrence Baker, she would strike back at Stephen for his unnatural betrayal. This was the only logical thought that passed through her mind. All else was imagery—the picture of his fingers peeling away the buttons of her blouse, the way his hands slipped over and around her breasts, the tingle of his lips moving down her neck to her shoulders.

He placed her gently on the couch. She didn't even take off her coat. It served them like a shell, closing in around them after he had unfastened her slacks and slid them and her panties down over her feet. When he sat back to undo his own pants, she found herself intrigued with his look of concentration. He was more like a craftsman than a spontaneous lover now, concerned with every move, every stage of what had to be done. For a moment she felt like a third party watching the scene. Then, as if he could hear her thoughts, he directed his attention back at her, smiling for the first time since they had entered the house.

He kissed and nibbled at her breasts tenderly; he stroked her smoothly, moving about her body as though he could sculpt his private Venus and transform her into another woman to give her a new identity, one that would cut her away from the world and the people she now despised.

She did feel as though she were in the hands of an artist. There was no sense of exploration, no testing, no trial and error. Everything he did, he did with purpose and confidence. He brought her up by taking her to a point of maddening stimulation and then retreated to start on another part of her—to kiss her ankles, to work his way up her legs, moving gracefully between her thighs, erasing all the tension in her body as he went along; getting her to the point where she clutched at him, tugging him closer, driving him to move faster.

She had a climax almost the moment he entered her. Her head began to spin as she reached peak after peak, thinking she would pass out beneath him. Her cries overcame his groans and anything he whispered. She heard nothing anyway, nothing but her own demands for more. When she opened her eyes she saw him braced up above her, his head held back, his eyes closed, his face grimacing almost in pain. She could never recall such a look on Stephen's face. His lovemaking was polite compared to this, and she thought that somehow, when two people made love as much as she and Stephen had, they should be less tentative toward one another.

In the midst of all this she couldn't help thinking that what had been missing in her and Stephen's lovemaking was this aggressive call for pleasure that forced both parties to satisfy one another. Stephen never demanded any more of her. She should have realized he wasn't as fully involved with her as a man should be.

Finally spent, Terrence fell against her. Neither of them spoke until their breathing slowed. Then he pulled himself up and sat back. His look of satisfaction made her feel good; it made her feel significant and appreciated. This was another thing she felt was currently missing in her relationship with Stephen.

"Sometimes you just know something's going to be right," he said. "This was one of them."

"When did you know?"

"Back in the theater when you looked up at me on the stage. Don't laugh, I'm serious," he said. She held a smile, but it was a soft smile, a loving smile.

"Tell me about it."

"I had just finished what everyone seemed to think was a damn good performance. I felt the accomplishment. I was high on the applause, but then I looked down at you and all of the applause died away. All sound was shut off, and it was as if you were the only one out there. I forgot where I was for a moment. I actually forgot what I had just done. None of that mattered."

"Why is it I get the feeling that you might be reciting something from a play you were once in?" she said. She began to put on her clothes.

"It's that feminine distrust. You have more than your share of it."

"Do I?" She paused to give it a thought. "Maybe I do. Maybe that's my problem. One of many," she added.

"I don't care what your problems are," he said. "I'm not even going to ask you anything about yourself and your current marital situation. I want us to be like Adam and Eve and this to be our Paradise," he said indicating the house. She laughed, but he kept his serious expression.

"You're so dramatic. Is that part of being an actor?"

"I wish you could forget that I do acting."

"I can't. We all do it," she said, thinking about Stephen. She stood up and shook out her hair.

"Was this your act?"

She stopped and looked at him.

"No. I don't think I wanted anything as sincerely as I wanted this today."

"Will you want it again?"

"And again and again?" She couldn't help laughing. She felt wild, drunk, suicidal. "I don't know. It seems important that we have some spontaneity, don't you think? You really couldn't be sure that I would come here today, and I didn't decide to do it until nearly the last moment. That's part of the thrill. I feel like someone who has been a careful driver all her life, but who decides one day to go a hundred miles an hour. Yes," she said, anticipating his question, "I liked it. And yes, I might want to do it again."

She stopped because she heard the hysteria in her voice. He heard it, too, and his expression changed from one of quiet amusement to one of deep concern.

"You do have some major problems, don't you?"

"Me? I'm Carl Palmer's daughter. I'm a successful businesswoman. I have money, prestige, power, respect. Major problems?"

"I'm going to break one of my own rules. This isn't just a fling for me. I want to help you."

"You already did," she said, and started out.

"Wait a minute." He grabbed her wrist before she reached the front door. "This is quite a reversal. Usually the woman feels like she's been used."

"I'm sorry. Am I hurting your male ego?"

"That's a low blow, Cynthia," he said. She studied him and then let herself relax. He released her wrist.

"You're right. I'm sorry. Look, I'm having trouble putting things into perspective right now. I'm terrified of commitments. But you were right—I had to be here today. I don't know if I have to be here tomorrow or the next day or the next." She turned away from him. "My world is crumpling."

He reached out to put his hand on her shoulder. She stiffened at his touch until he stroked her hair and brought her back against him.

"Can't I help you? Seriously. I want to help you."

She turned to look into his eyes. Was there really any way to tell about someone by looking at him?

"If you're just acting," she said, "you're really good. But we knew that already, didn't we?"

"I'm not just acting," he whispered. She closed her eyes. He kissed her forehead and then lifted her chin gently so their lips could meet. The kiss was gentle, soft, loving. It was a convincing kiss, but she told herself perhaps she wanted to be convinced. What did it matter anymore? she thought.

"Our spirits have linked and I think there's a reason."

He studied her for a moment.

"Are you serious?"

"As much as I could ever be." She turned away from him again because the tears were coming. "My husband... my husband is having an affair with my brother," she said.

"What?"

"Just what I said. My brother has always been... been somewhat different, but none of us faced up to it—least of all me. I'm famous for ignoring reality. Maybe that's why I am so distrustful. I have another, more rose-colored view of things. Ironically, my brother, and now my husband, are always chastising me for being too optimistic. I should have turned their cool, practical view of things on them."

"Are you saying that your husband is a homosexual?" He still looked dumbfounded.

"My brother, despite his strangeness or maybe because of it, is a powerful man. He has ways of gaining control over people, winning them to his point of view. He's successful at most anything he wants to do, and he has a quiet ruthlessness about him."

"But you can't turn someone into a homosexual, can you?"

"I don't know as he's done that exactly, but what he has done is terrible enough."

"And you never realized any of this until now?"

"As I said, I have a way of ignoring whatever reality displeases me."

"Jesus."

"Maybe you shouldn't have broken your rule," she said. She wiped her cheeks with the back of her hand and smiled at his look of incredulity.

"Maybe not." He smiled. "What are you going to do now? Does your husband know you know?"

"No."

"When exactly did you find out about this?" She didn't reply, but he saw the answer in her face. "You mean . . . right before you came here today?"

"Yes."

"I see. Then I guess I have been used in a way."

"You probably won't believe me now, but I think I would have come here anyway."

"Why shouldn't I believe you? Listen, are you positive about this thing?"

"Practically."

"There's only one thing for you to do then—confront him," he said, "and see if you're right. Then, if you are, get out."

"You make it sound so simple."

"Most things are a lot simpler than we first think. I know it's easy for me to say, but..."

"No, maybe you're right."

"What was this other thing you said—something about our spirits?"

"It's complicated," she said. "It has to do with someone who was murdered in one of the houses I sold."

"Murdered? When?"

"About fifty years ago."

"I don't understand. Why would that affect you so deeply?"

"If you saw her picture, you'd understand. I have to get going."

"I want to see you again," he said. "And soon. Very soon."

"Despite all this?"

"Maybe because of it. You're more exciting than a three-act suspense thriller."

"Thanks a lot. I'll call you."

"Listen...this spirit thing...could it be that you're using it as a way to escape the reality you detest?"

"It doesn't lead me out of it.... It leads me to it," she said, and she started out again. He followed her.

"Oh. Sid Jaffe called. I'm going to his office tomorrow to sign the lease."

"Good. Then I won't feel like a trespasser."

He laughed and closed the door behind them. She paused on the steps to look out over the lawn. The weakened sun rays just passed through the tops of the trees in the woods across the street. She pulled her coat closed.

For a moment the image of Karla Hoffman passed before her. She saw her as she was in the picture by the gazebo, only this time she turned to look directly forward.

"Hey," he said, "you all right?"

"What? Oh, yes. It's just a lot cooler now than when I came. It gets kind of nippy toward evening this time of the year."

"Right."

He followed her to the car and knelt down when she got in and lowered the window.

"I'll call you," she said.

"Promise?"

"Yes."

"Look. I'm sure you have a lot of people you can turn to, but don't be afraid to move me up the list."

"Maybe I will. I don't think either of us have a choice about it anymore," she said.

Reflection

She started the engine, put the car in gear and backed out of the driveway. He stood there watching her, and she wondered if he thought she was totally out of her mind. She couldn't blame him if he felt that way. If someone had told her the things she told him, she realized she might very well have that kind of reaction. And yet he seemed concerned and sincerely interested. When she looked back at him he waved.

She drove away feeling like one who had just slipped in and out of a dream, but she thought it might have strengthened her enough to face whatever reality now awaited.

9

ON HER WAY HOME, Cynthia did feel another presence with her in the car. It was an eerie sensation, like the one a person has when she knows she's being watched. It wasn't that she really believed Karla was beside her; it was more like being under someone's heavy influence. After all, she thought, she wasn't herself. What she had just done with Terrence Baker was completely out of character for her, even though it made her feel good to have done it.

There was a new voice in her mind, the voice of someone with more experience, more self-assurance. This voice challenged her feelings of guilt and challenged her hesitation and weakness. In fact it even chastised her for it. And then a debate was started concerning Terrence Baker's advice.

Should she do what he suggested and confront Stephen directly? What would she say? She envisioned the dialogue between them, with her sounding like a detective summing up her solution to the crime. "You told me you were at a meeting. You told me you had lunch in a restaurant, but I went past Jason's house and you were both there."

What if he came up with one of their logical explanations? she thought. The other voice said, "Tell him that you saw Jason in his bathrobe taking coffee upstairs. It was coincidental that you came by the house and saw their cars. You were about to go in to see what was doing when Jason appeared."

What if he said, "What does that mean? Can't we have coffee? We took a break. So what?" What should she say then?

"It's crystal clear," the other voice told her. "You can lay it out for him. He changed his hairstyle to look like Jason's, to fit what Jason liked, didn't he? He went to Jason's tailor to buy the clothes Jason favored. He shaved off his beard to please Jason, not you. He uses Jason's cologne because that's the scent Jason likes. Jason rewards him. He gave him your father's ring, and now he bought him an expensive gold watch."

But was it all so crystal clear? How clear would it be to someone else, someone who was not involved and couldn't react based on instincts developed after years of their living together? Most everything on that list of accusations could be seen as innocent. Some of it was supposedly even done to please her.

No, she thought, it wasn't time for a direct confrontation, not the kind of confrontation Terrence was suggesting. Besides, there was the nagging possibility, actually the hope, as slim as she thought it was, that maybe, just maybe, she was wrong in what she believed.

"What do you need to be, a hundred percent sure?" the other voice asked. "Do you want to catch them in the act?" God no, she thought.

And yet, how small all her circumstantial evidence seemed now that it was laid out before her. She definitely needed something more, something very close to catching them in the act. In the interim, how was she to behave? Could she act? Oh Terrence, she thought, I should have asked you to lend me some of your technique.

Before she reached the house the other voice described a plan to her. It was so simple and so natural she was surprised it didn't come to her right away. She blamed her failure to think of it quickly on her good nature, on her tolerance. "It's your own fault," the other voice said. "You should have been more jealous right from the start." She had to agree. Perhaps she was also at fault to a degree because she had been so dedicated to her own work, she thought. "Don't do that," the voice said. "Don't rationalize their behavior and Stephen's betrayal."

Reflection

Who was this voice? Was it a deeper, stronger part of herself, or was it Karla Hoffman reaching across half a century? It didn't matter to her now. It had given her the strength to go on, so she welcomed it no matter what it was.

It was totally dark by the time she got home. There wasn't a light on in the house, but she remembered that Stephen was going for Chinese food on the way back from the office. "That's good," the other voice told her. "That's perfect."

She went directly to the bedroom after she pulled the car into the garage and found the matchbook cover she had discovered on the floor of the closet. It was still where she had left it on the dresser, undisturbed. She was happy he hadn't come upon it. Her other voice wouldn't tolerate such an indirect approach. It was time to turn things back at them; it was time to test them and their relationship. She had to know where she stood.

She took a shower and changed into a pair of designer jeans and a flannel shirt. She put on her tennis sneakers and twirled her hair so she could pin it up. Then she set the table, made some tea and sat waiting for him in the kitchen. A little after six she heard the garage door go up and she thought, tonight he had done exactly what he said he was going to do. Apparently Jason hadn't interfered. Sure enough, he entered carrying a bag of still-warm containers of Chinese food.

"Hey, you're all set. Great. This stuff smells so good I nearly ate it through the bag on the way home."

"Do I have to warm anything?"

"I don't think so. It still feels hot enough. I'll just change quickly," he said, placing the package on the kitchen table. It was then that he took note of her. "Hey, you look great, sort of pure farm girl. I like it."

"Thank you. Don't be long."

She got the food into the dishes and poured the steaming tea into their cups as he returned.

"Smells wonderful, doesn't it? I'm sure Jason was right about this place. There was quite a line for takeouts." He sat down and started to eat. "I don't know how he does it. You would never think he gets around that much, would you?"

"Oh, I don't know," she said. "Jason often surprises me. According to him, he gets around a great deal. In fact," she said, reaching into the breast pocket of her shirt, "he gave me this and said I should make you take me there whenever we go to Atlantic City." She threw the matchbook cover across the table. Stephen looked down at it and paused in his eating.

"What's that?"

"What does it look like? It's a matchbook advertising a place you two were at, right?"

"He gave you that?"

"Jason has a habit of collecting business cards, matchbooks, whatever whenever he goes anywhere. Haven't you noticed? It's his way of keeping a record of things. He's so precise about his time. But I'm sure you realize that."

"Sure, but..."

"So why do you seem so surprised? Oh, that's right," she said, smiling and waving her right forefinger at him, "you fibbed. You told me you two hardly had any time to breathe while you were there. That's not exactly the way Jason described it," she said, trying to sound more like she was teasing him than reprimanding him. She continued to dish herself some food from the containers. He stared and then looked down at his plate.

"We were busy," he said. "Very busy. I don't care what impression you might have gotten from talking to Jason."

"Oh, I'm sure you were. Jason has a way of belittling so many things, doesn't he?"

"I can't believe that Jason would recommend this place to you," he said, picking up the matchbook and turning it around in his fingers. His eyes narrowed in a way that was unfamiliar to her. It brought a chill to the back of her neck.

"Why not?"

"We were in and out of it rather quickly. It wasn't what you would think it would be from reading this."

"What's the difference?" Her heart was beating rapidly. "This food is very good. You're right about this place. Rather I should say, Jason knows his Chinese food."

"Yes."

"I don't recall him being very fond of Chinese food, though," she said. "I know he hates MSG. Did you order this without the MSG?"

"Yes, I did."

"Jason must have taught you that. You never do it when we're out together."

"I never thought about it."

"I did, but I never made a point about it. But," she said, smiling, "I'm glad you realize it now. It always gives Jason a headache. He probably told you that. Does it give you a headache now, too?"

"I've had headaches, but I never connected the two."

"Um. You'd better continue eating before your food gets cold," she said.

"Huh? Oh, right, right."

They both ate quietly for a few moments. She watched him out of the corner of her eye and thought she heard the other voice within her urge her to go on.

"So your meeting went well today," she said.

"Yes, it did. It was a good day for the Palmer Agency."

"That's what Jason said, too. He almost used those exact words."

"When did you and he do all this talking?" Stephen asked, a half smile on his face.

"I don't know. Before I left the office sometime. Why?"

"No reason, except I was with him most of the time."

"I guess you weren't with him then. You were with him enough anyway, Stephen. He told me you even stopped at the house on the way back to the office," she added. She didn't think herself capable of saying it that quickly and directly, but it was as though the other voice within her had taken over for the moment. Stephen's reaction was what she thought it might be for the moment. The smile left his face, and he froze in position. She continued to eat as though she had said nothing unusual.

"What do you mean?"

"Mean? Mean about what, Stephen?"

"You just said 'stopped at the house.' Which house?"

"Why, Jason's house, silly. What other house could I have meant?"

"He told you we stopped there?"

"Well, didn't you? You're acting as though it were some kind of sin for you two to stop there."

Stephen stared at her for a moment. She felt the chill again, but she didn't look away, even though his face seemed to turn right before her eyes. His expression became harder; his lips thinned and whitened. There was a tightness around his eyes and through his forehead.

"No, it's not that it was a sin to stop there," he said. She heard the battle for control in his voice. "Jason's usually not that talkative about our business trips, is he?" he asked.

"No, he's not. He's certainly not as talkative with me as he is with you. Maybe he was just in a good mood because of your successful meeting," she said. "Don't you think that might be it?"

"Yes," he said, looking pensive. "I suppose so."

"This food is fantastic," she said again. "I'm so glad you thought of it. I mean, that Jason thought of it. Why didn't you invite him over, too?"

"Huh? Oh, he was going . . . going out to dinner with a client of ours, the Bentons."

"Jason's amazing," she said. "He'll never be lonely even if he doesn't marry. Actually, you might say he's married to the business."

"Yes," Stephen said.

"You've slowed down, Stephen. I thought you said you were ravishingly hungry."

"Oh, yeah, sure," he said, and he dug into his food.

When she was finished eating she put her fork down and folded her hands as she watched him eat. He drank his tea and looked at her curiously.

"You have a funny look on your face," he said.

"I was just thinking," she said, "how glad I am now that you shaved off your beard. You do look younger."

"What about my plumpness?"

"You're not really that overweight," she said, impressed at how convincing she could sound when she lied. It wasn't something she considered herself skilled at before. If anything, she was usually more brutal with the truth when it came to criticizing and complimenting people. "Of course it won't hurt you to lose a few pounds. You're still going to join the health club, aren't you?"

"Sure, but I'll have to go there in the evenings."

"Too bad you can't get Jason to go with you," she said, but before he could respond the phone rang. It was Paula. She was feeling kind of blue, and she wanted to know if Cynthia would go with her to a movie.

"We can see that new psychological terror film, *Pin*. I know you like that stuff. I just want to get out. I'd see anything, even a Walt Disney. Robert and I had a bad fight. He's thinking of leaving me again."

"I'm sorry to hear it, Paula. Just a moment." She held her hand over the receiver and turned to Stephen who was beginning to clean off the table. "It's Paula," she said. "She had a fight with Robert and she's feeling low. Mind if I go with her to a movie?"

"No, no problem. I'm just going to go over some accounts in the den and get an early sleep anyway."

"Fine. Okay, Paula, I'll pick you up in a half hour." She hung up and helped clean off the table. "Sure you don't mind?"

"Why should I mind?"

"We seem to be spending less and less time with each other these days. I mean, just the two of us."

"Well, if you want me to mind..." He smiled and she thought, God how can this be? How could this be happening?

"That's all right. We're going to have a vacation soon you said, right?"

"Right."

"Maybe you'll wait up for me," she said.

"Maybe I will." He leaned over to kiss her, and she closed her eyes before his lips reached hers. The kiss was so soft it hardly existed. She left him to get ready to go out. He was in the den by the time she started for the garage.

"See you later," she called. He acknowledged her and she left. The moment she started the car and backed out, she felt relief. It was as though she could slip back into her true self. Her heart was beating madly because she knew what was about to occur. He would call Jason and ask him why he had told her all those things and Jason would deny it, just the way he had denied the things she had accused him of doing, like telling Stephen about Karla Hoffman.

"He's trying to torment you," the other voice said. "Because he's been jealous of you and Stephen. It's something he has been doing all these years. You should have seen it from the start."

I know, she admitted. I know.

"You're two of a kind, you and your brother Jason. You're not any less Palmer than he is. That's something you're about to discover about yourself and he's about to discover about you. I hope you can handle it."

I will. I can.

She looked back at the house after she had backed completely down the driveway. You'll hate each other before I'm finished with you two, she thought.

She heard laughter in the car and realized it was coming from her, but it wasn't her. It was the other voice. She accelerated to get away quickly.

In the short space of a few hours she had moved from horror and shock to passion and strength. Now she turned all of her emotions into a mad, feline anger.

I was glad I turned you in to Mother that day, Jason, she thought. Glad I got you into trouble for carving a dead cat in our basement. You were always the distorted one, and I was always tired of your condescending manner toward me.

I'll turn you in to Mother again, she thought.

The resulting wild laughter, as alien as it sounded to her, filled her with energy and determination. She drove on, anxious to carry out her plans.

IT WAS NEARLY MIDNIGHT by the time she returned home. She and Paula had gone for ice cream after the movie and talked for nearly an hour. She liked the picture, but since part of the terror came from an incestuous relationship between a brother and a sister she found the plot unnerving. In the end the sister destroyed the brother mentally. Once again she felt there were messages for her personally in the events happening around her. It was as though some inner force was directing her toward answers.

Paula didn't like the picture, but Paula wasn't really in the mood to like anything. Actually Cynthia was glad she didn't want to talk about it. She didn't want to expose it to the armchair criticism of amateur reviewers. She thought that might destroy the magic it held for her. Paula's only comment was "It makes *Psycho* look like a Walt Disney production."

Cynthia couldn't remember a time when Paula had been as maudlin and so full of self-pity. Robert had finally exploded at the way she ran the house and organized their lives. He said the marriage was all take on her part and all give on his, and he felt she was incorrigible. She thought he had found another woman.

"He's comparing me to her," she said. "He must have discovered some 'Stepford Wife,' a subscriber to *Good Housekeeping* and *Family Circle* who probably impressed him with all the coupons she cuts out before going to the supermarket. I always knew he was a male chauvinist pig, but I thought I could live with that. I've always been able to ignore it." She paused and waited for Cynthia to react, but Cynthia was concentrating on her sundae. "I'm talking, talking, talking," Paula said, "and you're just filling your face."

"Sorry."

"Well? What do you think of all this, or didn't you hear a word I said?"

"I heard you. Why do you assume he's found another woman?"

"I know the look when I see it. Sometimes he sits there staring at nothing, but there's this half smile on his face. He's probably reliving some tumble at a motel. I don't believe he has to work late all the times he claims he does."

"Check up on him."

"I don't want to show him I care."

"But you do. That's obvious."

"Well, I'm not a spring chicken, and I'm not God's gift to men."

"No one would believe that from the way you act."

"Jesus. You know you sound harder tonight, a lot harder than I even remember you. I don't think you feel a bit sorry for me."

"Just tired, I suppose. I do feel sorry for you. Really." She reached across the table to pat Paula on the hand.

"Oh, I'm not looking for sympathy. Yes I am," she added quickly. "That's why I invited you out. Was Stephen angry?"

"Stephen? Stephen is...understanding." Paula didn't see Cynthia's wry smile.

"He is, isn't he? At least he gives that appearance." Paula toyed with her ice cream for a moment, turning the spoon around in the mound of butter pecan and chocolate supreme. "I looked at my horoscope today," she said, making it sound like a confession. That brought a smirk to Cynthia's otherwise somber face. "Before you pooh-pooh it let me tell you what it said. It read, 'Avoid conflicts at home.' What do you say to that?"

"I've told you before—horoscopes are so general they have to come true at one time or another."

"Well I shoulda listened anyway." She studied Cynthia for a moment. "You always seem so damn sure of yourself, but tonight you sound even more so. I wish I had your confidence."

"Things are not always what they seem."

"Right. I like your hair that way. What did Stephen say about it?"

"He liked it."

"Oh? Are things better at home? You're acting like a woman who's had some satisfaction."

"Not yet, Paula, but soon . . . soon."

"And what's that supposed to mean?" Paula asked. Cynthia was quiet. "You know you're acting damn peculiar tonight, Cynthia Warner. You're not yourself."

"Very perceptive. I'm not myself. I'm someone else," she said, and laughed. The laugh was so unexpected, it frightened Paula. She thought for a moment and then narrowed her eyes as she leaned forward.

"Wait a minute. Does this have anything to do with Terrence Baker?"

"Why do you ask that?"

"What happened after you grilled me at my house?"

"Nothing."

"You're not telling me the truth, are you?" Paula asked after a moment.

"No."

"Cynthia Warner, you lucky little bitch. I want all the erotic details—everything and retold with passion. The least you could do is let me have a romantic affair vicariously. I talked you into going to the play that night. You owe it to me."

"All right," she said, "I'll tell you something."

"Good." Paula leaned forward again, expectantly.

"But it won't be about my love affair. It'll be about someone else's love affair."

"Someone else's?" Paula got that knowing look on her face. "I thought so. Didn't I tell you so when you came to my house to ask me what I had told Terrence about you? I knew it, I knew it," she repeated as a way of congratulating herself.

"It's not what you think, at least, not exactly."

"It's about Stephen, right? He's having an affair, right?" Cynthia nodded. "What did I say? Didn't I say so? Didn't I recognize the symptoms? This new girlfriend probably wanted him to shave his beard, so . . ."

"His new girlfriend is a man," Cynthia said.

"What? I thought you said, 'man.'"

"I did. My husband and my brother are having a homosexual affair." She said it slowly and carefully as though she was very concerned about her diction. Paula just stared for a moment, but Cynthia didn't change her expression.

"Are you serious? My God, you are serious. This is what you meant when you said that Stephen was becoming too much like Jason?"

"I didn't realize the extent of it at the time."

"You know, this doesn't surprise me. I mean, the part about Stephen surprises me, but there's always been a lot of talk about Jason. I never told you most of it. I figured, why put you through all that nasty gossip."

"I saw, but I would not see," Cynthia said. "When I think about it, I suppose my parents did the same thing."

"But to think that Stephen...people have the wrong idea about gays, I suppose. We tend to see them as limp-wrist types."

"Despite it all I still don't think of Stephen as gay. I think of him as seduced."

"What do you mean?"

"My brother is a powerful, persuasive and intelligent person. I used to admire the way he manipulated my parents. As long as I can remember he always seemed to be in control." She thought for a moment and then scraped the bottom of her ice cream bowl.

"I don't understand how you can just sit there and calmly eat ice cream after telling me all this."

"Oh, I wasn't this calm all day, but I've simply settled into it. Now I know I can and will do whatever I have to do."

"What are you planning to do?" Paula asked. Her eyes were wide. The smile came back to Cynthia's face, but it wasn't a smile that gave Paula a sense of relief or calm; it was a smile that reminded her of the terror film they had just seen. It sent a chill through her. This wasn't the Cynthia Warner she knew.

"I'm going to drive both of them mad, and then I'm going to leave him," she said.

"Drive them mad? What do you mean?"

"My brother would love me to simply disappear, quietly retreat. He knows I'm not going to announce it to all the world. But he's about to discover that we are the same kind of people," Cynthia said, her eyes filled with determination. Paula shook her head.

"He knows that you know?"

"Not yet."

"I feel like such an idiot, crying to you about my problems, telling you I suspect Robert might be having an affair with another woman. What's that compared to your situation? How did you find all this out? You didn't actually..."

"Catch them in the act? Just about. I could have, but I couldn't let myself do it."

"Competing with another woman is one thing, but competing with a man... I don't think you're going to handle this right, Cynthia. I think you should confront Stephen directly."

"That's what Terrence said."

"Terrence? Terrence Baker? You told him about this? When? Where?" Cynthia smiled at Paula's enthusiasm. "There's more to tell, isn't there? My

God, you've had quite a day or so. Well? Don't leave me hanging."

"Let's get out of here," Cynthia said. "We'll talk in the car."

She told her all of it on the way to Paula's house. It felt good to let it out, and she was grateful that she had at least one friend in whom she could confide. They sat for a while in the car parked in Paula's driveway.

"Robert's home," Paula said, indicating the lit rooms. "You've influenced me. I'm going to have a sensible conversation with him... no shouting, no name-calling, just quiet, reasonable talk."

"I wish you luck."

"It's funny," Paula said, "but a few days ago, even yesterday, if someone would have asked me to describe you, I would have said things like 'stable, conservative, a life of perfection.'"

"Which only goes to show you how often things are not what they seem to be. That's a painful lesson, believe me."

"Promise me you'll call me for lunch and not a week from now."

"I promise."

"And call me if you need me for anything, anytime."

"I will."

"I don't want to miss the next episode. This is better than *Dynasty*."

"You might be right. Thanks for being such a good friend."

They hugged and Paula got out. She turned back to wave as Cynthia started out of the driveway. On the way home Cynthia had the eerie feeling that she had just seen Paula for the last time. She shook it off before she reached her house, but it left her in a melancholy mood. As she pulled up she was surprised to see almost all the lights were off, but then she remembered that Stephen had said he was going to get an early sleep. She wondered how he could after the things she had said to him.

After she pulled into the garage and entered the house, she saw that there was a small light on in the den, so she went directly to it. The den was directly off the front entrance. When she got there, she found Stephen in the soft leather chair waiting for her. With only the small lamp on at his side, he looked pale and ghostly. He was in his robe and slippers, and he had a book in his lap. He looked up as soon as she appeared in the doorway.

"I thought you'd be asleep," she said.

"Long movie?"

"Paula and I went out for some ice cream," she said. "What happened to your early-to-bed bit?"

"I tried, but Jason called. He came in from dinner with the Bentons and called to tell me some business news."

Reflection

"It's interesting how you two can't wait until you see each other to tell each other things. Does everything that you two do have the same degree of intensity?"

"It's not that. We're just dependent on each other. We respect each other's advice and ideas. I suppose we have a lot more trust in each other than most partners do."

"Partners!" she said disdainfully. She walked into the den and took off her jacket.

"That's why," he said, choosing to ignore her disparaging remark, "when we tell each other something and say it's so, we believe each other completely."

"Really?"

"Yes, really. Actually he called a few hours ago, but I waited up to talk to you."

"Oh?" She sat on the love seat, enjoying the fact that she was cloaked mostly in darkness.

"He said he didn't give you that matchbook cover, and he said he never told you we went to his house."

She laughed. It was a strong and convincing laugh with not a note of uncertainty or fear in it. The laugh even surprised her. It was as though it had come from another part of her, a part of her that she never knew existed. She welcomed it, though; she welcomed the courage and the strength.

"Just like Jason to do something like that," she said. Her nonchalance threw him off. He raised his eyebrows and leaned forward.

"Something like what?"

"Play with you. He's been doing it to me for some time now, or haven't you noticed?"

"I don't understand. What are you saying? You're saying that Jason told you something and then pretended he didn't? Why would he do that?"

"You'll have to ask him. Whenever I questioned some of the differences between you two and your stories, you told me he was joking; it was part of his weird sense of humor. Didn't you tell me that? Didn't you even say, 'that's Jason's way'?" she asked, speaking in a tone of voice an elementary teacher might use to deal with a problem child. He sat back and stared at her for a moment.

"That was different," he said.

"Why?"

"Because . . . because it was harmless stuff. This is . . ."

"Well, isn't this harmless? You didn't pick up any women when you were at this place in Atlantic City, did you, Stephen?"

"Of course not."

"And you didn't have any women with you at Jason's house today, did you?"

"You're being ridiculous. If I were going to be an adulterer, do you think I'd have your brother in on it?"

"So why isn't this harmless? It's just Jason's weird sense of humor," she said. "Only this time he's turned it on you. Now you know how I often felt." She got up. "I'm tired. Paula wore me out with her problems. Coming to bed or are you going to let Jason's little joke keep you up all night?"

"I'll be right along," he said. She saw the confusion in his face, and she heard it in his voice. It warmed her heart.

"Fine," she sang out. She left him sitting there and wondering under the small light.

It was nearly twenty minutes before he finally came to bed. She pretended to be fast asleep, but she heard him toss and turn for quite a while before his breathing became regular and subdued. Then she peered into the darkness as though she could hear another voice whispering to her.

She thought it said, *This is the way. Go on. Go on.*

It comforted her, and she was able to find sleep herself. It came on the heels of a series of images—pictures of Karla Hoffman sitting on the swings at the Rose Hill House; Karla Hoffman walking alone over the front lawn, her head down, but her face locked in an angelic smile; and Karla Hoffman climbing the steps to her room, the room in which Cynthia had been. Before she reached it the images faded, and Cynthia gratefully accepted darkness and sleep.

10

CYNTHIA KNEW she couldn't avoid Jason the next day, but she deliberately made him wait for as long as she could. She went to the office late, but as soon as she arrived Judy Dobbs told her Jason wanted to see her.

"He said I should tell you to go directly to his office," she said.

I've been summoned, she thought, and ignored it altogether. About twenty minutes later Sally Kaufman buzzed her to repeat the message. She thanked her, but she ignored that, as well. She busied herself with her work and when Sally Kaufman called again, she was on the phone. The next time she called, Cynthia said she was too busy at the moment. Actually she snapped at her, and the seasoned secretary stuttered an apology and hung up. It was the first time she had done something like that to one of the employees. She was truly acting like a different person. Finally Jason came to her.

"Cynthia, how about a few minutes for me?" he asked after he poked his head in the doorway. She could see that his impatience had tightened him into a fist. His jaw was stiff; his eyes wide. When he came forward his posture was more stonelike than ever. She thought he looked somewhat peaked, and even the bright maroon cravat didn't compensate for the paleness in his cheeks. As always, when he kept his anger contained, the small blue veins in his temples became emphatic. She remembered thinking about that when she was a little girl. She used to wonder what it would be like to put the tips of her fingers on those veins to feel the blood pulsating through them. But for her to touch Jason, even for only a few seconds, would have been a major accomplishment.

"One moment," she said, and went to her file cabinet. She wanted to turn her back on him, so she pretended to be looking for a document. She heard him shut the door behind him and come to the chair at her desk, but she didn't turn around. She flipped through file after file, and then she slammed the door shut and went to her seat behind the desk. She didn't look at him right away, however. Instead she wrote something in a notebook and then, finally, she sat back. "What's so important this morning? Another real estate venture you two cooked up, I suppose."

"I received the strangest phone call from Stephen last night," he said. Another inconsistency, another twisting of the truth, she thought, but she didn't say anything. "He insisted on bringing it up again this morning. He's quite upset."

Jason's back was straight against the back of the seat. His hands were on his knees and his head was so stiff and so still, she thought he looked like a chalk doll. There was a controlled fire in his eyes; they burned like embers that needed only to be fanned.

"Is that why he was out of the house like a flash? I don't think he even had his breakfast. By the time I was out of the shower he was gone. He usually makes the coffee, too, and he didn't. Did he have some breakfast with you?" she asked innocently. Jason was obviously confused by her tone of voice, indeed, by her entire demeanor.

"He stopped by, yes."

"Oh, he went directly to your house. I thought you two might have had a breakfast meeting. You have just about every other kind. Did you serve demitasse?"

"Pardon?"

"Oh, you wouldn't have demitasse in the morning, would you?"

"Hardly."

"So you say he's upset. Well, if he's angry because I went to the movies with Paula Levy..."

"Paula Levy? No, that's not it. Look, why did you tell him I gave you a matchbook advertising that nightclub in Atlantic City? And why did you say I told you he was at my house yesterday? You and I didn't have any conversation about any of these things."

"What? He said I said that *you* told me that?" She sat forward, a dazed smile on her face. Jason studied her, his look of indignation turning to a look of astonishment.

"Yes."

"It must be a joke. I didn't tell him you told me anything, Jason. Why would I say such a thing?" She sat back again, and smiled as she shook her head. "I found a book of matches on the closet floor, and I asked him about it. I guess it fell from his pants pocket. Since he told me you two were so damn busy every moment in Atlantic City, he looked like a kid caught with his hand in his parents' cocaine jar; and as far as his being at your house... Paula Levy told me about that when she called to ask me to go with her to the movies last night. She rode by your house yesterday and saw the car there and thought I was there, too. Since it was during business hours she wanted to know if anything was wrong. You know Paula—she could work for the local newspaper. In fact she ought to work for the local newspaper."

"Paula Levy told you?"

"Uh-huh. So I asked Stephen about it before I left for the movies. He told me you two had a quiet lunch there. I didn't mean to make it seem as though I had my spies out or something, but he did resent my asking, I suppose. I know he wasn't eager to tell me about it. Did he think you'd be angry because he told me? Is that it?"

"Of course not, but why would he say you said I told you all this?"

"I don't know. As I said, maybe he didn't want you to know he told me. You two are so secretive sometimes—more often than ever lately," she said. She looked away and pretended interest in another document. "What's the big deal anyway, Jason?" She looked up sharply. "Is this something to carry on about here? The secretaries have enough to buzz about."

"I'm not carrying on," he said. His voice cracked. It was unusual. He was rarely on the defensive this way and very rarely put on the defensive by her. She knew that frustrated him more. "I just wanted to know...."

"Know? Know what?" She sat back again, filling her face with anger. Her eyes widened like his; her lips grew thin with tension. His own posture softened, and for the first time since he had entered her office he noticed that she wasn't her immaculate self. Her hair wasn't brushed as nicely as it usually was, and she hadn't put on any makeup, not even any lipstick. She looked as though she had simply thrown on some clothes and come directly from the bedroom. "What's there to know?" Her eyes became smaller as she apparently grew more inquisitive. "Did you two do something you're ashamed of when you were in Atlantic City? Is that why Stephen said you two couldn't reach me on the telephone?"

"Of course not," he said, but she thought he looked guilty.

"I don't understand any of this then. If it's so important to everyone, maybe we'd better have a family conference or something. Where is Stephen now?"

"He's at the credit union." Jason seemed to wilt before her. His upper body sagged, and he put his fingers between his neck and the cravat to loosen it. "No, no, that's all right. I'm sure it's just some stupid misunderstanding. I'll straighten it out."

"Well, do so. I don't want either of you to have a nervous breakdown over it. Jesus, what if something serious happens around here?"

"You're right." He stood up. "So," he said, and she recognized his desire to change the topic quickly, "you've made a few more sales, I hear."

"Yes."

"And a rental agreement?"

"Yes." She lowered her eyes.

"Since when have you started being a rental agent?" he said, his customary sarcasm creeping back into his voice.

"It was just a favor... a favor for Sid Jaffe. He's frustrated with his failure to sell the house he unfortunately assumed and he's tired of paying out on it. It's just a year's lease with an option to buy, of course. Hardly the kind of deal that I would think would interest you. After all, you guys are moving in pretty big circles nowadays."

"I heard that good actor rented it," he said, unabashed by her hard reply.

"My secretary ought to write a newspaper for the Palmer Agency."

"Apparently this man is quite attractive," Jason said. "The women are very taken with him." She stared expressionless. "I guess I will see his play this weekend."

"Good."

"Now that he's a client of ours," he added, and smiled coldly. He is back to himself, she thought. She had made only a small dent in that armor of arrogance. But she had only just begun.

Before either of them could say anything else, the phone buzzed. It was one of her new clients, so Jason left her office. Afterward she sat back to consider what her scheming might have accomplished. She thought she would love to be able to listen in on Jason and Stephen's next conversation. How adamantly Stephen would deny things she had said, but she felt she had been very convincing, especially when she became aggressive and accusatory. The more emphatically Stephen denied the things she had said, the more suspicious Jason would become. She was sure of it. If she could continue to drive this wedge between them...

Jason didn't like to be crossed and nothing angered him as much as betrayal. If he was to believe that Stephen confided in her about the intimacy that had developed between them, perhaps she would gain her revenge. Now, more than ever, she felt she wanted that.

This morning, almost as soon as she had awakened, that goal was on her mind. Perhaps it was only another reaction, another way to avoid the pain of what she believed Stephen and Jason had done to her. Whatever, it gave her some satisfaction to think of it and to plan for it. It made her feel stronger and significant again. Paula was right— how does a woman compete with such an abnormal betrayal? What did she do to turn Stephen away? The blame couldn't lie with her; it had to lie with Jason. Therefore her anger was directed mostly toward him.

None of this took away her attention from the Karla Hoffman affair. If anything, it helped to whet her interest even more. She recalled the new information Miss Weintraub had given her, and she took out her phone book and looked up the number for the River Tavern in Woodbourne. Then she called and spoke to Lucy Morganstern, explaining that Miss Weintraub had given her the information. Once she mentioned Miss Weintraub, Lucy Morganstern told her it was certainly all right to come over to talk to Liza Glenn.

"He's in the kitchen, but he can take a few minutes off to talk to you. We don't get a very big lunch crowd anyway, so don't worry about it. I'll tell him you're coming. He loves to talk about the old days. Sometimes we can't shut him up for hours."

"That's wonderful. Thank you," she said. She hung up and gathered her things together quickly. She had no patience for her work now and no interest in it anyway. There were a number of calls for her to make, but she didn't give them a second thought.

Although she couldn't see it in herself, she had become a driven woman. Jason had been correct in his appraisal of her appearance. Her determination and eagerness to do what she had been doing to Stephen and him was so strong now that she didn't even think about her appearance before she left the house. She had run the brush through her hair only a few times, and she didn't notice that the pants outfit she was wearing was the one she had set aside for the cleaners. None of this mattered; none of this occurred to her, because she had the exciting feeling that things were coming to a head.

Soon all the secrets of the Karla Hoffman affair would be known and whatever meaning it had for her would be understood. She would know what had to be done and how to do it. These thoughts had taken complete control of her, but rather than feeling like someone possessed, she felt grateful.

It was during her ride to Woodbourne that she lit the first cigarette for the week. She very rarely smoked; a pack could last her for a week or more sometimes. Suddenly, though, she felt as though it were the right thing for her to do because it was something she would do all the time. It struck her as curious, but she did it anyway. A question passed through her mind vaguely—did Karla Hoffman smoke?

Woodbourne was one of the bigger hamlets in the township. She had sold a number of properties here over the past few years, and now with the new state correctional facility being built, she anticipated a great many more sales. The hamlet really consisted of only one main street that ran from one end to the other. It led her to the bridge over the Neversink River and the River Tavern, which was located at the far end of the town. She had never been in the tavern, but that wasn't unusual. There were a number of small taverns with which she was unfamiliar, even though she had lived her entire lifetime in the community.

She had heard of Lucy Morganstern, but she had never met her. The fifty-four-year-old tavern owner was at the bar when Cynthia entered. She knew Cynthia immediately and greeted her moments after her entrance. There were a half-dozen men seated at the bar, and all of them turned to look in her direction. She saw a couple at one end of the tables to the right, but other than that, the tavern was empty.

The tavern consisted of one long, wide room. It was poorly lit. The gray skies did not send much illumination through the windows that faced the river, and Lucy hadn't turned on all her lights. Nevertheless, Cynthia could see that this had been a very attractive place once. Its view of the Neversink River and its spaciousness recommended it. She made a mental note of the property's potential. Under the right management it could be developed into a successful restaurant once again, she thought. Now it was simply a tap room with insignificant food. A hand-written sign advertised deep-fried chicken on Fridays and fish and chips on Saturdays.

"Come in, come in," Lucy said, moving around to the front of the bar. Her hair, which was practically all gray, hung in loose strands to her shoulders. She wore a pair of tight jeans, even though she had wide hips and a wide rear. Her flannel shirt was opened down to her bra, and the sleeves were rolled up to her elbows. She wore a set of cheap, gold-leaf costume jewelry earrings that looked tarnished at the edges.

"Hi," Cynthia said. "I never realized how big it is in here. It's deceptive from the outside."

"Oh yeah. They used to hold square dances back there," Lucy said, pointing to the rear of the room. "That small platform is where the band was. Have a seat. I'll get Liza. He's eager to meet you. You wanna beer or somethin'?"

"Er... diet soda, if you have."

"I have diet Coke."

"Fine." She took a seat close to one of the windows and looked out at the Neversink. The gray sky seemed to take the life out of the water. Without sunlight the river looked dark and polluted. She thought it moved lethargically, without music, without energy, without life.

"Hello there," Liza Glenn said. She looked up at the seventy-two-year-old handyman, who put her glass of diet Coke on the table. The wrinkles in his forehead and his temples cut deeply and darkly. His thin gray hair was nearly all gone, but tuffs of it grew wildly in spots on the sides and rear. The bald areas were covered with age spots—deep brown circles that made for a random design from the back to the front.

She thought the thinness in his face brought out his bone structure. It was as though the skeleton within were trying to emerge free and clear of flesh and skin. He had a sharp nose with narrow nostrils. There was a dip at the bottom of his jawbone, which had the effect of drawing his mouth down so that his lower lip was habitually turned outward, revealing his two remaining bottom teeth. When he smiled she saw that he had a few more of his own teeth on top.

Only his eyes disguised his age. The stubborn will to live on, to struggle against tomorrow, showed itself in the twinkle of energy and interest. His bushy, untrimmed eyebrows diminished their intensity some, but Cynthia was still able to detect a gentle, quiet quality in him when he sat across from her.

"Hello," she said. "Thanks for coming out to talk to me."

"Lucy says you want to know somethin' about the old days at the Rose Hill?"

"Yes."

"It was a beautiful place, beautiful. We had some lovely gardens and hedges. That lawn would get so damn green in the spring, I swore there were underground springs keeping those roots moist. Ben Hillerman usta tease his wife and say he was thinkin' of givin' it all up and turnin' the place into a golf course." He smiled widely, pulling his lips back so far in the corners his face looked as though it were made of rubber. She smiled, too, and sipped some Coke.

"You were there in 1935?"

"1935? Oh sure. I was eighteen when I started. I had been there four years by then. The Hillermans were good to me. I liked workin' for 'em, especially Mrs. Hillerman. She was a tough one, but fair. And she was always concerned about me gettin' a good meal. That was important. She nursed me when I came down with the flu, too. More like a mother to me. I dug her grave," he added. "Went to the cemetery up in Glen Wild and dug it that mornin', cryin' inside all the while."

"In 1935 there was a murder at the Rose Hill House, a stabbing."

"Oh," he said, sitting back, "that's what you wanna know about, huh? I thought you was doin' research on the old hotels."

"You don't like talking about the murder?" she asked. She saw the way he pulled himself in and looked away.

"Ugly thing. I don't know why people always got to bring up the ugly things."

"You don't happen to remember what she looked like, do you?"

"Who? Karla Hoffman?"

"Yes," Cynthia said, impressed that he had the name on his fingertips even after fifty years.

"Sure I do. Sure..." He stared at her for a moment as she shifted in the seat so that her face would be more in the light. "You ain't a relation of hers, are ya?"

"No, but I do remind you of her, isn't that so?"

"There's a resemblance, sure. Her hair wasn't always your color, but it was the year she was killed."

"This isn't really my color, either," she said, smiling. "Can I buy you a beer or something?"

"Oh no, Lucy wouldn't want me to do any drinkin' while I was workin'. I've had my bouts with the sauce. I know who's the boss when it comes to that, and it ain't me." Cynthia laughed, and he appeared to relax again.

"It's important that I learn as much as I can about Karla Hoffman and what happened. It's worth some money to me," she said, going to her pocketbook. She took out two twenties and put them on the table.

"I see that."

"What kind of work did you do around the Rose Hill House?"

"Oh, just about everything Mr. Hillerman wanted me to do. I did gardenin', maintenance, paintin', carpentry, plumbin'. You had to be a jack-of-all-trades in those days."

"Did you have much contact with the guests... talk to them much, that sort of thing?"

"Some. Some of the older women could outtalk me," he said, smiling at his memories, "but I had to limit it or I wouldn't get much work done."

"What kind of contact did you have with the Hoffmans? How well do you remember them?"

"You're talkin' quite some time ago, so if you're lookin' for some details..."

"I realize that, but whatever you might remember might help."

"Help what? She's been dead so long."

"It would help me understand some things," she said. He heard the tone of pleading in her voice and shrugged. "I've learned that Mrs. Hillerman didn't like Karla's brother, is that so?"

"She didn't like any of 'em. I didn't, either."

"Why not?"

"The men were strange, if you get my drift."

"No, I don't. Please be more specific. How were they strange?"

"They were standoffish, snobby, and there was somethin' about the way they hung around each other. Most of the time she was left to herself. I'd see her walkin' alone or readin' off by herself. They'd be takin' rides or playin' tennis, and she wouldn't be with 'em. She was lonely, I guess. It sorta explains why she was what she was."

"What was she?" Cynthia asked, but he looked away again. He shook his head.

"I don't like talkin' about the dead. My mother usta say, you do that and they'll come back and haunt ya. I got enough things hauntin' me these days without addin' the ghost of a murdered woman."

"I understand. I'm just trying to know her better, know what she suffered," she said. Liza Glenn's eyes widened with a new surge of interest.

"Suffered? Yeah, I suppose you can say she suffered. Another thing my mother usta say was 'idle hands get into mischief.' All these rich people havin' nothin' to do but play croquet and sit and talk nonsense all day or eat themselves sick. It didn't surprise me some of them got into trouble. Or got other people into trouble," he added.

He looked out at the river and then wiped his face in the stained apron that hung about his neck and over his faded flannel shirt down to his gray corduroy pants. Some of the men at the bar broke into a loud laugh. By the way they were looking at her and Liza, she imagined that the joke was about them. He looked uncomfortable and eager to get up, so she pushed on with more urgency.

"There was something else, wasn't there? Something the police never knew. Maybe something no one but you knew. Isn't that right?" She sounded like a prosecutor now, but she couldn't help it. Once again she felt as though she were being taken over by another force. She couldn't even explain why she asked him what she did; how she had come up with such an idea. Whatever it was, it filled her with an uncharacteristic aggressiveness.

"It was a long time ago," he said softly. He looked terrorized by her approach.

"I know. But people can't be hurt by the truth now. They're gone." Her points seemed well-taken. He nodded and turned away from the window.

"Old man Hillerman, he ain't dead yet, I hear. Must be close to ninety."

"He's been taken to a nursing home. He's senile, and he can't take care of himself any longer."

"Oh, too bad. But he's alive. My mother was right about somethin' else, too, 'only the good die young,'" he added.

"What do you mean?" He didn't respond. "I know sometimes it's painful to remember things," she said, and pushed the twenties across the table. He looked down at them.

"I suppose it really doesn't matter anymore," he said, and he took the bills and stuffed them into his shirt top pocket.

"Not to anyone but me, believe me."

"Rose Hillerman, she was a good woman. I hated to see her hurt by anyone, even him."

"You mean, Mr. Hillerman?"

"Yep. I seen him with her a few times, but I didn't say nothin'. I figured it wasn't my business, although it bothered me plenty that I kept it to myself."

"Seen him with... with Karla Hoffman?"

"Ben Hillerman was a strong, good-lookin' man. I never wanted to tangle with 'im. As for her... I can't blame her, I suppose, seein' the way her husband treated her, leavin' her to herself all the time. But I blame Mr. Hillerman. He shouldn't a betrayed a woman that good."

"Did anyone else find out? Anyone else know?"

The old man stared at her a moment. His eyes of youth and energy suddenly seemed tired and gray, reflecting the dullness of the river that flowed by just outside the window. He folded his hands on the table, the large knotty fingers clutching each other firmly, and leaned in toward her. She couldn't pull her eyes from him, and she suddenly felt as though there was nothing beneath her. She was falling, falling, falling through time itself. The heat rushed up her neck, and her face took on a pink flush. She brought the glass of diet Coke to her lips almost defensively.

"Her brother," he said softly, "he knew."

"How do you know that?" she asked, barely speaking above a whisper now. A weakness settled into her chest as the old man's eyes narrowed with the scenes from the resurrected past. All the sounds around the two of them were shut out.

"I came upon him one night. We had this shed in the back, to store tools, machinery, lounge cushions and the like. I came out because I remembered I forgot to put away the rakes and I thought it was goin' to rain that night, and I seen 'im leanin' against the shed, peerin' through the small window."

"The brother?"

"Yeah. So I got curious, too, and I came around the other side. There was a full moon that night, and the glow was so bright they coulda had lights on in there."

"So the brother saw you, too?"

"Nope, I don't think so. When he was satisfied he stalked off. I figured, oh boy, there's goin' to be trouble now, but it went on like that for a while and then..." He stopped and sat back, a far-off look coming into his face. "Maybe if I woulda told someone after what I had seen that first night..."

"You couldn't know what it would come to," she said.

"Sick, the three of 'em, way before this stuff started out there," he added, waving toward the front of the tavern.

"Stuff?"

"Drugs and sex and fags proud they're fags, and women sleepin' with women..."

"But Mrs. Hillerman, she never found out what really went on?"

"I couldn't say no for sure. Like I said...I never told nothin' to nobody. But like you said, what does it matter now?"

"It matters to me. There's no doubt about how it happened, is there?"

"The brother confessed. I came up to the room soon after it happened, way before the police arrived. She was sprawled out over the bed facedown, and her brother was sittin' there on a chair, his hands coverin' his face. The husband was standin' by the window lookin' down. When he turned to me I got the shivers. They were both so calm it was like nothin' was wrong. I had to look twice. Weird, boy, weird," he added, and shook his head. "You know he didn't take her body back to Brooklyn and plant it in a family plot."

"What do you mean?"

"She ain't buried in Brooklyn. I guess he thought it would have been too much of a reminder or some sacrilege or somethin' to put her with the rest of the relatives. I don't know."

"Well, where... is she?"

"She's buried up here, in Glen Wild, in a plot not far from where the Hillermans rest. Maybe it was some sick joke, huh? Keep her in the shadow of Mr. Hillerman's future grave site," he said, his voice fading off. She started to open her pocketbook to get another cigarette and stopped.

"Did Karla Hoffman smoke?" she asked.

"Smoke? I don't recall. You ask some strange questions all right. What's that got to do with it? She didn't die from lung cancer, believe me."

"It's not important," she said, and held her pocketbook open for a moment. She took out a business card and handed it to him. "If you should think of anything else relating to the murder or to Karla Hoffman, anything that might be important, please call me. I'd appreciate it."

"Sure, but I don't know what you think's important and what's not anymore."

"If it's important, you'll know," she said. He shook his head at her cryptic remark and got up with her. "Thanks again," she said. She offered him her hand. He shook it quickly and then watched her walk to the bar where she thanked Lucy Morganstern and paid for her Coke. After she left Liza looked at Lucy and shrugged. Then he went back to the kitchen, feeling that even though he made an easy forty bucks, there was something terrible about it.

SHE STARTED to ride around aimlessly, like someone in a daze. It hadn't turned out the way she had hoped. The mystery wasn't solved; the questions weren't answered; things had become even more confusing. Of course, now she understood why Karla Hoffman had told Ben Hillerman she thought she was going to die. She must have felt threatened because their affair was known. Ben was unable to tell Sam Segar everything that day, but part of what shook him up must have been his own sense of responsibility, his own guilt. Maybe Mrs. Hillerman did know more than Liza Glenn thought she did, and that was the primary reason for her wanting the murder forgotten as quickly as possible. It wasn't only her worry about the effect it could have on their resort business, although admittedly, that had to be a concern. She didn't want to be reminded of her husband's infidelity and what that infidelity had brought.

Infidelity was so much a part of what had happened and what was happening now, Cynthia thought. She couldn't ignore the obvious parallels. Weren't they what she was looking to discover anyway? She drove on, now with purpose. She knew her destination. Almost any place in the township could be reached within a half hour's time. Once again she wove her way over backroads to save time.

Because of the brightness in the leaves in these more heavily wooded areas, the grayness of the day did not seem as oppressive. Yet she had no real sense of the scenic beauty because once again she felt numb and ethereal as though she were moving on a shelf of dreams, guided by images and sounds that made her feel quite apart from herself. She never lost her sense of direction, but when she arrived at the scene, she was surprised as she would have been had someone blindfolded her and taken her here in secret.

She turned into the old Glen Wild cemetery and parked her car in the clearing left for that purpose. Stones in this section dated back to the middle and late 1800s. These older stones were ghostly white; the letters and the numbers of many were unclear, having been worn down by time and the weather. However, cemetery caretakers had kept them straight and the plots around them trim, since they were the first stones anyone approaching the cemetery would see. Behind them was the section peopled by the dead of the early and middle twentieth century.

She got out of her car and looked around. The stillness was comforting, seductive; she was lulled into a sense of calm, and the wildness and the frenzy that had been in her face since she had begun the morning left her. Loose strands of her hair danced in the breeze, but despite the overcast the air was still warm for this time of the year. She closed her eyes and felt her heartbeat become quieter, softer. Then she opened them and headed for the gravestones.

Moving slowly but determinedly, she walked past the stones and saw the familiar names of families she had known all her life. She stopped when she came to the Hillermans. She had heard Rose Hillerman's name so often these past few days, the dead woman seemed like a lost old friend. Then recalling what Liza Glenn had said about "...some sick joke...keeping her in the shadow of Mr. Hillerman's future grave site," she looked around. A stone off to her left caught her interest. It was a simple, rectangular granite and the name was large enough and clear enough to read from where she stood, but she approached it anyway. It read:

KARLA HOFFMAN
Born: October 27, 1905
Died: July 12, 1935

There was nothing else—not an inscription, not a prayer.

Suddenly she felt terribly sorry for her because she was buried in a strange land without any relatives nearby to comfort her soul. It was as though she had been discarded. It wasn't as though she was a soldier buried in another country, surrounded by soldiers. The names around her were the names of people she never really knew. It was as though she had been doomed to eternal loneliness. Perhaps that was why her spirit lingered behind.

Standing there and staring at the stone, Cynthia had a fascinating idea—even if the physical resemblances that linked them together were coincidental, the spiritual ties seemed to be part of some design, perhaps Karla Hoffman's penance. Cynthia represented Karla's last chance to do something good and now had the facts to prevent her from experiencing the same fate. In this sense they would be helping each other, as long as Cynthia didn't fail to read and understand the omens.

She reached forward and touched the stone. It should have felt cool, but it was warm, as if she had touched Karla Hoffman's hand. Perhaps they had made a pact.

When she left the cemetery she carried the promise away with her.

11

WHEN CYNTHIA ARRIVED BACK at her office she found that Stephen had left a note on her desk. It read:

> Waited lunch for you, Judy didn't know where you had gone. We're going to Charlie W's and then down to Middletown to see Bill Plotkin of Prudential. If we're not back before you leave for the day, don't make anything for supper. We have the Sullivan County Chamber of Commerce dinner at the Skytop.
> Love, Stephen

She had forgotten about this dinner; she hadn't even written it in her calendar. She couldn't tolerate the thought of going to it. If there was one thing she didn't want now, it was sitting at another affair with Jason and Stephen. She didn't have the patience to remain in the background while they dominated conversations and monopolized everyone's attention. She knew they would, especially since they had accomplished so much during the past few weeks. Their business adventures were the kind of drama that excited the type of people who attended the county dinner. She made up her mind she would pretend to have a terrible headache and stay home. The way things were, she didn't expect that it would bother either of them very much anyway.

When she continued to go through her pile of phone messages, she found that Terrence had called an hour and a half ago. She dialed the bank's number and requested to speak with him.

"I went to Sid Jaffe's and signed the lease," he said. "We've got to find a way to celebrate."

She told him about the county dinner, and her plans to get out of going to it.

"So I'm going to leave work early and play my role," she said. "Wish me luck in my performance."

"Hey, wait a minute," he said, sensing she was about to hang up, "I've got to see you."

"Maybe this is a bad day for it. I've got a lot on my mind."

"That's the best time to see me. I assume you haven't said anything to your husband about the other matter?"

"No, not yet."

"After they leave for the dinner, come to the house."

"I couldn't do that. Besides, you probably don't have the electricity turned on yet and..."

"They're supposed to do it this afternoon. And what if they don't? We'll sit by candlelight. I'll bring a bottle of wine, and we'll celebrate the lease then. Will you do it?"

"No," she said weakly.

"I tell you what," he said. "Even if the electricity is on, there'll be a single candle lit on the floor of the living room when you drive up."

"I can't promise."

"I'll be there," he said. "Just keep thinking about it," he added.

After she hung up she did sit there for a few moments thinking about it. She wanted to go, and yet she couldn't help thinking about Liza Glenn's description of his coming upon Karla and Ben Hillerman in the toolshed with her brother peering in.

As she thought about it she realized that the only way to get at the heart of the truth would be to talk to the one surviving member of the threesome, assuming he was still alive, that is. Where and how could she find Borris Hoffman, and if she did find him, what guarantee was there that he would talk to her? Perhaps the physical resemblance between her and Karla Hoffman would be so striking to him that he would feel a need to talk. There was a chance; it was a hope. But how did you begin to look for someone who was alive fifty years ago, someone who had a factory somewhere in Brooklyn? She didn't even know the name of the factory.

Of course her first thought was to call Ralph Hillerman again. When she got him on the phone and asked him if he knew any of the information, she had the distinct impression that if he knew it he wouldn't tell her.

"No," he said, his voice colder, more formal than ever, "I don't know anything about him. I had nothing to do with the guests in those days. My mother kept the accounts. I was too young for that." There was a long pause and then he added, "I was hoping you'd kind of leave this thing alone now, Cynthia. I don't like what it's doing to you."

"Thanks anyway, Ralph," she said, and hung up before he could say another word.

For a few moments she sat there filled with a sense of depression and frustration. Then she took out the news clipping and looked at the picture once again. Almost immediately an idea occurred to her. The section of the Glen Wild Cemetery in which Karla Hoffman was buried was owned and maintained by the Woodridge Synagogue. She called Rabbi Dorfman, and he told her that the cemetery committee was headed by Murray Bauman, who also owned and operated the large dry-cleaning business she herself patronized. She had suspected that he had something to do with the synagogue and the cemetery. When she phoned him he was most cooperative.

"Hoffman? Yeah, I know the stone," he said. "The old section."

"The plot is still well maintained, so I thought someone might still be paying for it."

"Well, we wouldn't let it go even if they didn't. How would that look? Let me check my books and call you back."

He promised he would get right to it, so she waited by the phone. She couldn't have been more nervous had she been waiting for the results of a medical exam. For her this was like life and death anyway, so naturally ten minutes or so seemed like an hour or so. Finally the phone buzzed and Judy announced Murray on the line. She picked it up quickly without even acknowledging her secretary.

"Murray?"

"Yeah, you're in luck on this. I got a check just a little more than a month ago."

"Was it from a Borris Hoffman?" She held her breath.

"Yes, it was."

"I need the address," she said. "I've been trying to locate him."

"Oh, I see. Okay, he lives at 7 Diamond Square, Rye, New York. You want the zip code?"

"No, that's fine. Thank you." After she hung up she began mumbling to herself. "Rye, New York. That's only a little more than an hour away from here. I could go down there today. I could go down there tonight. I should call him. I've got to call him." She picked up her phone and dialed information to get his number, but once she had it she hesitated. "How am I going to introduce myself? What am I going to tell him I'm after? He probably won't want to talk about the murder. Even now, all the years later, it has to remain a painful memory."

She began to panic again. She had done so well and tracked him down so quickly. She couldn't lose it now. I can't take a chance and tell him what I'm really interested in, she thought. There has to be another way. Deceptions, deceptions...she looked around the room as though the answer might be suggested by one of the plaques. It was. Her gaze settled on the plaque she had received three years ago from the Herald's business editor as "Businesswoman of the Year." She recalled how proud Stephen was, but how disdainful Jason seemed. In any case, the plaque gave her an idea for a disguise. She phoned him.

When he answered there was such a familiar ring to his voice that she couldn't speak for a moment. It was confusing; it was as though she had made a mistake and dialed someone she had known all her life.

"Is this Mr. Hoffman . . . Borris Hoffman?"

"Yes, it is."

"My name is Warner, Cynthia Warner," she said. No sense in giving a false name; he won't know me anyway, she thought. "I'm a free-lance writer for the *New York Times*."

"That so?"

"Yes, sir. And we are preparing a series on the early clothing industry in New York City."

"I see."

"You were the owner of a clothing factory in Brooklyn, were you not?"

"Yes, I was. We were in business right through the fifties and into the mid-sixties."

"Is there any chance, sir, that I might come to see you for some information?"

"What kind of information?"

"Oh, background information, true-to-life experiences concerning the difficulties and the successes of those early days."

"I suppose so, sure. When do you want to come? I want to warn you, though, we weren't a major clothing manufacturer. We did well, but . . ."

"We're not interested in the majors," she said quickly. "We're looking for human interest. Would tomorrow morning about nine-thirty be all right?"

"Nine-thirty? Sure."

"Thank you, sir. I'll see you then," she said, and hung up quickly before she did anything to lose it. As soon as she hung up she put her right palm against her chest and began taking deep breaths. Her heart was beating madly. She realized that she had been holding her breath during most of the phone conversation, and his voice had a definite, strange effect on her. She felt as though she had phoned the other world and spoken to one of the dead. In this case she had really traveled back through time.

She opened her pocketbook and took out her face mirror to look at herself because her skin felt so hot. Her face was flushed and her eyes were glassy, but what struck her the most was her entire look—the way her hair fell over her forehead and temples, the way her mouth turned and the tip of her nose lifted, and even the way her eyebrows sloped. She put the news clipping on the desk again and studied the photograph. Whatever strong resemblances there were before, she thought, were nothing to the resemblances now. In her mind she was becoming more and more like Karla Hoffman every passing moment and especially now, after speaking to Borris.

A second idea chilled her. This was why she didn't spend as much time on her coiffure and her makeup this morning. She no longer had any interest in her "modern-day look." She was avoiding any of the clear-cut differences between her present appearance and the appearance of the woman in the newspaper pictures. Was it a form of possession or was it her own subconscious desire to escape into another identity, one that was accommodating, one that easily fit her? Maybe I want to be Karla Hoffman so much, I'm starting to find the similarities, she thought; maybe I'm finding them where they don't really exist.

Although these questions bothered her, they didn't frighten her as much as she would have thought they would. They put her into a kind of semiconsciousness, a half daze that made her feel light and free. The office was suddenly too confining, even somewhat threatening. She didn't want to be bothered with anything that would take her attention away from Karla.

It occurred to her that she had someplace else to go and someone else to see. There were links with the past that still had to be completed before she walked into the home of Borris Hoffman and faced him. She put everything back into her pocketbook, got up slowly and walked out of the office. Judy looked up from her desk, the puzzled expression on her face reflecting the way Cynthia appeared to her.

"Are you leaving the office, Mrs. Warner?"
"What? Yes."

"Did you find the note from Stephen? He wanted me to be sure you saw it."

"Yes," she said. "Thank you," and continued on out of the building. There was a picture in her mind all the way to Liberty. She drove directly to Monica's Boutique because she knew the kind of clothing, the styles and the fashions she kept in stock. Styles had changed so radically over the past few years. The unique thing about Monica Decker, however, was she didn't give up on anything. A dress fashionable in the 1930s could be seen in her window right beside something that had come out last week.

Usually, when Cynthia went shopping for clothes, she went at it the way most women might—unpressured, browsing, casually looking for something that might stand out, a discovery. It was possible to shop for hours and buy nothing. But today it was different. When she arrived at Monica's she went right to the section that contained the style and the color she was hoping to get. Her mind locked in on a garment. The salesgirl was impressed with the way Cynthia slid the garments over the rack, searching as though she had seen something she had wanted hanging there some time ago. When she found it she seized it with such force, she pulled it off the hanger and sent the plastic device bouncing on the floor. The salesgirl scooped it up, but before she could say anything Cynthia was in the fitting booth.

She emerged with the dress on, but not to seek out comments and criticism from the sales force, even though the girls at Monica's were famous for their honesty.

"I'll take it," Cynthia said before the salesgirl could utter a word.

"It's been here a while," she said, feeling she had to make some statement. She wanted Cynthia to understand that it wasn't one of the more popular old-fashioned items. Cynthia didn't seem to hear or care. She took her charge card out of her pocketbook and handed it to her. She took it and went behind the counter to the cash register, but when Cynthia went back into the fitting room and emerged with her own dress folded and in her arms, the salesgirl stared in confusion.

"You're going to wear that now?" she asked.

"Yes. Put my dress in a bag, please, and cut the tags off this one."

"Sure," the salesgirl said. She looked to the rear of the store to see if anyone else had been watching or if Monica was out of her office in the back. Then she processed the card, packaged and bagged Cynthia's dress, and came around the counter to cut off the tags. "It's a very nice dress," she said.

Cynthia didn't acknowledge the remark. She went to a full-length mirror and stared at herself for a very long moment. In her own mind, the store's backdrop disappeared. She was standing on the lawn next to the gazebo at the Rose Hill House. It was a bright sunny day, and off to the right of the big house Ben Hillerman paused in his work to look her way. His naked, muscular back gleamed in the sunlight. His hand, holding the hammer, froze in midair. He looked like a statue created to celebrate the joy of honest, manly labor.

"Mrs. Warner? Mrs. Warner?"

Cynthia turned to look at Monica Decker, who stood by with a curious smile on her face. Her salesgirl had filled her in quickly.

"Yes?"

"Are you sure you want to wear that right now?"

"Of course," Cynthia said. She went to the counter, picked up her charge card, picked up the package containing her original dress and left the store quickly, leaving Monica and her salesgirl behind, amused but a little dumbfounded.

SHE DIDN'T HEAD FOR HOME. Instead Cynthia turned and drove on until she reached the Walnut Nursing Home. It was a large, homey structure that disguised its institutional nature well. The grounds were quiet and serene with well-trimmed hedges and lawns and clean walkways. At this time of the day the stillness created a look of dreamlike slumber that seemed to fit well with Cynthia's mood. As she walked from the car to the front of the building she felt as though she threaded her way in and out of the present. Minutes, hours, days, months had formed a soft shell that folded back gently to permit her to enter the past.

The lobby was small and furnished with a half-dozen soft-cushioned couches and a dozen or so easy chairs. There were tables covered with magazines and books. At this time of the day, a little less than an hour before the dining room was to open, the more independent and agile residents had gathered in anticipation in the lobby. All of them turned to her with curious eyes, their attention easily directed to anything new that entered their world. A quick perusal of the inhabitants told her that Ben Hillerman wasn't present. She went directly to the front desk and asked to see him. The receptionist called for an aide to escort her.

"He's in the game room," the aide told her. "He likes to watch the other men play gin rummy. Follow me," she said. She couldn't help directing a look toward the receptionist, who already wore an expression of curiosity because of Cynthia's dress.

"Thank you," Cynthia said. She smiled at the old folks and walked just behind the aide. "How's he been?" she asked. The aide, a woman in her early twenties, turned and smiled.

"Actually, quite good. He seems to be more alert and even more lucid. And when he's not so sharp he thinks he's in his own hotel back in the old days. He says some funny things."

"Oh."

"Are you a relative?"

"No, just an old friend."

"Uh-huh," she said, and walked on.

They paused at the door of the recreation room, a twenty-by-forty room with tables covered with arts and crafts supplies, a television set in the rear, couches and chairs, and a card table to the left of the entrance. The light brown paneled walls and the two large windows made it airy and bright.

Ben Hillerman was in his wheelchair just behind a group of men playing gin rummy. He wasn't making comments, but he was shaking his head with obvious displeasure at the way one of the elderly men was handling his cards. He didn't look up at them in the doorway.

"You can sit on that couch right behind him," the aide said. "Should I tell him who you are?"

"No, let it be a surprise. I want to see just how lucid he is."

"Okay. There he is," the aide said, and shrugged. She started away as Cynthia entered. Ben Hillerman didn't notice her until she was right beside him. When he looked up she smiled and he simply stared, his eyes blinking rapidly.

"Hello, Ben, how are you?" she said. He didn't reply so she knelt beside the wheelchair and took hold of his arm. "I remind you of someone, don't I, Ben?" His nod was so slight it looked as if it was more involuntary than deliberate. "I'm Carl Palmer's daughter. You remember Carl Palmer, don't you, Ben?"

"Carl Palmer? Sure. Carl Palmer," he said, but she didn't think he knew whom she was talking about. He looked lost in thought.

"I look like Karla Hoffman, don't I, Ben? Karla Hoffman," she repeated slowly. He studied her, his face taking on a look of fear. "Come, talk to me a little while," she said, and stood up to turn his wheelchair to the couch. The men at the card table paused to look and then went right back to their game. She sat on the couch and faced him. "You remember Karla, don't you, Ben?" He shook his head, but she could see he was pretending. It's harder to lie when you get older, she thought. Your face betrays you faster. "Sure you do, Ben. You couldn't forget Karla."

"I'm tired," he said.

"Just a moment more, Ben. Tell me a little about Karla. Tell me about her brother. Did they look alike?" He shook his head. "Did she like him? Were they close?"

"No," he said. This time he looked as though he couldn't help but answer her questions. She was encouraged.

"Did she think he was too close to her husband? Did she hate him for taking her husband's attention away from her?" At first it looked as though he didn't understand her question. Then his eyes grew small, and she could practically feel him reaching back through time.

"Her husband was a fool," he said. "A fool."

"For letting things go too far. Is that it, Ben? He let things go too far?"

He nodded slowly.

"Did she hate her husband, too, Ben? Is that why she turned to you? Please, try to remember. Did she hate him?"

"I don't remember," he said. "I'm tired."

"She was beautiful, Karla, wasn't she, Ben? Beautiful and lonely."

"Yes," he said.

"But why did her brother kill her, Ben? What did it matter to him if she had an affair with someone else? He was driving her husband away from her anyway. Ben, can you understand me?"

"He loved her," he said. He looked as if he was under hypnosis.

"Who loved her? Her husband really loved her?"

"No."

"Her brother? But..."

He lowered his head until his chin touched his chest and closed his eyes. The effort at reaching back into the past had exhausted him, even for that short time. She leaned forward and touched his hand but he didn't stir.

One of the men around the card table yelled, "Gin," and the others raised the voices in unison. Three other elderly people, two women and a man, came into the recreation room followed by the young aide. She looked over at Cynthia.

"He conk out on you?"

"Looks like it."

"He nods off like that every once in a while. Sometimes it's only for a short time, and sometimes it's for a few hours."

"That's okay." She stood up.

"Did he remember you?"

Cynthia looked down at him.

"Yes, he remembered, but I think he's locked me up securely in his mind again."

"Well, that's something anyway," the aide said. Cynthia nodded.

"Thank you."

"I'll try to remind him you were here," she said.

"Yes," Cynthia said. She studied him a moment and then knelt down again to kiss him on the forehead. "Goodbye, Ben," she said. She started out.

"Wait," the aide said. "Who shall I say was here?"

"Tell him, Karla, Karla Hoffman," she said, and left. It wasn't until she got back into her car that she caught her breath.

Reflection

It was the kiss, she thought. Karla Hoffman had made her do it. It was a kiss that traveled decades and crossed the line between past and present. For Cynthia it was emotionally exhausting. She started away, tears streaming down her face.

It wasn't until she was back on a main highway that she began to think clearly again. What had she done? What had she learned? If anything, things were more confusing than ever for her. Why did Ben Hillerman say Karla's brother loved her? How could he have loved her if he killed her?

Jason could kill, she thought. If I took Stephen away from him completely, he could kill. It had to be the same for Karla. Was she winning her husband back? Did the incident with Ben Hillerman convince him that he was losing his beautiful wife, and did he reject her brother because of it? That made more sense. The old man must have gotten confused, she thought.

"I'm right, aren't I?" she asked, and waited for the other voice but her mind was silent. "I have to be right," she muttered. "Tomorrow, when I meet Mr. Hoffman, I'll know for sure," she thought.

She got home before Stephen did, and she took off the dress and put it away. She wanted to wear it again in the morning when she went to see Borris Hoffman. Then all she did was make herself some warm milk and go to bed. She really did have a headache. Stephen found her there when he arrived. When she didn't wake up he woke her.

"Sorry," he said, "but it's getting late if you want to go to the county dinner."

"I don't want to go, Stephen. I'm tired and I have a headache."

"Did you take anything?"

"Yes. I just want to sleep for a while."

"Okay. I'll try to be back early."

"It doesn't matter," she said. "I'm just going to sleep." He nodded and went on to shower and dress for the dinner. Just before he left he looked in on her again, but she was really asleep. Terrence Baker's phone call woke her.

"You're not going to come tonight, are you?" he said.

"No. I'm tired," she said. "I'm mentally exhausted."

"How are things at home?" he asked.

"Same. The truth is, I haven't thought about it."

"What have you been doing then, selling houses?"

"No."

"That spiritual sister?"

"Yes," she said. He was very quiet for a long moment.

"All right," he said. "If you change your mind, I'll be here at least another hour."

"Okay." She hung up without saying goodbye. Then she turned over on her back and looked up into the darkness. It had to be that Karla Hoffman's fling with Ben Hillerman wasn't that significant for her. Whatever satisfaction he provided wasn't substantial. It couldn't be. Ben Hillerman wasn't going to give up his world for her. What could she have hoped to gain in the long run?

What can I hope to gain from an affair with Terrence Baker? she wondered. Perhaps Karla Hoffman had decided to battle for her own husband. Maybe that was where the message was in all this. Maybe deep inside herself, Cynthia knew she would do the same. Was the prediction then that if she did what Karla did, she would have Karla's destiny?

"There's a difference between you and I, though, isn't there?" Cynthia asked the darkness. "I can see the possible future by studying the past. That's why you're here, isn't it?"

The silence didn't discourage her. She turned on her side and closed her eyes. She was in pursuit of a good night's sleep. Tomorrow she would meet the man who could see just how close the similarities between her and Karla really were.

12

SOMETIME DURING THE NIGHT, she wasn't sure how late, she awoke to the sound of voices and laughter. She knew it was Stephen and Jason, but her curiosity about what they were up to wasn't strong enough to keep her awake. She was too tired, and it seemed that their talk and their laughter was part of some dream anyway. In the morning when she awoke and looked at the clock, she was surprised to see that Stephen was still asleep beside her. She remembered hearing Jason's voice late at night, but now she wondered if it had really happened.

Stephen didn't wake when she got out of bed. She slipped on her robe and went out to the kitchen. The coffee cups they must have used and a half a pot of remaining coffee were on the counter by the sink. She thought about it for a moment and then sensed that she and Stephen were not alone in the house. Her curiosity whetted even more, she went to the closer of the two other bedrooms. The door was half opened. She pushed it the rest of the way and stepped in.

Jason was asleep in the bed, his arm dangling over the side. She stood there studying the exposed portion of his face. He looked dead to the world, but even in this state he appeared ominous to her. She wished she could somehow slip in mentally behind his sleeping visage and listen in on his conniving thoughts. She suspected that even in his dreams he plotted ways to take control of people and their lives.

And yet when she took a step closer and saw how deeply asleep he was, she was forced to be more compassionate and less resentful. There was an unassuming, babylike softness in his face, too. It was easy to see something of herself in his bone structure, in the way his forehead rose above his eyebrows and in the way his mouth settled in repose. She recalled the times their mother looked at Jason with such pleasure in her eyes. There was something unique about him. He appeared so mature. His life was always in such good order.

Why did it come to this? Cynthia wondered. What twisted avenue of fate did he wander down? She stared at him as though the answers might be written somewhere on his face. He didn't wake, but his eyelids fluttered. Did he sense her presence? She didn't trust him. He could easily know she was there, but pretend he was still in a deep sleep. She turned and left the bedroom quickly.

Stephen had turned over in bed, and although his eyes were still closed, she sensed that he was close to waking. She went to him and nudged him. He woke with a start and looked up at her. She was amused at his look of confusion.

"What time is it?"

"Late for you," she said, "and very late for Jason. What's going on?"

He sat up and rubbed his cheeks vigorously. Then he looked at the clock.

"Why is Jason here? What happened?"

"I couldn't let him drive home. He got polluted last night."

"Jason did?"

"We stuck around after the dinner. Bob Haskins was there and Sam Crammer from United National. I didn't realize how many drinks Jason had until he started getting a little nasty. You know how he can be when his sarcasm goes unchecked. There was nearly a fight."

"What?"

"He doesn't like Crammer. Everyone knows he screws around—except his wife who either knows and doesn't care or really doesn't know. Anyway, Jason went at him a bit."

"For being unfaithful to his wife?"

"Jason can be quite puritanical when he wants to be."

She thought about it for a moment. All kinds of statements were on her lips but she held back.

"I thought I heard the noise and the laughter last night."

"Yeah. He'll be feeling it today," Stephen said. He started to get out of bed. "You'll have to go to the office ahead of us. We'll be late."

"I'm not staying there," she said. "I have things to do."

"Just open up, that's all. Oh," he said, pausing at the bathroom door, "we met Ralph Hillerman at the dinner. He's very concerned about you. Something about a murder that took place at his place fifty years ago? Jason seemed to know something about it."

"It's not important," she said quickly. "I've got to get moving if I'm going to open the agency."

He shrugged and went on into the bathroom. She went to the main bathroom to shower. Stephen was still in the shower when she came back to their bedroom to put on the old-fashioned dress. He didn't see her until she was just about ready to leave. When he came out of the bedroom she was just finishing a cup of coffee. He stood there staring, a half-amused, half-curious smile on his face.

"Where the hell did you get that?"

"Monica's," she said.

"Since when do you wear your hair that way?"

"There are a lot of things about me you haven't noticed lately, Stephen."

"I guess you're right." She put her coffee cup in the sink and started out. "Wait a minute. Wait."

"What is it?"

"How about we have lunch today? I want to talk to you."

"I don't think so. I'm tied up until the afternoon."

"What are you doing?"

"What are *you* doing, Stephen? That's more important," she said, and she paused at the second bedroom. Jason was still asleep. She looked back at Stephen, who now wore a look of total confusion. Then, without another word, she left.

She went directly to the agency to open the doors. Judy Dobbs was waiting in the parking lot. Cynthia was surprised that she was there so early, but then she suspected that the girl probably looked forward to these few minutes when she could be relatively alone with Stephen. She saw the disappointment on her secretary's face when she drove up, but instead of being annoyed at her Cynthia suddenly felt very sympathetic. How pathetic it was to love someone who barely knew you existed, she thought. Love could be a cruel thing.

"They're right behind me," Cynthia told her after she unlocked the front door. "I'm not even

Reflection

going in. I have a morning appointment some distance from here."

"Oh. When do you expect to be back?"

"After lunch," she said.

"I like your dress," Judy said. "It's different."

"Thank you."

"And those earrings are pretty."

"What?" Cynthia reached to her lobes slowly, a sense of shock settling in her. She hadn't even realized she had put them on. They were the earrings that looked so similar to the ones Karla Hoffman wore in the picture. "Yes," she said, and went to the car. She drove off quickly, heading for Rye, New York.

All the way down she rehearsed the questions she would ask. She tried to decide what she would do if Borris Hoffman was belligerent. She knew there was no way to force him to talk, but she hoped he would sense how important it was to her.

She had been to Rye, New York, before, but she wasn't familiar with its streets. She was lucky, though, because she met a policeman at the first intersection and he gave her explicit directions. The street was set back and quiet and in an obviously expensive area. Borris Hoffman's house was a quaint, fieldstone-faced gingerbread with cone-shaped hedges bordering the short narrow sidewalk that led to the front door. She parked beside the Mercedes sedan in the driveway, but after she turned off the engine she just sat there. Her heart was beating madly.

Out of habit she opened her pocketbook and took out her face mirror. When she looked at herself it struck her that she did look odd, that she was like someone dressed in costume. In a real sense she was preparing for a performance. That partially explained the butterflies in her stomach. It brought her back to an idea she had after she had met and become involved with Terrence Baker. We're all playing roles of one kind or another every day, she had thought. So what was real? What was true?

She got out of her car slowly and then, clutching her pocketbook to her body, she made her way up the sidewalk to the front door. She hesitated a moment, took a deep breath and then pushed the buzzer button. The chimes rang within. A few moments later Borris Hoffman opened the door. The look of shock on his face was so great that she thought her mere appearance might have the effect of a death blow. He did look as though he were about to crumble.

Although he was a man in his late seventies, he had the physique of a man twenty years younger. He was still muscular and broad shouldered. His cheeks were pale but full. There was no sallowness in his face; none of the sunken cheeks and bony facial structure that often accompanied old age. Somehow she knew that before Borris Hoffman had opened this door to face her that he would be a man of a strong, virile appearance.

For her there was something about him that complemented the familiarity she had heard in his voice when she phoned him. Once again she had the eerie sensation she had known him all her life. The aloofness, the impersonality that usually characterized a meeting between two strangers, did not occur here. She felt as if she had come upon a long-lost relative, and they were about to revive the close relationship that had once existed between them.

Borris Hoffman was tall, a good few inches over six feet. Although his hair was filled with gray and thin, it looked like the battle to hold on to color and style was not yet lost to time. He had it brushed back neatly on the sides, but there was still something of a wave in the front. It dipped forward to the top of his forehead. She saw that there was a brightness in his blue eyes, which for now he kept open much wider than usual. She liked the turn in his mouth. It reminded her of Stephen's strong lines and the masculine power he could emit from his smile. Hoffman wore a light blue wool sweater and a pair of dark brown slacks, which did not hang from his waist in baggy fashion as the pants of many elderly men did.

He raised his right hand to his face as though to block away the sight before him. For a long moment neither of them spoke. Cynthia was both encouraged and frightened by his reaction. She knew it could go either way—he would close the door and flee from the scene or he would be so taken with her that he would drop all pretense and tell her only the truth.

"I'm Cynthia Warner," she said, "but I'm not a reporter from the *Times*."

"Who are you? Are you . . . a relative?"

"No, Mr. Hoffman, but you can see why I have come." He nodded slowly, but he didn't step back to permit her to enter. "Can I come in? I want to talk to you. I've got to talk to you."

How, she wondered, was she going to get him to understand her need to know things? Would she have to draw up all the parallels? Would he think her mad?

"Come in," he said. "I don't mean to be impolite, but you took me back fifty years. You're sure you're no relative of my wife's?"

"I'm pretty sure."

"Come in, come in," he repeated, and stepped farther back. She entered the house and looked about. There was a five-foot-high grandfather clock in the small alcove. Without even knowing Borris Hoffman, she thought it was characteristic of him that the clock had the time accurately. He led her to the living room, a small but uncluttered room furnished in French Provincial. Everything looked clean, untouched, frozen in time. The rug was immaculate, the furniture polished. Her eyes were quickly drawn to the portrait of Karla Hoffman above the mantel. The resemblances between them could not be more striking. She stared up at it and felt the spiritual presence. Hoffman looked from her to the portrait and back to her. "Forgive me for staring," he said when she turned to him.

"I understand. That's why I'm here."

"How... why..."

"Let me start at the beginning," she said. "May I sit down?"

"Of course." He indicated the small love seat. After she sat down he sat in the chair directly across from her. The intensity of his gaze filled her with confidence. "I'm a real estate agent," she began, and she told him about her sale of the Rose Hill House and how she had come upon the newspaper clipping. She described the way she had pursued the story and her terrible need to know as much as she could. She didn't go into her personal problems. He listened intently, nodding from time to time, and always wearing an expression of amazement.

"Ben Hillerman is still alive then?" he asked.

"Yes, but his memory is erratic at best."

"Fifty years is a long time," he said. "For anyone, even someone who still possesses his mental health. Why did you come to me? What is it you want to know now?" he asked, but she could see in his face that he already knew the answer. It was almost as if he had expected her.

"Most of all I want to know why he did it, why your brother-in-law killed his sister. It never came out in the trial, did it?"

"No, not really." He looked hesitant.

"I'm not going to do anything terrible with the story. I'm not selling it to anyone who might write it up and put it in one of those sensational newspapers. What I need to know, I need to know for myself. I feel your wife's presence. I feel...driven. It's as though we'll never be free... she'll never be free, until I know the truth. Do you believe me? Do you understand?" He stared at her a moment and then he nodded.

"Karla and her brother were first generation," he said. "Children of immigrants. It was hard during those early days. They lived in the ghetto in New York, and both their parents worked to scrape up a living. I'm not trying to justify anything," he said, pausing, "I'm just describing it the way I understand it. The way I understood it much later."

"You mean after you were married awhile?"

"Yes. They were quite dependent upon one another. They were very close. I think their closeness was...unnatural."

She took a deep breath. She had to look up at the portrait. Its presence was so strong.

"You mean there was incest?"

"I don't think so. I never believed it went that far. Maybe," he said, shrugging, "it was something I refused to believe."

"Then wouldn't her brother resent you when you married her and resent her for marrying you?"

"Maybe. Maybe he did. I'm not a wise man. I'm no prophet. I've done well for myself, but if there's one thing I've learned living this long it's that things are never as simple as they first seem. There are layers upon layers."

"Yes," she said.

"If you know that already, you are wise beyond your years. Anyway," he went on, "whatever was between them, Leon, my brother-in-law, was never really able to develop what they call today a good heterogeneous relationship. You understand?"

"Yes."

"He devoted all of his energies to the business and to us." He leaned back in his chair. "I realized too late that the relationship developing between Leon and myself was just as unnatural. At first I was flattered by the attention he gave me. We were inseparable, Damon and Pythias."

"I understand," she said, "more than you could know."

"Um. I suppose I deliberately blinded myself to what was truly happening all those years."

"What was happening?"

He looked at her, the debate as to whether he should say it or not quickly ended.

"He was making love to Karla through me. She was as much a part of him as she was a part of me. In his eyes, that is." He looked up at the portrait and shook his head. "She had an extramarital affair," he added, almost like an afterthought.

"I know." She told him about her talk with Liza Glenn, and what Liza Glenn claimed he had seen."

"Then now you know," he said. "Now you know why Karla and her brother got into that terrible argument and why he . . ." He swallowed and looked away.

"Why?" Cynthia asked, not grasping. Hoffman looked up at her, his eyes filled with pain. For him, even after all these years, the incident was as fresh as ever, Cynthia thought, especially because she bore such a resemblance.

"He believed she was betraying him, don't you see? She betrayed me, of course, but to him it was as though she betrayed him because to him we had become one. He was as hurt as I should have been. When I came upon the scene he was ranting and raving like the abused husband. That's when it was clear to me, when I understood how far things had gone. Of course, it was too late," he added sadly. "There was nothing I could do then. He was pathetic. I couldn't have felt more guilty had I driven the knife into her myself."

"So that's why you were so kind to him afterward, why you cared what happened to him?"

"Yes, but I couldn't very well explain it, could I?" The tears were coming now. She felt sorry for what she had forced him to do and to say, but she had to know.

"I suppose this explains his suicide shortly afterward."

"Yes. I never went to see him. I couldn't get myself to face up to it. When I heard he had killed himself I felt both relief and sadness. You see," he said, leaning forward, "Leon made the ultimate sacrifice for me. He took on my guilt," he said. There was still a look of pride and satisfaction in his face, and for the first time since she had entered Hoffman's house, she wondered if he weren't more responsible than she thought for the way things had turned out.

"But what about Karla?" she asked, and paused. There was no way to be euphemistic about it. "In a sense, didn't you drive her into her infidelity?"

He sat back and looked up at her portrait. Then he did something she didn't expect—he smiled.

"Karla was a very strong-willed and independent woman, perhaps years ahead of her time. I'm not saying I don't share some of the blame, but somehow, someway, she always maintained her separate identity. Oh, she wasn't career-minded the way your modern day woman can be," he said, "but she saw every aspect of marriage, of compromise, as a chipping away of her own special identity. Although we were married for a number of years, we never had children, you see. She wasn't ready to give anything up yet," he added. There was some bitterness in his voice.

Cynthia blanched. In many ways it was as if someone fifty years from now was describing her. She lowered her head as if the thoughts were literally too heavy to hold up. Did Karla bear some of the guilt? Was she now being unfair to Stephen? What was it Jason had said—"It's harder to be objective about things close to you"? Could it be that she couldn't see herself for what she was, for what she had been?

"You have a remarkable resemblance to my wife," he said as though he knew everything about her life with Stephen. She looked up sharply, but he was talking only about her physical similarities. "And when I saw you in that doorway... in that dress... I thought for a moment that she had actually come back from the dead."

"Maybe she has," Cynthia said.

"Oh, I see. You're very serious about this being something of a spiritual experience for you."

"Yes."

He nodded and looked up at the portrait again.

"If anyone could do it, Karla could." He smiled at a thousand small memories. "But you know," he said, "I never told anyone the things I told you. Not really. If there is a spiritual purpose to all this, perhaps it was to give me the relief that comes with confession. What do you think?"

"I don't know," she said. She stared at him. He looked as selfish to her now as he might have looked to Karla fifty years ago.

"I see. You still think it has something to do with you personally."

"There are other parallels," she said.

"Oh?"

"But I've got to work them out for myself," she added, and stood up. "Thank you for what you've told me."

"Looking at you makes me feel young again. It brings back all the music. We had a beautiful romance in the early days. I've never known another woman like her." He stood up, too. "I can be very envious of your husband. But," he added, "if he were here I'd have to tell him that I can be very fearful for him, too. Do you understand? I don't mean any disrespect, but..."

"I understand," she said quickly. She went to the living room doorway and then turned back to look up at the portrait. He looked at it with her. "Why did you bury her in the Catskills, away from the rest of the family?"

He took a deep breath.

"There was no room by her parents, and I thought she would want her independence, even after death." He started to smile and then stopped. "I couldn't bury her in my family plot...I thought that every time I went to visit my parents' graves she'd haunt me. I suppose it was another way I tried to escape my own guilt, to leave it up there with her."

"Did it work?"

"No, not at all. And if there was ever any doubt in my mind, your presence has ended it."

"Maybe that was one of the reasons for this," she said.

"Knowing Karla, I'm sure."

He sat down again, looking much weaker and older than when she had first come in.

"Goodbye," she said, and left him staring up at that portrait.

THE RIDE BACK went much faster. She felt as though she were fleeing from something, bursting out of that cocoon of the past that had closed in around her these past few days. It gave her a new sense of freedom; she breathed better. When she looked into the mirror she saw a face with more life. It was as though she had moved out of a black-and-white movie into a color film. Even the sounds around her were clearer, sharper. That dreamy haze that had fallen over everything and that made her feel like a sleepwalker was gone.

Perhaps Borris Hoffman was right. Perhaps Karla Hoffman's only purpose in reaching out to her and through her was just achieved: to help her husband find inner peace through confession. He faced up to things he had kept hidden in his heart all these years, and all these years it ate away at him. It could be that whatever jurisdiction passed sentence on him now believed he had suffered enough. Cynthia had helped to provide his redemption.

But how could she ignore the parallels in her own life? There had to be some reward in it for her, too. The difference now was she felt she had the power to see things better, even about herself. The gift was that she could be objective. Distortions, half truths, all subterfuge would fall away. She felt invincible because she was not only armed with her own improved vision, but the vision of someone who had lived a similar life fifty years ago.

She didn't go directly to the office. She drove home instead and there changed from the old-fashioned dress to one of her own pantsuit outfits. She changed earrings and worked on her hair and her makeup. When she stepped back to look at herself, she felt renewed and revived. Confident and eager for any challenge, she headed over to the office. When she arrived her secretary's mouth dropped open stupidly. She was so taken with the change that she couldn't help speaking out.

"What happened to your other outfit?" she asked.

"What other outfit?" Cynthia said, but she didn't wait for an answer. She went right into her office to work.

Not long afterward Stephen knocked on her office door and entered. It was obvious to her that Judy had already filled him in on the change of clothes. He wore an amused smile.

"What have you come up with—a new plan to sell houses?"

"What do you mean?"

"Dressing according to the age and style of the house? Jason just said he thought that might be a great idea. When you want to sell a farm, you dress like a farmer's wife; when you want to sell a restaurant and bar, you dress like a sexy waitress."

"Very funny."

"Who knows, maybe you'll start something significant."

She sat back.

"How is my brother feeling?"

"Like a fool. He was hoping you'd still be home when he awoke. He wanted the sympathy."

"From me? That would have been a first."

"Uh-huh." He stared at her, the smile still on his face.

Reflection

"What are you up to now, Stephen?"

"How busy are you?"

"Just bringing the paperwork up to date."

"Can you get it all done by the end of the day?"

"I suppose. Why?"

"I want you to pack."

"Pack?"

"I made reservations for us. We're taking that vacation I promised. Now don't disagree," he said, holding his hand up like a traffic cop. "I've seen how you've been these past few days and I think you were right—we've got to take a break, both of us."

"Where are we going?"

"You're not going to believe this," he said, "but I found something you should love. It's right up your alley."

"What?"

"An old-fashioned Catskill-type resort and not that far away."

"Old-fashioned?"

"Just the way the Rose Hill House must have been fifty years ago," he said. "Simple things to do, home-cooked, family-style meals, unpretentious rooms, a family-run resort. What do you think? What could be more romantic?"

For a moment she just stared at him.

"It sounds . . . nice," she said.

"Nice? I thought you'd be more excited. Christ, there's even a gazebo on the back lawn!"

13

STEPHEN'S RESORT WAS in the upper Delaware Valley, actually only a little more than an hour and a half away. She was impressed with his efforts to find it. Apparently, from what he told her, he had been searching for something like it for some time. He had been determined to find something that would please her. She liked that. The only part of his statement she didn't like was that he said he did this because she needed the vacation even more than he did.

"Not that we're both not overworked," he added quickly, seeing the change in her expression. "It's just that I don't see it in myself as easily as I see it in you."

Jason couldn't have said it any better, she thought; but she accepted his explanation. Besides, she wasn't in any mood to fight. The prospect of a romantic holiday outweighed other considerations. It could bring things back to the way they were; it could straighten out their lives. For the moment she was convinced of this, and this was why she was so adamant when Terrence Baker suggested otherwise.

She called him back toward the end of the day. She didn't know whether it was just her imagination or not, but it seemed to her that Judy Dobbs wrote the message darker and bigger than most of the others. She had strong reservations about calling him because she had come to believe that this side romance was distracting her from seeing the realities of her own life clearly. This romance was truly a fantasy; it was immature to continue it.

And yet the hunger for the fantasy still continued. We all need romance, she thought. And if Stephen and she couldn't find it, revive it and rectify their lives, then Terrence Baker would become even more attractive to her than he was now. Perhaps it was unfair to keep him dangling, but she couldn't help it. She couldn't turn him off completely. Not yet.

"I half expected you would come last night," he said. "No matter what you said."

"I don't think it took me five minutes to fall asleep after I spoke to you."

"I nearly finished the bottle of wine myself, waiting."

"Sorry, but I told you I wasn't coming."

"What about tonight?"

She hesitated a moment, and then she told him about the vacation. He was silent so long, she thought he had left the phone on his desk and walked away.

"I think you're making a big mistake," he finally said.

"Why?"

"There are reconciliations and there are reconciliations. This won't work."

"How can you be so sure?"

"If he's doing what you think he's doing, it's sicker than you think."

"There are things you don't understand. I didn't... I couldn't tell you all of it...."

"You can't blame it all on your brother," he said, "if that's what you're thinking."

She was, but she didn't want to admit it.

"No, I'm not, but..."

"How long are you going to be gone?"

"Three, four days."

"And if you work everything out?"

"I don't know. Do I have to decide everything at once?"

"What is your spirit telling you?" he asked, but she heard the note of disdain.

"That all men are sons of bitches," she said. He laughed. "I've got to go."

"Hey."

"What?"

"Good luck."

"Thanks."

"Don't worry, I don't mean it," he said, and she laughed.

Surprisingly, the conversation with him left her feeling good. Her spirits were high at the end of the day when she went home to pack.

DURING THE TRIP to the New Prospect, the resort, the name of which she thought was apropos, Stephen became more and more like his earlier self. It was as though the farther they went from Jason, the more he returned to being the Stephen with whom she had first fallen in love. His voice was filled with warmth and excitement; he took a childlike pleasure in every new sight, every beautiful aspect of nature.

And the natural sights were beautiful, exceptionally so on this trip. Maybe that was because she was seeing things through optimistic eyes again. She couldn't say, but whatever the cause, she enjoyed it. She enjoyed the long stretches of country highway that passed through acres and acres of low flatlands still covered with the stalks of Indian-summer corn. She enjoyed wave after wave of crimson and orange and yellow leaves, a veritable sea of color undulating in the warm but brisk autumn breeze. She loved it when they came upon a large pond or lake and saw the geese pausing for a rest after completing a leg of their journey south.

Stephen was like a tour guide, announcing everything just before anything appeared. She was impressed with his familiarity with all the landmarks and sights. Could he have memorized it all from only one exploratory trip? She saw him as remarkable again—bright, perceptive, alive.

"Every time I see this little farmhouse coming up on the right here, Cyn, I think of you. I don't know why. There's something about it that reminds me of you."

As soon as they completed the turn and came upon it, she knew why. The house was obviously old, turn-of-the-century vintage, but whoever owned it doted on it. The white siding, which looked as if it was the original wood, was scrubbed clean. The flat black shutters had a richness in texture that bespoke of daily maintenance. The hedges and the walkway were trimmed and immaculate. Stephen slowed down as they went by it, so she saw that the porch had been carefully jacked up and restored to its original state. But the little wishing well to the right with its shiny tin pail stole her heart.

"Oh, Stephen, you're right. It's beautiful. I wish it were for sale."

"Don't think I didn't stop to ask," he said, and laughed.

"And?"

"Naw, it's one of those family-owned properties, deeded down through the generations, passed on as firmly as their genes. The people appreciated my interest, but they looked at me as if I were totally whacked-out."

She laughed. They crossed a small wooden bridge that spanned a tributary stream off the Delaware River, and once again she felt as though they had moved over some boundary to leave the darker, sadder and uglier aspects of their life behind. In a way they had found a "fountain of youth." Stephen looked younger and more energetic. They spoke to each other in tones reminiscent of the early days of their romance, and she felt swept away. She could close her eyes and open them and not be afraid of what lay ahead. The sky couldn't be any bluer, the clouds any more billowy and white.

When the small hotel came into view she lost her breath. It lay back on a small hill couched in the center of the valley. As they descended toward the house she saw the small lake to the right and to the rear of it. People were out on the lake in rowboats, moving so slowly they looked painted on the water. Off to the left were the stables where two pairs of guests were preparing to mount their horses and follow the trails deeper into the valley and toward the river. The warmer air of the valley had kept the grounds, the trees and the foliage lush and green. The hotel looked as though it had been frozen in time. The fingers of the seasons never touched it; the claws of inclement weather couldn't take hold and damage the scenic splendor. It was definitely a place in which to fall in love or recapture a love lost.

"What do you think?"

"Stephen, it's magnificent. What a location. How did you find it?"

"Actually Jason knew about it," he said. She looked at him, but even a reference to Jason couldn't detract from her state of euphoria. This place looked impenetrable. Evil, depression, sorrow in any form was turned away at the gate. "Wait until you meet the owners," he said, "they're straight out of the nineteenth century."

They drove directly to the main building. It was reminiscent of all the old tourist houses that were built throughout the Catskill resort area—a three-story structure with a long, wide front porch. She could see where the building had been expanded as the business grew. Yet somehow, maybe because it was significantly away from the main tourist region, the New Prospect looked unique. She saw it with virgin eyes. It would be a richly novel experience.

Almost as soon as Stephen turned off the engine, Clarence Smalls, the owners' thirty-year-old son, came out of the main building and down the steps. He was dressed in a T-shirt and jeans and a pair of well-worn work boots. His thick, dark black head of hair flowed over his ears and down his neck almost to his shoulders, but it was brushed and orderly, obviously washed and blow-dried. He had a face of strong and distinct features, almost Indian because of the high cheekbones and deeply set dark brown eyes. His nose was Roman straight, and sharp at the end. He had a wide, strong mouth set in an almost square jaw. Cynthia saw that he was muscular and hard, like a true farm boy shaped by the labor on the land.

"Hi," he said, his warm smile diminishing his cold, tough appearance. She sensed a gentleness beneath the surface, but it was a gentleness that came from a slow-witted good nature. "You're Mr. and Mrs. uh..."

"Warner," Stephen said.

"Yeah, Warner. I'll help with your bags."

"Thanks." Stephen got out and opened the trunk. Cynthia got out, took in a deep breath of air and studied the building. A few moments later Lillian Smalls appeared in the doorway. She wiped her hands in her apron and waited for them to come up the short stairway. Cynthia estimated her to be in her sixties. She was a short but strong woman of obvious energy and grit. Her handshake was firm, and her voice was warm but businesslike. Cynthia saw that Clarence had inherited his sharp facial features from her, but her dark eyes were keen and perceptive. In a moment she had sized up these two guests and determined whether or not they would truly enjoy a stay at her resort.

"Hello again, Mr. Warner."

"We couldn't have picked a better day to come out."

"Oh, the weather's been kind to us this season." She smiled at Cynthia.

"This is my wife, Cynthia."

"Pleased to meet you. Your room's all ready. You've got the one right above us. Choice view. Don't just stand there, Clarence," she said, pausing. "Get their stuff up to four." He moved quickly inside. "Well, you missed breakfast. If you want a cup of tea and some biscuits, come right into the kitchen after you settle in. Lunch will be outside today in the rear of the house, smorgasbord style."

"We know about your food, Mrs. Smalls," Stephen said. "That's why we've come."

"Oh, call me Lillian, and if you don't call my husband Charley, he won't answer you," she said. Stephen laughed.

"This is one of the most beautiful places I've seen," Cynthia said. "It's kept so well, too."

"Thank you. I hope you enjoy your stay with us. Just go right in and follow the stairway up," she said.

The entrance room wasn't as wide as the Rose Hill House's, but the interior structural design was similar. There was a sitting room to the right and the kitchen was straight ahead, down the corridor.

From what she could see of it, it looked larger than the one at the Rose Hill.

They followed the circular stairway up to the second floor. The door to their room was open, and Clarence had just put their bags on the colonial-style double bed. It was a small but quaint room with true warmth and personality, more like a room found in a country inn than a room in a hotel. There was a clean, heart-shaped mirror in a pine frame that matched the texture of pine in the bed headboard and posts, as well as the dresser and small night table. The window shades were up and the brown-and-white curtains drawn, but since their window faced the west side the sunlight wasn't direct and bright. The room had a hard oak floor that looked as though it had been recently polished. Cynthia went right to the closet to hang up her jacket.

"Thanks, Clarence," Stephen said, and took out two dollars. But Clarence held his hand up.

"No tips, thanks. My mother don't believe in that."

"Really? Well, okay. Thanks."

They both watched him leave, closing the door behind him. Then they looked at each other. Stephen shrugged, and they both laughed.

"And this place isn't what you would call expensive, either," Stephen said. "Just an all-around great find."

"I love it."

"And I love you," he said. He looked from her to the bed and back to her again.

"Oh, Stephen," she said, "we can't just hop right into the sack. What would Lillian think?"

"That we're honeymooners, what else?" he said. He embraced her and they kissed. They did kiss like honeymooners. When they parted, neither spoke. They undressed quietly, pulled back the quilt on the bed and slipped under it to make love as gently but as passionately as they ever had. When it was over they still moved softly around one another, barely speaking. It was as if neither of them wanted to break the spell. They dressed in more comfortable clothing and then went down to enjoy the grounds and explore the hotel.

They met Charley Smalls down at the dock by the lake. He was repairing the oarlock on one of the rowboats. Cynthia could see that whereas Clarence inherited his facial features from his mother, he inherited his body size and shape from his father. Although Charley Smalls was closing in on seventy, he looked as straight and as firm as a man in his late forties, early fifties. His neck was still wide, his shoulders broad. He had his hair trimmed short, and there were still dark black streaks running through it.

He shook their hands firmly and smiled, but Cynthia sensed that he was far more withdrawn than his wife. It was apparent that he left the dealings with guests to her. He and his son kept the place going; he wasn't interested in the business end or the socializing. He did take the time to tell them about the horseback riding, the boating, the horseshoe game and the hiking trails.

"And there's great fishin' in the river if you've a mind to do that."

"It's enough just to sit back and enjoy the scenery," Cynthia said. Charley Smalls nodded, but he looked as though he didn't believe she was sincere.

The first thing they did do was go for a boat ride. She was surprised at how warm the lake water still was. After they pushed off Stephen rowed hard for a good five minutes, acting like a teenage boy determined to show off his strength and endurance. She laughed at him when he stopped out of breath.

"I told you you were getting too fat and too out of shape."

"Maybe you should . . . row. If I got a heart attack rowing my wife in the middle of a lake, it would be too embarrassing."

She laughed and they changed places. He pretended to be a rich nobleman being pampered by a servant girl. They passed another couple in a rowboat and the man yelled over, asking Stephen how he had gotten Cynthia to do it.

"Women's lib," Stephen replied. Everyone laughed.

For Cynthia these were magical moments. She didn't want to question why or how it was happening; she was just glad that it was. She had made plans to get into some deep conversations with Stephen, to bring up all her suspicions and hates, but now she wondered if that wouldn't break the mood and destroy the moment. To lose this—this long weekend in paradise—would be a sin, she thought. She decided to let things take their natural course. If the subjects came up she would discuss them; if not, she'd leave them for another time. She had dreamt of these romantic days too long to let them slip away. In the back of her mind was the idea that if their love had any power, if she had any power as a woman, this time together should be significant enough to solidify their relationship once again and strengthen Stephen enough to reject Jason for what he was and what he could do. Perhaps she was being too optimistic, she thought, but she had to give it a chance.

At lunch they met the other guests. Four couples had come up together from the city. The husbands were all members of the same law firm. They said that they made a trip to the New Prospect an annual thing for the past three years. They were all about Stephen's and her age, intelligent and witty people, well schooled, well traveled, what she often called, "Jason's kind of people." As they all sat around talking, she enjoyed observing Stephen's behavior. Here, without Jason, he was different. There was no ridicule in his voice, no sarcasm; he could tolerate being subdued, being laid-back, not being the center of attention. There was a warmth and a friendliness to him that was reminiscent of the old days. The New York couples took to them and invited them to help form teams for a horseshoe tournament. She couldn't remember having as much fun doing such simple things.

Afterward they all went for a short hike to search for the abundant blackberry patches Clarence Smalls described. When Cynthia asked him to lead the way, he looked flattered but frightened. He told her it was easy to find and went through a detailed description of the way once again. Then he fled as though in fear she'd insist he come.

"Maybe his mother doesn't want him to mingle with the guests," Stephen said. One of the young lawyers told him that he thought that was the case.

"Maybe he hurt someone once or got into trouble once. I don't know," he said. "It's obvious he's a little retarded."

"But he seems too gentle to be harmful," Cynthia insisted. After they started away she caught him watching them from a window in the rear of the house. He was peering between the curtains.

The hiking trails took them uphill, and Cynthia could see that Stephen was a little annoyed at himself for being so tired so quickly while the young lawyers appeared undaunted by the difficulties of the journey. There was a lot of horseplay, and sometimes they broke out into runs. Before long she and Stephen were falling behind.

"They all belong to a health club," she explained. "They have regular workouts, something I've been telling you to do for some time now."

"Yeah. I meant to start this week."

"You always mean to start, Stephen, but somehow something always gets in your way."

"Um."

"Maybe it's not so hard to figure out why," she said, but she had already gone beyond what she wanted to say. They were having too much fun to get into an argument now, she thought.

They found the berry patches, but Stephen didn't want to tackle the thorny bushes. They stayed back and watched the other couples go at it, filling a two-pound coffee can. "So Mrs. Smalls can make a pie," someone said. Afterward, on the trip down, Stephen kept up with the men and she lagged behind with the women. They were surprised to discover that she and Stephen lived only an hour and a half from the New Prospect in the Catskills, where there were so many similar resorts.

"Similar, but not the same," she explained. "This place is like a jewel. It's hard to find places like this still in existence. Our hotels are sophisticated, complex; some of them are little cities unto themselves, with clothing stores, drugstores, barbershops and beauty parlors, all within the hotel proper. Oh, they have horseback riding and rowboats and hiking trails, too, but somehow... this is different. It's like taking a jewel out of a jewelry store; it stands out more. I just..."

She stopped because she realized they were all looking at her, quite taken with the way she had wrapped herself in the explanation. She laughed.

"I can go overboard sometimes."

Everyone smiled and they walked on, but she felt terribly self-conscious. She had to wonder if these women could see through her, see how hard she was trying to recapture love. It was true she was going at it all with such intensity. Maybe they would think she was a romantic, she thought.

As soon as they got back, she and Stephen went up to shower and rest before dinner. He was really tired, but he tried to hide it, putting all his hopes into the medicinal and therapeutic effects of a long, hot shower and a short nap. She sat by the small table and brushed her hair, looking at him from time to time, watching him sleep. He seemed contented, and although he was physically tired, she thought she read a deep satisfaction in his face. She got herself dressed before waking him and then decided she would go down to the sitting room to wait for him to join her.

"This is a switch," he said, "you're going to be waiting for me."

"Don't spend all day deciding what to wear," she teased. He threw his pillow at the door when she stepped out.

There was a couple out on the porch, but she went into the sitting room and browsed through some of the books on the shelves and looked at the knickknacks. She heard the screen door open and close, but she didn't turn around until she sensed someone looking at her. It was Clarence. He stood in the doorway.

"So many nice things here," she said. She felt herself blush because he was staring so hard.

"Yeah. My mother dusts everything once a week."

She laughed.

"Have you been busy all summer?"

"Oh yeah, very busy. I've been going in and out of town for supplies all the time. Just came back now."

"That berry patch was all you described," she said, embarrassed by the long pause after he spoke. He smiled.

"Told ya. Well, I gotta get goin'. See ya later," he said, and he was gone. A few minutes later Stephen appeared. She half expected he would be wearing one of the shirt and pants outfits he had bought when he was with Jason, but instead he was dressed in the light blue, cotton short-sleeve shirt she had bought him when she had been up at the town of Fallsburg golf club at the beginning of the summer. He had worn it once or twice at the most. She was also surprised that he was wearing jeans. That was something else he hadn't done for some time.

"You got a little color today," she said. "Your arms look brown."

"I thought I did." They heard the voices of the others as they came down the stairs. "Shall we join them?"

"Gladly. I could eat through the table, I'm so hungry."

"It's all the fresh air," he said. Then he smiled and added, "and activity."

She took his hand and they walked to the dining room, a long, wide room paneled with what looked to be old barn wood. There were two chandelier ceiling fans above the great table that presently had twenty-two place settings. Two teenage girls were bringing out large platters and bowls of food.

"Reminds me of the Amish restaurant," Cynthia said. "Family-style."

The young couples they had spent the day with called to them, and they joined them at the far end of the table. It was a true feast—home-baked bread, thinly sliced roast beef, homemade potato salad and cole slaw, steamed vegetables and cold spring water. For dessert there was homemade apple pie and ice cream, as well as rice pudding.

There was a great deal of chatter throughout the meal. The informality of the dinner, the casual, rustic setting and the delicious food helped Cynthia to relax more than she had in months. She knew that the four couples had obviously discussed them, and they apparently all agreed that they liked them. She had to admit that Stephen was as personable and as pleasant as she had ever seen him. She liked the other women. Each couple was well on its way toward an affluent life, yet none of them were pretentious or snobby. Perhaps it would come later on, she thought, but for now, or maybe because of this place, they were all warm and friendly and excited with the interchange of friendship.

They never saw Lillian Smalls during the meal, but they understood that she was chiefly responsible for the preparation. Charley and Clarence did not appear, either. However, after it was over, Lillian Smalls did come out of the kitchen. The table of guests gave her a loud round of applause. Cynthia thought it really was something of a performance, and for a moment she thought about Terrence. But even thinking of him for a moment seemed wrong, now that she was beside Stephen and they were having such a warm, romantic time.

"Everything all right?" he asked.

"What? Oh, yes, yes. Everything's wonderful," she said, and blanched from guilt.

"I imagine this was what the Rose Hill House was like in its heyday," he said. His remark had the effect of a sharp slap in the face. From what she could see he didn't say it to be sarcastic or cruel, but it jerked her out of her dream time for a few moments. She looked about like someone who had gone unconscious, fallen back through time and awoken fifty years ago. Was this all really happening? The laughter continued. Some of the men and women lit cigarettes. Someone made a suggestion they all go for a walk in the moonlight and she thought, yes, yes, that's what they used to do after the meal—walk in the early-summer evening.

"What do you say? Cynthia?"

"What?"

"Jeez, you are in a daze, aren't you?"

"No, I was just..."

"Everyone's going for a walk. You want to go along or are you feeling tired?"

"No, no, I'm fine. Sure."

She took his hand again, and they followed the other couples out the front door. They all went down the driveway and onto the country road. There were no streetlights, and traffic was practically nonexistent. Someone up front in an extra loud voice said, "I didn't read a newspaper all day, and I didn't hear or see any news program and I don't give a damn." There was a lot of laughter in agreement.

"It is as if we dropped out of reality, isn't it?" she said.

"That's what we came here to do," Stephen said. "Right?"

"Yes," she said, but she wasn't altogether sure that was exactly what was happening. In any case it was a warm evening; they were in pleasant company; they had just had a great, old-fashioned meal, and she didn't want anything to destroy the moment. She would force herself not to think any serious thoughts, if she had to.

After the walk she and Stephen and the four couples went into the sitting room and played Trivial Pursuit until nearly eleven o'clock. When they went up to their room, both of them couldn't believe how tired they were. For the first time in weeks she fell asleep moments after she put her head to the pillow. There was no tossing and turning, no struggle against terrible thoughts, no replay of innuendos or suspicious activities.

They woke to the sound of voices in the hallway. Breakfast ran from seven to nine, but with the prospect of another beautiful day ahead, most everyone staying at the hotel wanted an early start. They didn't get right out of bed, though. When Stephen and she turned to face each other, she felt the old excitement build quickly. He was looking at her the way he had in the early days, his eyes filled with a hunger so obvious it brought tingles into her breasts and thighs. Their embrace and their kiss were longer than usual, and they went at their lovemaking with a wilder, more demanding attitude. Afterward they showered together and laughed about the Smalls turning them both into "country folk."

Cynthia couldn't believe that Stephen would return to the man he was before they arrived. Surely their renewal of their love already had had a significant effect. She was buoyed by the speed at which they had come back to each other. Her mind was reeling from all sorts of possibilities. Maybe she would change the design of the agency and have her office adjacent to Stephen's. They could even have a door adjoining them. She wanted to seriously rethink her career, as well. Perhaps she had been foolish to separate herself entirely from the insurance end of things and turn Stephen completely over to Jason. Sure, she thought, if she went back into it and all the decisions that had to be made had to be made by the three of them instead of only Jason and Stephen, her influence over Stephen would be that much stronger. She would defeat Jason at his own game.

She didn't want to discuss any of these ideas with Stephen yet. She recognized that there was a magic in their stay here; it was important to keep the real world out for as long as possible. Anyway, the hotel and the other guests made that easy to do. Their new friends were already down at breakfast by the time they arrived. They kidded them about their lateness, and someone quickly nicknamed them "the honeymooners." Cynthia blushed from happiness.

After breakfast they all went horseback riding. Clarence was the wrangler. He was obviously a good rider. In fact he and the horse looked like a part of each other. Although he led the group, he continually went to the rear of the line and worked his way to the front by giving the guests pointers about the handling of their horses. Both she and Stephen had done some riding in the past, and Stephen seemed determined to show up his New York friends. She could almost read his thoughts: they might be in better physical shape, but they didn't have his skill and confidence. He rode ahead, egging the other men on. It was a display of arrogance that reminded her of Jason.

On the other hand, Clarence spent a great deal of his time at her side. She sensed that he was enamored of her. When he talked he reminded her of a teenage boy. He was determined to win her admiration. He told her that when he didn't have the guests to care for, he would ride on his own, specially made trails. He could give the horse its head and go for miles and miles. She listened, a gentle smile on her face that he took for evidence of how impressive he was. From time to time he broke away and did some fancy riding.

The other guests who had been at the New Prospect before told her the ride went a lot longer than usual. In the back of her mind, she thought that might have been because Clarence wanted to keep her out there with him as long as possible. She felt indirectly responsible for the saddle sores and fatigue. She knew Stephen was suffering a little, even though he wasn't one of the complainers.

By the time they returned it was nearly lunchtime. Everyone cleaned up for it, but after they ate they were all content to merely sit around on the lawn chairs and watch some of the men play horseshoes. Later on Stephen retreated to their room to take a nap, and she sat talking with some of the other women on the front porch. The more they talked, though, the more she became aware of how little she had in common with them. The main reason came from the fact that they all had children. When they got on that subject she was completely left out. It led to the first long note of depression since she had arrived.

She excused herself from the group and went up to the room to get ready for dinner. When she arrived she was surprised to find Stephen already in the shower. She had hoped to make love and take their shower together again, but he had his clothing all laid out and was obviously anxious to get back downstairs.

"My wife isn't going to show me up this time," he said.

"Oh, Stephen, is that really important?"

"Naw. I'm just tired of lying around in this room. Take your time. I'll be down on the front porch smokin' my corncob pipe."

She sat on the bed and watched him dress quickly. After he brushed his hair he gave her a quick peck on the cheek and left. She sat staring at the closed door and then got up and slowly began to undress for her shower. The water revived her. She shampooed and blow-dried her hair, regretting more than ever her decision to change her color. After she brushed it out she went to the closet to choose something to wear. She settled on a frilly white cotton blouse and a light green skirt she hadn't worn all summer. She brought them to the bed and laid them out. Then she slipped into her panties and clipped on her bra. She was standing by the window and gazing out at the way the late-afternoon sun turned the leaves of the trees that were still green into a translucent emerald. For a few moments she was hypnotized by it.

Then her attention was drawn to the long circular driveway in front of the hotel because the silver Audi 5000 S that came onto the resort grounds was familiar, too familiar. Her heart skipped a beat. She

Reflection

pressed her blouse close to her body and stared down in disbelief.

Jason emerged from the car, and in his hand he carried his valise.

14

WHEN SHE OPENED HER DOOR to step out, she confronted Clarence carrying Jason's suitcase and Jason walking right behind him. She smiled back at Clarence who gave her a big hello, but her smile faded quickly when she saw him stop at the door of the adjoining room.

"Hi," Jason said. "God, you look great, too, and only after a day or so here. This must be the place," he said.

"Why are you here, Jason?" She couldn't disguise her displeasure, but he chose to ignore it.

He waited a moment as Clarence came back out of the room and handed him the key. He didn't even make the attempt to give him a tip.

"Stephen told me no tips," he whispered. "So you went horseback riding."

"That's right. We've been having a great time. Why did you come here?"

Jason kept his smile a moment and then shrugged.

"I wasn't going to," he said. "Despite its obvious pastoral beauty and romantic innocence, this isn't my idea of a vacation. I like to be pampered. I like..."

"I know what you like, Jason. That's why I repeat, why are you here?"

"Your husband practically threatened to have me kidnapped and brought here if I didn't come," he said. She felt the color leaving her face. "We're all working too hard," he said. "We need to be away from it, away from our driving ambitions and our modern-day complexities. I must say it appears he has chosen an adequate escape from all that. Am I right?" She just stared at him.

"Where is he?" she asked.

"Downstairs in conversation with a group of arrogant attorneys from the big city."

It's starting, she thought. He's not here a half hour and it's already starting.

"They're not arrogant, Jason. They happen to be very nice people, and we've been having a wonderful time with them. I don't want anything to interfere with that."

"To each his own," he said. "Well, I'd better shower and change. I understand dinner is a veritable frontier experience. See you soon," he added, and went into his room. She waited until he closed the door behind him, still refusing to believe he was actually here and only a thin wall away. Would he have his ear against it when they made love? If they made love?

She went down the stairs slowly, feeling like someone who had just been struck in the head. Clarence was at the bottom of the stairway, looking up as though in anticipation.

"How are ya?" he asked. "You ain't sore from the saddle, are ya?"

"A little." She smiled. "It's all right."

"Some of them other ladies is really sore. My mother says I kept them out too long. It didn't seem that long."

"It is for people who don't ride regularly," she said.

"Yeah. Okay, see ya later," he said, and went toward the kitchen. She stopped at the screen door because the conversation on the porch was louder than usual. It was very close to being an argument. Stephen was defending President Reagan's new budget proposals.

"That's just what they are—giveaways," he was saying when she stepped out. "Reagan's the first one to expose those liberal bleeding hearts for what they are."

"Scrooge couldn't have said it any better," one of the lawyers replied, and there was a lot of laughter at Stephen's expense. She saw his face redden, and she knew he was about to snap back in anger.

"Stephen!" she said sharply, so sharply she turned all the heads her way. "I've got to talk to you."

"Sure. Excuse me," he said. "We're not finished."

She went down the steps to the walkway to draw him away from the others. When he caught up with her she turned on him.

"How could you tell Jason to come here? This was supposed to be our holiday, our chance to get away from it all. His coming ruins it," she said. She clutched her hands into fists and held them firmly against her thighs. Her entire body was stiff and poised as though to go into battle. He saw the intensity in her face and looked back to be sure the others weren't watching.

"Take it easy, will you. Jesus, you should see yourself."

"I'm upset, Stephen. I'm really upset."

"All right, all right. First of all, I didn't tell him to come out here. He had to know where we would be. He's familiar with the place."

"He says he hates this place," she interrupted. "He's implying that you practically forced him to come."

"I didn't say he stayed here. He knows of this place. He knew it was the kind of thing I was looking for."

"Why did you suggest he come?"

"I didn't. His coming is just as much a surprise to me as it is to you. Who'd ever think Jason would leave the business? We'll probably get a dozen calls, now that he's here," he added, looking away and shaking his head. "I'm sure he left the number."

"God, Stephen."

"Well, what do you want me to do, tell him to leave?"

"It wouldn't be such a bad idea, no."

"Really? I couldn't do that. I never realized you hated him so much." He looked at her as though the thought had actually just occurred to him.

"I hate what he's done to you," she said, her voice a little above a whisper.

"Aw, you're exaggerating. Look, he'll stay to himself and we'll..."

"You know he won't."

And then as if on cue to support her, Jason called to them from the porch. He was dressed in a sports coat and tie.

"Be right there," Stephen said.

"Christ, look at him. He looks like he's going to dinner at the Concord. Doesn't he know where he's at? This isn't one of those fancy hotels."

"Can't change him," Stephen said. He smiled. "He's what he is."

"What about you, Stephen? Can you be changed?"

"All right, all right," he said, taking her hand. "I'll work it out. I'll speak to him and keep him away from us."

"This place is too small, Stephen. That's going to be impossible."

"It won't. You'll see. Come on."

Reluctantly she followed him back to the porch. Everyone was starting to go in to dinner.

"You'd better be hungry," Stephen told him.

"I am. But," he added, looking at Cynthia, "probably nowhere as hungry as you two."

Stephen opened the screen door and she stepped back into the hotel, but he didn't walk beside her. He followed behind, walking with Jason. When they arrived at the dining room, she saw from the expressions on the faces of the young couples, that they were already a little turned off from socializing with them. She wondered how much time Jason had spent talking with Stephen and the others before Clarence had shown him his room. She imagined it was Jason who had started the argument that Stephen nearly finished on a very sour note.

This dinner was different. The food was just as delicious, if not more so than it had been the night before, but the mood was subdued. She sensed a new formality between them and the others. It took only moments for Stephen and Jason to dominate the conversation. Unlike the day before, Stephen had opinions about everything, and he made his statements almost as though he were throwing down a gauntlet. If anyone challenged or disagreed, Jason came in like a second-team debater held back as a secret weapon. Before long the couples were directing their conversations to one another, and a real schism between them and Stephen and her developed. By the time dessert was being served, Stephen and Jason were having their own conversation, a conversation she was barely a part of, both because they didn't really include her and she didn't want to be included.

Jason balked at going for a walk after dinner. He said it was behaving too much like Catskill-mountain tourists. There was nothing more revolting than riding along the highways and seeing this line of stuffed and bloated hotel guests walking along the roads.

"As if a twenty-minute stroll endangering themselves and the drivers of automobiles really had anything to do with digestion. Digestion depends on eating moderately," he added in his usual pedantic tone. The others looked at him as though he were someone from outer space. She saw that Stephen, despite what he had promised her, was reluctant to leave Jason behind. As an excuse he said that he hadn't eaten as much as he had the night before. Their decision was to simply sit out on the porch. She said nothing. She let them go ahead. She didn't join the others for the walk, but she couldn't sit out with Jason and Stephen, either. She excused herself to go up to the room for a few minutes and left them.

She didn't go to the room. She went out the back door and walked down to the lake. Except after the remark Stephen had made comparing New Prospect now to the way the Rose Hill must have been fifty years ago, Cynthia hadn't thought about Karla Hoffman. For a while it was as if a pressure had been lifted. But now it was different. Under the light of a three-quarter moon, the surface of the lake glittered. The water was so still, it looked more like ice. Standing on the dock, she looked out over it. The shadows, the reflected illumination and the stillness in the early evening filled her with a deep melancholy. Once again she sensed another presence; the darkness took shape at her side.

Turning, she started away, walking like one in a dream. She didn't head back toward the house, however. Instead she crossed the back lawn and went directly to the gazebo. When she got there, she stood by it the way Karla Hoffman had in the newspaper picture of her at the Rose Hill House. She postured as if someone was out there taking her picture, too. Visions of Stephen and Jason passed before her. She saw them talking together, whispering in the corners of rooms filled with people; she saw them laughing together at the dinner table; she saw them riding side by side in the car. They were together everywhere and everywhere they were, she was in the background.

As she looked out at the small hotel now, her view of it changed. It was no longer the idyllic, romantic spot Stephen had chosen in which to renew their love. With Jason's arrival it had taken on an ominous character. The darkness around the house was no longer warm and inviting. It looked as if it hid evil instead. The shadows were deeper, longer. A great dark hand had been placed over the windows, the shutters and the entrances. This would become just what the Rose Hill House had become for Karla Hoffman—the house of death.

Believing this, she reached a conclusion: the main reason Karla Hoffman's spirit and she crossed was to get her to see and understand a prediction. Now she was sure of it. The cycle was nearly completed. If she didn't take a strong, independent action soon, their destinies would merge, as well. She listened for the voice, for the confirmation, but she didn't have the patience to wait for it. More importantly, she was too afraid to wait for it. She thought she saw something move at the corner of the house. Everything around her had taken on a threatening appearance. She had to get away.

She returned to the house and reentered through the back door. When she came upon one of the girls who helped serve the dinner, she asked her to direct her to a phone.

"I have to make a very important call," she said. The girl smiled at Cynthia's urgency.

"There's a pay phone in the hallway off the kitchen," she said. There was no one in the kitchen or the hallway when she got there. A low-wattage bulb in a small ceiling fixture threw a dim, yellowish glow over the walls that were papered in a flower-print pattern. There was a small, dark pine table with a few phone books piled on it right under the pay phone. Without hesitation she went to the phone and dialed for information. When the operator came on she asked for Terrence Baker's number.

"It's a new listing," she told her. "A day or so old at the most," she added, but she didn't have to give more than his name. In a moment the computerized directory punched out his number, and the operator, in perfect robot voice, gave it to her. She pulled all the change out of her pocketbook and spread it on the table. Then she dialed the number and paid for the call. After the third ring she was about to give up; but Terrence answered in the middle of the fourth.

"Hello," he said, but the sound of a woman laughing in the background kept her from replying. "Hello? Hello? Who the hell is this?"

"Forget it," the woman shouted, "and come back."

He didn't hang up, though. She heard him listening. She was afraid that after another moment or so he would sense her on the line, so she hung up the receiver quickly.

She wasn't mad because he had another woman. When she thought it through fairly, she realized she had no claims on him. She didn't permit him any claims on her. She never promised him anything, and she had even turned down a rendezvous. That wasn't what angered her.

As irrational as it was, what angered her was the fact that he wasn't available when she needed him so much. Instantly he fell into the classification for all men—self-centered, undependable, creatures of the moment. She had been just as much a fool to place her trust in him as she had to place any trust or hope in Stephen.

However, this realization didn't leave her with a sense of defeat; rather it strengthened her resolve. I'm a Palmer, she told herself. I'm a Palmer, a Palmer. It went through her brain like some fanatical chant. Her father had battled forces that were seemingly greater than himself, and he had built a prosperous business and won the highest respect in his community. She believed she had inherited his grit and his perception.

She looked at the phone and for a moment considered calling Paula Levy. But then she thought Paula would never understand all this. It was why she never really discussed Karla Hoffman with her. Paula wasn't capable of comprehending the significances. She would merely see it all as another in a series of soap opera episodes. She was fond of Paula, but Paula wasn't the person to turn to at this moment.

The truth was she had no one to turn to, no one but herself and... Karla Hoffman. We've come this far together, she thought. We might as well go all the way. A shadow moved over the wall to her right as if in reply, but when she turned around sharply she confronted Clarence Smalls.

"Makin' a call?" he asked. She nodded. "The phone company wanted to take that outta here. They said it doesn't get used enough. My mother told 'em to come and get it, but no one's come yet."

"That's nice," she said. She was going to start away and leave him gawking at her, when the thought occurred to her that Clarence could help her. What was important now was to take an action that would clearly illustrate how disgusted she was with what had occurred. The things that went on, went on partly because she tolerated them or ignored them; but this wasn't going to be the case anymore. "Can you drive me somewhere?" she asked.

"Huh? Drive ya?"

"Yes." He looked as if he didn't understand the concept. "Take me away in your car," she added.

"Sure. Where'd ja want me to take ya?"

"I've got to get back to Woodridge. Take me someplace where I can hire a cab."

"Woodridge? Yeah, I know where that is. I'll take ya there."

"It's too far, at least an hour and a half."

"So what? I got nothin' else to do. I'm off," he said.

"Where's your car?"

"It's in the back," he said, obviously growing excited because she was going to let him drive her all the way. "It's the blue station wagon."

"I don't want anyone to know," she said. "Can you keep it a secret?"

"Sure."

"All right. I'm going to walk down the driveway and onto the road. Pick me up in about ten minutes. I'll pay you for the gas."

"You don't hafta pay me." He grew indignant.

"Okay. Thanks. Ten minutes," she said. He nodded, his face intense.

She was excited by her decision; her heart was beating rapidly. But she was confident, like one who had captured the future and knew exactly which way to go. She went back out to the front porch, expecting to find Stephen and Jason in another one of their tête-à-têtes. She imagined they'd be alone, that the others would stay clear of them now. She'd tell them that she decided to take the walk after all, and she'd leave them muttering about it back on the porch. Then she'd simply walk off into the darkness and get into Clarence's station wagon when he pulled up. Later she'd call them and tell them to enjoy their stay together. This had to be it; she'd bring it to an end.

But when she stepped out on the porch she was surprised to find that they were no longer there. She hadn't seen them in the sitting room, either. She went over to another couple, the one that had been rowing yesterday and got such a kick out of her rowing Stephen.

"Yes," the man said, "I overheard your husband say he was going to look for you. Your brother, is it?"

"Yes?"

"He sat there for a while, and then he went down toward the road, not more than a few minutes ago."

"Toward the road?" She looked into the darkness. Maybe they had split up to search for her and he had taken that direction, she thought. She dreaded meeting up with him, but she had given Clarence her request and she didn't want to run around looking for him to change it. "Thanks," she said, and started off the porch.

She could hear the other guests off to the right. Their voices carried clearly through the otherwise relatively quiet night. She was envious of the laughter of the women. There was a time, she thought, when she was like that. She had almost been like that here. As she walked on her bitterness and anger built. It was like some kind of monster feeding on itself and swelling in size. Her hands, folded into fists, were so hot she thought she could start a fire by merely touching something flammable.

Turning to the left, she stepped into the deeper shadows on the road and waited. Suddenly she saw Jason coming from the direction of the others. He was walking very briskly, his feet slapping the pavement. She stepped back farther out of sight to watch him take the turn up the driveway. For a moment he was caught in the light at the entranceway. Rarely had she seen his face so twisted in anger. His characteristic stoical expression was gone; he looked determined to do someone some harm. His hands were folded into fists, too, and his shoulders were raised, making him look like part hawk and part man.

She took a deep breath. Clarence was coming down the driveway, and Jason had to step aside to let him pass. She wasn't sure where Jason was in the shadows, but when Clarence drove out she had to come forward from the shadows or he would drive right by her. He stopped sharply.

"Hi," he said much too loudly. She hurried around to the passenger's side and got in quickly.

"Go," she said. "Drive."

"Sure." The urgency excited him. He floored the accelerator and they shot off into the darkness, leaving the happy laughter of the other guests dying behind them.

THEY RODE for nearly twenty minutes without talking. Then, to help pass the time, she began to ask him questions about himself. At first she wanted to hear his voice only to keep herself from thinking about what she was doing and what had to be done, but as he talked, describing his life and his work, she had the strange feeling she had heard it all before. It finally occurred to her that in many ways Clarence Smalls reminded her of Liza Glenn. She imagined that he was similar to Liza in her early days. After all, they did have the same kind of work in the same kind of resort. She remembered the way Liza described Mrs. Hillerman's mothering him, nursing him when he was sick, making sure he had good meals....

Perhaps during her loneliness and boredom, Karla Hoffman spent time talking with him. Perhaps he fancied her, but he was too embarrassed or ashamed to admit it now. Maybe he ended up disliking Ben Hillerman because Ben Hillerman did the thing he fantasized. She felt overwhelmed. There were parallels everywhere. She didn't know whether she was fleeing from them or fleeing toward them.

"I could go faster in the daytime," Clarence said, feeling a need to justify his cautious driving, "but there are loads of deer along here and they just come chargin' out."

"That's okay. I'm not in a terrible rush now," she said. She sat back to try to relax, but the automobile behind them closed in with its headlights high, flooding them with illumination. Clarence cursed and tried to adjust his rearview mirror. The car began blinking its lights on and off.

"What the hell...maybe it's a cop," he said. He pulled to the side. She sat forward as Jason in his Audi passed them and came to a stop a dozen yards ahead. "Who's that?"

"It's my brother," she said. He got out of his car and walked back to them. He came around to Cynthia's side.

"What are you doing? Where the hell are you going?"

She didn't answer. She looked at Clarence, who looked terribly confused, and then she opened the car door abruptly. Jason stepped back fast to avoid being hit with it.

"Thank you, Clarence," she said. "You don't have to take me any farther."

"You sure?"

"Yes. Thank you." She got out of the car. Jason stared at her, a look of astonishment on his face. "Where's Stephen?"

"Back at the hotel. He doesn't even know I came after you. When I saw you get into this station wagon, I just got into my car and followed. Where were you heading?"

"Home."

"Home?"

"Let's go," she said, and she walked toward the Audi. He followed slowly. After she got into the car Clarence pulled away.

"Can you tell me what this is about?" Jason said getting in.

"Yes. Drive."

"Where to?"

"I said home."

"Home? But..."

"Just drive, Jason," she commanded. The anger and aggression in her voice surprised even her, but she didn't regret it. She was glad she had found the strength. Without hesitation he started the car and drove on.

"Why do you want to go home?" he asked in a softer tone of voice. She recognized his retreat, but that only hardened her more.

"Just keep driving."

"But what about Stephen?"

"Clarence will probably tell him. Actually, my dear brother, I'm surprised you followed, surprised you cared. You could have remained at the hotel and had Stephen all to yourself."

"What are you talking about?" The thinness in his voice disgusted her, and strangely enough, even though she wanted to punish him and defeat him, a part of her didn't enjoy seeing the weakness in him.

"I'm talking about the way you've manipulated him, the way you've molded him all these years, the way you... you made love to him until you possessed him just like you possess everything else." Jason started to slow down. "No! Don't stop! Keep going."

"I knew it," he said. There was a sadness in his voice that confused her. "I knew he was starting to turn you against me."

"He was starting? That's a laugh, Jason. Do you think I'm a total idiot? Did you really believe that all this time I wouldn't understand what was happening?"

"I don't think you have, Cynthia. In fact I know you haven't."

"Is that so? You were insidious, taking him away from me first in little ways—changing his hairstyle to conform with yours, having him go to your tailor to buy your type of clothing, getting him to shave his beard, for crissakes, because you knew he looked more like a man with it on than you could ever look."

"I never told him to change his hairstyle. That was his own idea. And as for the clothing...we had some real arguments about it. I knew you didn't like my taste, but that didn't seem to matter anymore to him."

"I know, Jason. That's the point."

"But it wasn't because of me, because of what I was doing to him. It was because of him, because of what he was doing to me."

"Is that right, Jason? He was doing things to you? Is that why you gave him Dad's ring and bought him that expensive watch? You wanted to reward him for doing things to you?"

"He took the ring," he said sadly. He paused as if his throat were closing. She looked over in the darkness of the car. He took his right hand from the steering wheel and wiped his forehead. "As for the watch, I bought it for myself, but he took that, too."

"And you just gave it to him."

"That's right, Cynthia, I just gave it to him," he said, his voice tighter and stronger because of the resentment he evinced.

"Listen, Jason," she began in as controlled a voice as she could, "there's no sense in going on with the lies. I've caught you both in too many of them anyway. And," she said before he could reply, "I was at your house the other day when you and Stephen were supposedly away on some business trip."

"So that's how you knew. Then Stephen never said anything. You made that up."

"What's the difference now? I saw you going upstairs to him. I saw you dressed in your silk robe." She swallowed hard. "I know what you are," she said, "and I know what you've made him into."

"You don't really know anything, Cynthia," he said. His voice was so different, so young sounding that she felt they had fallen back through the years and he was giving her one of his famous pedantic lectures. "Actually, you and I are more similar than you'd care to admit. You're just as self-centered. You have as big an ego, and you're just as blind to anything that contradicts your view of things."

"Is that so?"

"Yes, I'm afraid it is. You see, Cynthia, everything that you described happening did happen,

Reflection

but not as recently as you think. What is between me and Stephen didn't just occur over the past year or so. It started a lot farther back than you know. In fact, Cynthia," he said turning toward her, "it began even before you got married."

"You seduced him," she charged. There was almost a hiss in her voice now. He was back to being his arrogant self; she could sense it. He would manipulate her if she let him; but she was determined not to be defeated, not this time. "That's what the truth is." He laughed.

"The truth is, I wish you were right," he said calmly. "I wish I was the one in control. I've been doing things his way for years. When he told me about the club in Atlantic City, claiming that I told you about it first, I thought he was conniving again, turning and twisting things to turn you completely against me. He never spared me one of your critical remarks."

She felt herself wanting to sympathize with him, but she fought it back. This is his clever way to turn things, she thought.

"Stephen would never do that."

"Really? Should I make a list for you? What should I begin with—your description of how I behaved after Mother's death, how you thought I hated her because I wouldn't look at her before they closed the coffin, how I played my music that night, much too loudly for someone who was supposed to be mourning...."

"Well, he was probably as revolted by the description of your behavior as I was witnessing it."

"No. He simply wanted me to know how much you disliked me, how it didn't matter what I did in the name of the family, because I had no family. In effect, he made me feel isolated."

"You did that to yourself."

"Maybe."

They were both silent for a while. She wanted to continue her hard line; she wanted to be as vicious and as biting as she could be, but something had begun to nag at her. Was she falling prey to Jason's clever tactics?

"If you're not the one in pursuit, why did you come up to the hotel? Why couldn't you leave us alone for a few days? I'll tell you why," she said before he could reply. "You were afraid I'd win him back. You were afraid I'd turn him against you and get him to see you for what you really are, Jason."

"You know," he said calmly, too calmly to please her, "some of the time, more often than not recently, I would wish for that to happen. I used to hope that you would find out and everything would come to an end, but then..."

"Then what?"

"From the beginning Stephen knew what to appeal to in me. It's like any other addiction, I suppose. I knew it was bad. It was leading to bad things but I couldn't help myself. Surprised that your brother has some weaknesses?" She didn't reply. She wasn't prepared for all this confession. "I don't expect you to forgive, but perhaps you can understand the conflict raging within me. That's why when Stephen asked me, rather demanded, I come to the hotel, I submitted. I thought perhaps this was it—there would be a face-off and it would end, whatever his motives would be. I suspect they're all financial."

"I know you're lying now," she said. "He told me he didn't know you were coming."

"He reserved the room. Ask the owners."

"I don't believe that." She thought quickly, frantically. "You probably called, using his name."

"I see it's impossible to get you to see the truth because you don't want to see it." He thought for a moment and then added, "Maybe you're better off. Maybe we should just leave it the way it is—you believing what you want to believe."

"I don't want to hear any more," she said. She put her hands over her ears.

"All right. You still want to go home?"

"Yes."

"Home it is," he said, and then he repeated, "Home," as if that contained more cryptic information.

Although there was a silence between them for the remainder of the trip, she felt something happening. The usual wall, the separateness that was always there began to vanish. She had to wonder just how much of what Jason said about her was true. Was she deliberately blind to anything that would upset the balance in her world? To what extent was the aloofness between her and Jason her fault as well as his?

Every once in a while he turned to her, and even though she couldn't see his face well in the darkness of the car, she sensed a warmth and a concern. Could it be that this, too, was part of his power? She tended toward believing that, because she had come to believe that all men were performers.

Yet she also sensed a desperateness in Jason. There were cracks in that otherwise well-polished facade. He was showing real pain. Was it the result of what she thought, even what she hoped—disclosure? No matter how he phrased it, he couldn't face her knowing what she now knew. Or was he now telling the truth and the pain came not only from the revelations about his personal sex life but also from the revelation that he was, despite everything, the weaker of the two? Was Stephen truly the one in control?

She was more confused than ever. Every time she thought she understood what was happening and what had been happening, something made it more complex. Never had she needed a confidant more. She feared loneliness. Oh, Karla, she thought, Karla, we have pursued one another so intently. Don't desert me now.

Thinking of her brought to mind a question that was like an answer to a prayer, for she believed that by posing it she would cut to the heart of the truth. Whatever related to Karla was special. Whether or not she wanted to believe they were mystical things, there was a spiritual power tied to them. Neither Jason's cleverness nor Stephen's intelligent rationalizations could penetrate that world.

She sat back firmly and looked straight ahead, once again feeling enhanced by Karla's spirit. Her house was right ahead. She waited until Jason pulled into the driveway.

"Now what?" he said. She didn't look at him when she spoke. She stared ahead as though the lines were written on the windshield.

"This is what I believe. I believe you've become insecure about Stephen recently. I believe you thought he was turning away from you, turning away from your control of him, and so you tried to turn him against me. You wanted us to have fights. You wanted us to have arguments. You built it up slowly, carefully, like a psychological hit man aware of the effects the accumulation of seemingly small things would have on me."

"God, Cynthia, what has Stephen done to us?" Jason said, shaking his head. Cynthia continued to stare ahead, not hearing him.

"But you made a mistake when you tried to use Karla Hoffman."

"Karla Hoffman?"

"Yes, it was just another one of those small things to you, so you felt secure in using it. I knew you were laughing at me all the time I was telling you about it in my office. I knew what you thought. Now I understand what you thought you could do with it—use it to make Stephen believe I was rapidly becoming an embarrassment to him and to you and to your precious agency. I was being flighty, foolish, even idiotic because I saw something significant in that newspaper story and picture."

"Oh, that again. I told you—I didn't mention it to him first. He mentioned it to me."

"Of course."

"And when you accused me of it I went back to him and asked him about it even though I didn't see why it was so important. I saw how important it was to you. He said he heard it from Ralph Hillerman."

"Ralph Hillerman did not . . ."

"Indirectly. He heard Ralph talk about it on your answering machine. It was Stephen who used it as another way to try to drive a wedge permanently between us."

She looked at him, a great feeling of excitement coming over her. She felt like a good trial lawyer who had just led the witness into a perfect trap. She remembered Stephen telling her there was a message from Ralph Hillerman on the answering machine. She remembered that he didn't ask her anything about Karla Hoffman then, and in fact he had come back to see what Ralph had wanted. He thought it had something to do with the sale of the Rose Hill. She could see him now, standing there, the towel wrapped around him. He was on his way to taking a shower. It was the night they went to Dede's for lobster.

But what excited her the most was the realization that she had turned off the answering machine without rewinding the tape. Stephen had come to dislike the machine. Now he was like Jason, refusing to talk to a recorder. "It's another part of our inane technological world," Jason had said once, "another way to dehumanize us." She remembered laughing about it, thinking who was he to talk about dehumanization. Nevertheless, in her mind, it was another way he changed Stephen.

So the machine was really only hers. Their phone number was unlisted, something else Jason had gotten Stephen to do. "It makes people feel special when you give it to them," he said. "And anyway, you don't want to be bothered by idiotic business calls all the time, especially after you leave the office."

She couldn't agree with that more so she agreed to a private number, and Stephen rarely got business calls at home. Consequently, the messages on the machine were usually for her. Now she was ecstatic about forgetting to rewind the tape and to reset the machine. What could she blame for her forgetfulness? Surely it had a lot to do with her intense interest in Karla Hoffman. She hadn't thought much about her current acquaintances and her current social life these past days. Was this ironic or was this another way in which Karla Hoffman reached across time to help her?

She turned, smiling at him. He saw her in the light from the driveway lamp. He narrowed his eyes and sat back. She looked so different, so threatening. She sensed his fear and that made her even more confident.

"You said, phone message, Jason?"

"Yes."

"Stephen told you the first time he had heard about Karla Hoffman was the time Ralph Hillerman left this message on my machine?"

"Yes."

"For once, Jason, I'm going to trap you clearly in one of your own lies. Come into the house," she demanded.

He followed her to the door. She went in and put on the lights. Then she went directly to the den and to the machine. Jason stood behind her in the doorway. His eyes widened. He looked as though the button-down collar of his shirt would choke him to death. As she reached out toward the controls she felt as though Karla Hoffman's hand was on hers, as though Karla Hoffman's finger was pushing down on her own. Then she rewound the tape, hit "play back" and turned to Jason. Ralph Hillerman's voice came on clear and loud.

"Hi, Cynthia, Ralph Hillerman. Talking to my wife just now, I remembered something else about Karla Hoffman. I'm still not crazy about talking about her. Remember what my grandmother said about riling up the dead, even though there is a remarkable resemblance between you and Karla. Anyway, give me a buzz and I'll add it to your bonus," he said, and laughed. "I'm at home."

It had the effect of a bullet. For a long moment she couldn't move. Jason went to the liquor cabinet and poured himself a snifter of brandy.

"You want anything?" he asked.

"What? No," she said softly. She watched him down it all in one gulp and pour himself a second shot. "How much have you given him, Jason?" she asked, a heavy note of resignation in her voice.

"I don't keep track anymore... stock options, outright grants. He owns seventy-five percent of whatever we've diversified into...."

For a long moment they looked at each other. Odd, she thought, but she never had as strong a feeling of affection for Jason as she had at this moment. He swallowed his second drink quickly.

"You and I have never been as close as we should have been," he said, "and I know it's my fault. I should have spoken up years ago."

"I'm not so sure who's responsible for what anymore," she said.

"But I want you to know that despite everything, even the things that I did that appeared to be done only for myself, I was thinking of you. I wish... I wish we had been closer."

"Me, too," she said.

"I did lie to you about something," he said, putting his empty glass down. He took a step toward her and put his hand on the top of the couch. "When I first came into your office and you first told me about Karla Hoffman and then showed me the picture, I made light of it by telling you of this girl I knew in college, this girl I said reminded me of you."

"I remember."

"I told you I had gotten to know her well and she was an airhead. That wasn't true. I knew her well, but she was an intelligent and sensitive person. She was really the first... the only woman... I wanted her because she reminded me of you, but it was also because of that that I couldn't... do you understand?"

She recalled what Borris Hoffman told her about Karla's brother. "Yes," she said, "I understand."

This moment of closeness took her back to a time before everything became complicated, a time when they were both very young and innocent. Jason was still the big brother, even then, but now she understood that when he was trying to tell her things and show her things he was doing so out of a deeper affection for her than she could have ever imagined. His pedantic and formal ways were only disguises, disguises he depended on because it was difficult for him to show emotion. He was afraid of it. But sometimes, when they were very young, it would break through. She should have thought about those times more often.

"I'm sure Stephen wants it all," he said. "I always knew, I suppose, but I didn't want to face up to it. In that way, you and I are very much alike."

She nodded, but she wasn't going to cry; she wasn't going to become hysterical and run away. She was right when she thought that Stephen was betraying her, but it was a different kind of betrayal, the betrayal of an even deeper trust. He had twisted her thoughts; he had gotten into her mind. She felt duped, used, perhaps more so than Jason.

"Go home, Jason," she said. She spoke like one in a coma.

"But I can't leave you now. Not after all this."

"Go home. It's between Stephen and me now. Go. Please."

"This isn't going to be easy. He's..."

"I know," she said, "but don't worry. I'll be Palmeresque."

"I bet you will be. Okay," he said, "but promise you'll call me no matter what. I'll be close by."

"I will."

He started out and then turned around at the door.

"I'm sorry, Cyn. You must feel terribly alone."

She wanted to kiss him, to go up to him and kiss him on the cheek, but she didn't. As soon as he was gone she regretted that she hadn't.

STEPHEN CALLED shortly after Jason left.

"Where the hell are you two? What the hell's going on? I can't find you. I can't find Jason. Clarence tells me he took you for a little ride, and you got out of his car and went off with Jason."

"Come home, Stephen," she said.

"What is it? What happened? Why did Jason leave? Is he coming back?"

"Come home," she repeated in a dry, unemotional voice. He was silent for a moment.

"Jesus. This isn't a five-minute ride. Whatever had to be done at home, couldn't it have been done afterward?"

She didn't reply. She just hung up the phone. He didn't call back, so she knew that he would soon be on his way.

She turned the lights down in the den and went to the bedroom. She changed into what she had now come to think of as her "Karla Hoffman dress," and she fixed her hair into the shape that Karla's had been when she took that picture at the gazebo. When she looked into the mirror she was positive she saw Karla. They had become a reflection of each other in every sense of the word.

Cynthia smiled and rose from the chair at the vanity table. She went to the bottom dresser drawer where Stephen kept his pistol. It was always loaded and ready; it was supposed to give them a sense of security. She had reluctantly agreed to his taking her out to the backyard a number of times to train her with it. She never liked it, but she did it for him.

Just like Jason, she was always doing things for him.

After that she went back into the den and sat in the chair facing the door, waiting.

The *Choice* for Bestsellers
also offers a handsome and
sturdy book rack for your
prized novels at $9.95 each.
Write to:

The Choice for Bestsellers
120 Brighton Road
P.O. Box 5092
Clifton, NJ 07015-5092
Attn: Customer Service Group